John R. Musick

The Witch of Salem

Credulity run mad

John R. Musick

The Witch of Salem
Credulity run mad

ISBN/EAN: 9783337387150

Printed in Europe, USA, Canada, Australia, Japan

Cover: Foto ©Andreas Hilbeck / pixelio.de

More available books at **www.hansebooks.com**

THE WITCH OF SALEM

OR

CREDULITY RUN MAD

BY

JOHN R. MUSICK

AUTHOR OF "COLUMBIA," "ESTEVAN," "ST. AUGUSTINE,"
"POCAHONTAS," "THE PILGRIMS," "A CENTURY
TOO SOON," ETC., ETC.

ILLUSTRATIONS BY F. A. CARTER

New York

FUNK & WAGNALLS COMPANY

LONDON AND TORONTO

1893

Printed in the United States.

PREFACE.

It is a difficult task to go back to ages by-gone, to divest ourselves of what we know and are and form a clear conception of generations that have been, of their experiences, objects, modes of life, thought and expression. It is a task better suited to the novelist than the historian, and even the former treads on dangerous ground in attempting it. One of the prime objects of the Columbian Historical Novels is to give the reader as clear an idea as possible of the common people, as well as of the rulers of the age. The author has endeavored at the risk of criticism to clothe the speeches of his characters in the dialect and idioms peculiar to the age in which they lived. In the former volumes, sentences most criticised are those taken literally as spoken or written at the time. Though it would seem that a few critics grow more severe the nearer an author approaches the truth, yet the greater number of thinking men and women

iii

who review these books are students themselves, and the author who adheres to the language of a bygone age has nothing to fear from them.

The "Witch of Salem" is designed to cover twenty years in the history of the United States, or from the year 1680 to 1700, including all the principal features of this period. Charles Stevens of Salem, with Cora Waters, the daughter of an indented slave, whose father was captured at the time of the overthrow of the Duke of Monmouth, are the principal characters. Samuel Parris, the chief actor in the Salem tragedy, is a serious study, and has been painted, after a careful research, according to the conception formed of him. No greater villain ever lived in any age. He had scarce a redeeming feature. His religion was hypocrisy, superstition, revenge and bigotry. His ambition led him to deeds of atrocity unsurpassed. Having drawn the information on which this story is founded from what seem the most reliable sources, and woven the story in a way which it is hoped will be pleasing and instructive, we send this volume forth to speak for itself.

JOHN R. MUSICK.

KIRKSVILLE, Mo., Oct. 1st, 1892.

TABLE OF CONTENTS.

CHAPTER X.

CHAPTER XI.

CHAPTER XII.

CHAPTER XIII.

CHAPTER XIV.

CHAPTER XV.

CHAPTER XVI.

CHAPTER XVII.

C.IAPTER XVIII.

CHAPTER XIX.

CHAPTER XX.

LIST OF ILLUSTRATIONS.

vii

THE WITCH OF SALEM.

CHAPTER I.

THE MAN WITH THE BOOK.

Through shades and solitudes profound,
The fainting traveler wends his way ;
Bewildering meteors glare around,
And tempt his wandering feet astray.
—MONTGOMERY.

HE autumnal evening was cool, dark and gusty. Storm-clouds were gathering thickly overhead, and the ground beneath was covered with rustling leaves, which, blighted by the early frosts, lay helpless and dead at the roadside, or were made the sport of the wind. A solitary horseman was slowly plodding along the road but a few miles from the village of Salem. In truth he was so near to the famous

"TAKE IT AWAY!"

1

Puritan village, that, through the hills and intervening tree-tops, he could have seen the spires of
the churches had he raised his melancholy eyes
from the ground. The rider was not a youth, nor
had he reached middle age. His face was handsome, though distorted with agony. Occasionally
he pressed his hand to his side as if in pain;
but maugre pain, weariness, or anguish, he pressed
on, admonished by the lengthening shadows of
the approach of night. Turning his great, sad,
brown eyes at last to where the road wound
about the valley across which the distant spires of
Salem could be seen, he sighed:

"Can I reach it to-night? I must!"

Salem, that strange village to which the horseman
was wending his way, in October, 1684, was a
different village from the Salem of to-day. It is a
town familiar to every American student, and,
having derived its fame more from its historic recollections than from its commerce or industries, its
name carries us back two centuries, suggesting the
faint and transient image of the life of the Pilgrim
Fathers, who gave that sacred name to the place of
their chosen habitation. Whatever changes civilization or time may bring about, the features of
natural scenery are, for the most part, unalterable.
Massachusetts Bay is as it was when the Pilgrim
Fathers first beheld it. On land, there are still the

craggy hills, with jutting promontories of granite, where the barberries grow, and room is found in the narrow valleys for small farms, and for apple trees, and little slopes of grass, and patches of tillage where all else looks barren.

The scenery is not more picturesque to-day, than on that chill autumnal eve, when the strange horseman was urging his jaded steed along the path which led to the village. His garments were travel-stained and his features haggard.

Three hunters with guns on their shoulders were not half a mile in advance of the horseman. They, too, evidently had passed a day of arduous toil; for climbing New England hills in search of the wild deer was no easy task.

They were men who had hardly reached middle age; but their grave Puritanic demeanor made them look older than they were. Their conversation was grave, gloomy and mysterious. There was little light or frivolous about them, for to them life was sombre. The hunt was not sport, but arduous toil, and their legs were so weary they could scarcely drag themselves along.

"Now we may rejoice, John Bly, that home is within sight, for truly I am tired, and I think I could not go much farther," one of the pedestrians remarked to the man at his side.

"Right glad will I be when we are near!" answered the fatigued John Bly. "This has been a hard day with fruitless result."

"We have had some fair shots to-day," put in a third man, who walked a little behind the others.

"Verily, we have; yet what profits it to us, Samuel Gray, when our guns fail to carry the ball to the place? I had as many fair shots to-day as would bring down a dozen bucks, and yet I missed every time. You know full well I am not one to miss."

"You are not, John Louder."

Then the three men looked mysteriously at each other. They were all believers in supernatural agencies, and the fact that such a faultless marksman should miss was enough to establish in their minds a belief that other than natural causes were at work. There could be no other reason given that John Louder should miss his mark, than that his gun was "bewitched." It was an age when the last dying throes of superstition seemed fastening on the people's minds, and the spasmodic struggle threatened to upset their reason. The New Englander's mind was prepared for mysteries as the fallow ground is prepared for the seed. He was busied conquering the rugged earth and making it yield to his husbandry. His time was divided between arduous toil for bread and fighting the Indians. He was hemmed in by a gloomy old forest, the magnitude of which he did not dream, and it was only natural, with his fertile imagination, narrow perceptions and limited knowledge, that he would see strange sights and hear strange sounds. Images and visions which have been portrayed in tales of romance and given interest to the pages of poetry were made by him to throng the woods, flit through the air and hover over the heads of terrified officials, whose learning should have placed them beyond the bounds of superstition. The ghosts of murdered wives, husbands and children played their part with a vividness of representation and artistic skill of expression hardly surpassed in scenic representation on the stage. The superstition of the Middle Ages was embodied in real action, with all its extravagant absurdities and monstrosities. This, carried into the courts of law, where the relations of society and conduct or feelings of individuals were suffered to be under control of fanciful or mystical notions, could have but one effect. When a whole people abandoned the solid ground of common sense, overleaped the boundaries of human knowledge, gave itself up to wild reveries, and let loose its passions without restraint, the result was more destructive to society than a Vesuvius to Pompeii. When John Louder said his gun was bewitched, there was no incredulous smile on his companions' faces.

The political complexion of New England at that time no doubt had much to do with the superstitious awe which overspread that country. Within the recollection of many inhabitants, the parent government had changed three times. Charles II. had lived such a life of furious dissipation, that his earthly career was drawing to a close.

The New England people were zealous theologians, and Massachusetts and Plymouth hated above all sects the Roman Catholics. Charles II. could not reign long, and James, Duke of York, his brother, would be his successor, as it was generally known that Charles II. had no legitimate heir. It was hoped by some that his illegitimate son, the Duke of Monmouth, a Protestant, might succeed him. Some had even hinted that Charles II., while flying from Cromwell, had secretly married Lucy Waters, the mother of the duke; but this has never been proved in history.

The somewhat ostentatious manner in which the Duke of York had been accustomed to go to mass, during the life of his brother, was the chief cause of the general dislike in which he was held. Even Charles, giddy and careless as he was in general, saw the imprudence of James' conduct, and significantly told him on one occasion that *he* had no desire to go upon his travels again, whatever James might wish. When it became currently reported

all over the American colonies that this bigoted
Catholic would, on the death of his brother, become
their ruler, the New Englanders began to tremble
for their religion. There was murmuring from
every village and plantation, keeping society in a
constant ferment.

The three hunters were still discussing their ill
luck when the sound of horse's hoofs fell on their
ears, and they turned slowly about to see a stranger
approaching them on horseback. His sad, gray
eye had something wild and supernatural about it.
His costume had at one time been elegant, but was
now stained with dust and travel. It included a
wrought flowing neckcloth, a sash covered with a
silver-laced red cloth coat, a satin waistcoat em-
broidered with gold, a trooping scarf and a silver
hat-band. His trousers, which were met above
the knees by a pair of riding boots, like the remainder of his attire, was covered with dust.

The expression of pain on his face was miscon-
strued by the superstitious hunters into a look of
fiendish triumph, and John Louder, seizing the arm
of Bly, whispered:

"It is he!"

"Perhaps——"

"I know it, Bly, for he hath followed me all day."

"Then wherefore not give him the ball, which
he hath guarded from the deer?"

"It would be of no avail, John. A witch cannot be killed with lead. He would throw the ball in my face and laugh at me."

The three walked hastily along, casting wary and uneasy glances behind as the horseman drew nearer. Each trembled lest the horseman should speak, and once or twice he seemed as if he would; but pain, or some other cause unknown to the hunters, prevented his doing so. He rode swiftly by, disappearing over the hill in the direction of Salem.

When he was out of sight the three hunters paused, and, falling on their knees, each uttered a short prayer for deliverance from Satan. As they rose, John Louder said:

"Now I know full well, good men, that he is the wizard who hath tampered with my gun."

"Who is he?"

"Ah! well may you ask, Samuel Gray, who he is; a stranger, the black man, the devil, who hath assumed this form to mislead and torment us. One can only wonder at the various cunning of Satan," and Louder sighed.

"Truly you speak, friend John," Bly answered. "The enemy of men's souls is constantly on the lookout for the unwary."

"I have met him and wrestled with him, until I was almost overcome; but, having on the whole armor of God, I did cry out 'Get thee behind me,

Satan!' and, behold, I could smell the sulphur of hell, as the gates were opened to admit the prince of darkness."

The shades of night were creeping over the earth, and the three weary hunters were not yet within sight of their homes, when the horseman who had so strangely excited their fears drew rein at a spring not a fourth of a mile from the village of Salem and allowed his horse to drink. He pressed his hand to his side, as if suffering intolerable anguish, and murmured:

"Will I find shelter there?"

Overcome by suffering, he at last slipped from his saddle and, sitting among the rustling leaves heedless of the lowering clouds and threatened storm, buried his face in his hands. Two hours had certainly elapsed since he first came in sight of Salem, and yet so slow had been his pace, that he had not reached the village; but on the earth, threatened with a raging tempest, he breathed in feeble accents a prayer to God for strength to perform the great and holy task on which he was bent. He was sick and feeble. In his side was a wound that might prove fatal, and to this he occasionally pressed his hand as if in pain.

He who heareth the poor when they cry unto Him, answered the prayer of the desolate. A farmer boy came along whistling merrily despite the approaching night and storm. Not the chilling blasts of October, the dread of darkness, nor the cold world could depress the spirits of Charles Stevens, the merry lad of Salem. In fact, he was so merry that, by the straight-laced Puritans, he was thought ungodly. He had a predisposition to whistling and singing, and was of "a light and frivolous carriage." He laughed at the sanctity of some people, and was known to smile even on the Lord's Day. When, in the exuberance of his spirits, his feet kept time to his whistling, the good Salemites were horrified by the ungodly dance.

Charles Stevens, however, had a better heart, and was a truer Christian than many of those sanctimonious critics, who sought to restrain the joy and gladness with which God filled his soul. It was this good Samaritan who came upon the suffering stranger whom the three Puritans had condemned in their own minds as an emissary of the devil.

"Why do you sit here, sir?" Charles asked, leaving off his whistle. "Night is coming on, and it is growing so chill and cold, you must keep moving, or surely you will perish."

"I cannot rise," was the answer.

"Cannot rise! prythee, what ails you, friend?"

"I am sick, sore and wounded."

"Wounded!" cried Charles, "and sick, too!"

His sharp young eyes were enabled to penetrate the deepening shades of twilight, and he saw a ghastly pallor overspreading the man's face, who,

"CANNOT RISE! PRYTHEE, WHAT AILS YOU, FRIEND?"

pressing his hand upon his side, gave vent to gasps of keen agony. His left side was stained with blood.

"You are wounded!" Charles Stevens at last declared. "Pray, how came it about?"

"I was fired upon by an unseen foe, for what cause I know not, as, being a stranger in these parts, I have had no quarrel."

"Come, let me help you to rise."

"No, it is useless. I am tired and too faint to go further. Let me lie here. I will soon be dead, and all this agony will be over."

At this, the cheerful mind of Charles Stevens asserted itself by inspiring hope in the heart of the fainting stranger.

"No, no, my friend, never give up. Don't say die, so long as you live. It is but a few rods further to the home where I live with my mother. I can help you walk so far, and there you can get rested and warmed, and mother will dress your wound."

"Can I go?" the traveller asked.

"Men can do wonders when they try."

"Then I will try."

"I will help you."

The boy threw his strong arm around the man and raised him to his feet; but his limbs no longer obeyed his will, and he sank again upon the ground.

"It is of no avail, my good boy. I cannot go. Leave me to die."

Charles turned his eyes about to look for the

stranger's horse; but it had strayed off in the darkness. To search for him would be useless, and for
a moment the good Samaritan stood as if in thought;
then, stripping off his coat and wrapping it around
the wounded man, he said hopefully:

"I will be back soon, don't move," and he hurried away swiftly toward home. On reaching the
threshold, he thanked God that he was not a wanderer on such a night.

The New England kitchen, with its pewter-filled
dresser, reflecting and multiplying the genial blaze
of the log-heaped fire-place, its high-backed, rush-
bottomed chairs, grating as they were moved over
the neatly sanded floor, its massive beam running
midway of the ceiling across the room, and its many
doors, leading to other rooms and attics, was a
picture of comfort two hundred years ago. The
widowed mother, with her honest, beautiful face
surrounded by a neat, dark cap border, met her son
as he entered the kitchen and, glancing at him
proudly, said:

"The wind gives you good color, Charles."

"Yes, mother," rubbing his cheeks, "they do
burn some;—mother."

"Well?"

"I heard you tell Mr. Bly, the other day, that
you could trust me with all you had. Will you
trust me with old Moll and the cart to-night?"

"What do you want with Moll and the cart?"

"To go to the big spring under the hill for a poor man who is sick and wounded."

"And alone?"

"Yes, mother."

"It is a freezing night."

"Yes, mother, and he may die. He is unable to walk. Remember the story of the good Samaritan."

After a long pause, the widow said, "Yes, you may have old Moll and the cart. Bring him here, and we will care for him; but remember that to-morrow's work must be done."

"If you have any fault to find to-morrow night, don't trust me again!" and the boy, turning to the cupboard beneath the dressers, buttered a generous slice of bread, then left the room with a small pitcher, and returned with it brimming full of cider, his mother closely noting all, while she busied herself making things to rights in her culinary department. Charles next went out and harnessed the mare to the cart, then returned to the kitchen for his bread and cider.

"Why not eat that before you go?" queried the mother.

"I am not hungry, I have had some supper, you know. Good night, mother. I will be back soon; so have the bed ready for the wounded stranger."

"God bless you, my brave boy," the mother exclaimed, as he went out and sprang into the cart. She now knew that he had taken the bread and cider for the sick man, under the hill.

Charles hurried old Moll to a faster gait than she was accustomed to go, and found the stranger where he had left him. Leaping from the cart, he said:

"I am back, sir! You said you were faint. Here's some of our cider, and if you will sit up and drink it and eat this bread, you will feel better, and here is old Moll and the cart ready to take you home where you will receive good Christian treatment until you are well enough to go on your way rejoicing."

So he went on, bobbing now here and now there and talking as fast as he could, so as not to hear the poor man's outpourings of gratitude, as he ate and drank and was refreshed. With some difficulty, he got the stranger into the cart, where, supported by the boy's strong arm, he rode in almost total silence through the increasing darkness to the home of the widow Stevens. He was taken from the cart and was soon reclining upon a bed.

His wound, though painful, was not dangerous and began to heal almost immediately. Surgery was in its infancy in America, and on the frontier of the American colonies, every one was his own surgeon.

The widow dressed the wound herself, and the stranger recovered rapidly. Charles next day found a horse straying in the forest with a saddle and holsters, and, knowing it to be the steed of the wounded stranger, he brought it home.

As the wounded man recovered he became more silent and melancholy. He had not even spoken his name and seldom uttered a word unless addressed.

One night this mysterious stranger disappeared from the widow's cottage. He might have been thought ungrateful had he not left behind five golden guineas, which, the note left behind said, were in part to remunerate the good people who had watched over and cared for him so kindly. Charles Stevens and his mother were much puzzled at this mysterious stranger, and often when alone they commented on his conduct.

Their home was outside the village of Salem, and for days they did not have a visitor; but two or three of their neighbors had seen the stranger while at their house, yet they told no one about him. His mysterious disappearance was kept a secret by mother and son. Little did they dream that in after years they would suffer untold sorrow for playing the part of good Samaritans.

John Louder and his friends had almost forgotten their day of hard luck in the woods. Their more recent hunts had proven successful, for the witches had temporarily left off tampering with their guns. The stranger whom they had met on that evening was quite forgotten.

A fortnight after the stranger disappeared, John Louder was wandering in the forest, his gun on his shoulder. The sun had just dipped below the western hills and trees, and he was approaching a small lake at which the deer came to drink.

It was a dense forest through which he was pressing his way. In places it was so dense he was compelled to part the underbrush with his hands. Centuries of summer suns had warmed the tops of the same noble oaks and pines, sending their heat even to the roots. Though the early frosts of October had stricken many a leaf from its parent stem, enough still remained to obscure the vision at a rod's distance.

Night was approaching, and John Louder, brave as he was to natural danger, had a strange dread of shadows and the unreal.

He pressed his way through the wood, until a spot almost clear of timber was in sight. This little area, which afforded a good view of the sky, although it was pretty well filled with dead trees, lay between two of those high hills or low mountains into which the whole surface of the adjacent country was broken.

2

Dashing aside the bushes and brambles of the swamp, the forester burst into the area with an exclamation of delight.

"One can breathe here! There is the lake to which the deer come to drink. Now, if Satan send not a witch to lead my bullets astray, perchance I may have a venison ere an hour has passed."

He gathered some dry sticks of wood and, with his flint and steel, quickly kindled a fire.

His fire was to keep off the mosquitoes, which were tormenting in that locality. The fire did not alarm the deer, for they had seen the woods burn so often that they would go quite close to a blaze.

Hardly had he lighted his fire, when he was startled by the tramp of feet near, and a moment later a horseman rode out of the woods and drew rein before him.

Louder was surprised, but by no means alarmed. A man in the forest was by no means uncommon, yet he felt a little curious to know why he was there. He reasoned that probably the fellow had lost his way, and had been attracted by his camp fire; but the stranger's question dispelled that delusion.

"Are you John Louder?" he asked.

"Yes."

"You live at Salem?"

"I do."

"Are you a Protestant?"

"I am."

"You do not believe in the transubstantiation of the body and blood of Christ into the bread and wine of the Sacrament?"

John Louder, who was a true Puritan and a hater of the Papists, quickly responded:

"I do not hold to any such theology."

"Nor do you believe in the infallibility of the pope?"

"I believe no such doctrine."

"Then there can be no doubt that you are a true Protestant."

"I am," Louder answered with no small degree of pride.

"So much the better."

The stranger dismounted from his horse and slipped his left hand through the rein, allowing the tired beast to graze, while with his right hand he began searching in his pockets for something.

"Would you have a Catholic king?" he asked while searching his pockets.

"No."

"You prefer a Protestant."

"I do."

"I knew it," and he continued, "King Charles is nearing his end. But a few months more must see the last of this monarch, and then we will have another. The great question which appeals to the heart of every Englishman to-day is, shall it be a Protestant or a Catholic?"

"A Protestant!" cried John Louder, in his bigoted enthusiasm.

"Then, John Louder, it behooves the English people to speak their minds at once, lest they have fastened upon them a monarch who will wrench from them their religious liberties."

Louder was wondering what the man could mean when the stranger suddenly took from his pocket a book. It was a book with a red back, as could be seen from the fire-light. The stranger drew from another pocket a pen and an ink horn and, in a voice which was solemn and impressive, said:

"Sign!"

John Louder was astonished at the request, or command, whichever it might be, and mechanically stretched out his hand to take the book. At this moment the camp-fire suddenly flamed up, and he afterward averred that the face of the stranger was suddenly changed to that of a devil, and from his burning orbs there issued blue jets of flame, while the whole air was permeated with sulphur. With a yell of horror, he started back, crying:

"Take it away! take away your book! I will not sign! I will not sign!"

"Sign it, and I promise you a Protestant king."
"Away! begone! The whole armor of God be
between me and you."

Quaking with superstitious dread, Louder sank

SEIZING A FIREBRAND, HE SEARCHED FOR THE PRINT OF A
CLOVEN HOOF.

down upon the ground and buried his face in his
hands. For several minutes he remained thus

trembling with fear, and when he finally recovered sufficiently to raise his eyes, the stranger was gone.

He and his horse had vanished, and John Louder, seizing a firebrand, searched the ground for the print of a cloven foot. He found it and, snatching up his rifle, ran home as rapidly as he could. It was late that night when he reached his house and, rapping on the door, called:

"Good-wife! Good-wife, awake and let me in!"

"John Louder, wherefore came you so early, when I thought you had gone to stalk the deer and would not come before morning?"

"I have seen him!"

"Whom have you seen?"

"The man with the book."

This announcement produced great consternation in the mind of good-wife Louder. To have seen the man with the book was an evil omen, and to sign this book was the loss of one's eternal soul.

"Did you sign it, John?" she asked.

"No."

"God be praised!"

were fined and imprisoned for contempt of court, in wearing their hats in the presence of that body. At this time William Penn was only twenty-four years of age.

A great many Friends had emigrated to America, and two had become proprietors of New Jersey. The first event that drew Penn's particular attention to America was when he was called upon to act as umpire between the two Quaker proprietors of New Jersey. Having the New World thus thrust upon his attention, the young convert to the new religion began to look with longing eyes across the Atlantic for a home for himself and his persecuted brethren. Shortly afterward, he ob-

WILLIAM PENN.

tained from the crown a charter for a vast territory beyond the Delaware. This charter was given in payment of a debt of eighty thousand dollars due to his father from the government. The charter was perpetual proprietorship given to him and his heirs, in the fealty of an annual payment of two beaver skins. In honor of his Welch ancestry, Penn proposed calling the domain "New Wales;"

but for some reason the secretary of state ob-
jected.

Penn, while endeavoring to think up an appropriate title, suggested that Sylvania would be an
appropriate name for such a woody country. The
secretary who drew up the charter, on the impulse
of the moment, prefixed the name of Penn to Sylvania in the document. William Penn protested
against the use of his name, as he had no ambition
to be thus distinguished, and offered to pay the
secretary if he would leave it out. This he refused
to do, and Penn next appealed to the king—"the
merric King Charlie," who insisted that the province should be called Pennsylvania, in honor of
his dead friend the admiral. Thus Pennsylvania
received its name. The territory included in
William Penn's charter extended north from New
Castle in Delaware three degrees of latitude and
five degrees of longitude west from the Delaware
River. William Penn was empowered to ordain all
laws with the consent of the freemen, subject to the
approval of the king. No taxes were to be raised
save by the provincial assembly, and permission
was given to the clergymen of the Anglican church
to reside within the province without molestation.

The charter for Pennsylvania was granted in
March 14, 1681, and on the following May, Penn
sent William Markham, a relative, to take posses-

sion of his province and act as deputy governor. A large number of emigrants in the employ of the "company of free traders" who had purchased lands in Pennsylvania of the proprietor, went with him. These settled near the Delaware and "builded and planted."

With the assistance of Algernon Sidney, a sturdy republican, who soon after perished on the scaffold for his views on personal liberty, Penn drew up a code of laws for the government of the colony, that were wise, liberal and benevolent, and next year sent them to the settlers in Pennsylvania for their approval.

William Penn soon discovered that his colony was liable to suffer for the want of sea-board room. He coveted Delaware for that purpose, and resolved if possible to have it. This territory, however, was claimed by Lord Baltimore as a part of Maryland, and for some time had been a matter of dispute between him and the Duke of York. For the sake of peace, the latter offered to purchase the territory of Baltimore; but the baron would not sell it. Penn then assured the Duke that Lord Baltimore's claim was "against law, civil and common." The duke gladly assented to the opinion, and the worldly-wise Quaker obtained from his grace a quit-claim deed for the territory, now comprising the whole of the State of Delaware.

As soon as William Penn had accomplished his purpose, he made immediate preparations for going to America, and within a week after the bargain was officially settled, he sailed in the ship *Welcome*, with one hundred emigrants, in August, 1682. Many of his emigrants died from small-pox on the voyage; but with the remainder he arrived, early in November, at New Castle, where he found almost a thousand emigrants. In addition to these, there were about three thousand old settlers— Swedes, Dutch, Huguenots, Germans and English —enough to form the material for the solid foundation of a State.

There Penn received from the agent of the Duke of York, and in the presence of all the people, a formal surrender of all that fine domain. The Dutch had long before conquered and absorbed the Swedes on the Delaware, and the English in turn had conquered the Dutch, and it was by virtue of his charter, giving him a title to all New Netherland, that the duke claimed the territory as his own. The transfer inherited for Penn and his descendants a dispute with the proprietors of Maryland, which might seem incompatible with the views of Quakers. William Penn, in honor of the duke, attempted to change the name of Cape Henlopen to Cape James; but geography is sometimes arbitrary and refuses to change at will of rulers, and Henlopen and May preserve their original names given them by the Dutch.

It was the earliest days in November when William Penn, with a few friends, set out in an open boat and journeyed up the river to the beautiful bank, fringed with pine trees, on which the city of Philadelphia was soon to rise.

On this occasion was made that famous treaty with the Indians, with which every school-boy is acquainted. Beneath a huge elm at Shakamaxon, on the northern edge of Philadelphia, William Penn, surrounded by a few friends, in the habiliments of peace, met the numerous delegations of the Lenni-Lenape tribes. The great treaty was not for the purchase of lands; but, confirming what Penn had written and Markham covenanted, its sublime purpose was the recognition of the equal rights of humanity, under the shelter of the forest trees, barren of leaves from the effects of the early frosts. Penn proclaimed to the men of the Algonkin race, from both banks of the Delaware, from the borders of the Schuylkill, and, it may have been, even from the Susquehannah, the same simple message of peace and love which George Fox had professed before Cromwell, and which Mary Fisher had borne to the Grand Turk. He argued that the English and the Indian should respect the same moral law, should be alike secure in their

pursuits and their possessions, and should adjust
every difference by a peaceful tribunal, to be com-
posed of an equal number of wise and discreet men
from each race. Penn said:

"We meet on the broad pathway of good faith
and good-will. No advantage will be taken on
either side; but all shall be openness and love. I
will not call you children, for parents sometimes
chide their children too severely, nor brothers only,
for brothers differ. The friendship between me
and you, I will not compare to a chain, for that
rains might rust, or the falling tree might break.
We are the same as if one man's body were divided
into two parts. We are all one flesh and blood."

The sincerity of the speaker, as well as his sacred
doctrine, touched the hearts of the forest children,
and they renounced their guile and their revenge.
The presents which Penn offered were received in
sincerity, and with hearty friendship they gave the
belt of wampum.

"We will live," said they, "in love with William
Penn and his children, as long as the moon and the
sun shall endure."

Mr. Bancroft says: "This agreement of peace
and friendship was made under the open sky, by
the side of the Delaware, with the sun and river
and the forest for witnesses. It was not confirmed
by an oath; it was not ratified by signatures and

seals; no record of the conference can be found, and its terms and conditions had no abiding inscription but on the heart. There they were written like the law of God. The simple sons of the wilderness, returning to their wigwams, kept the history of the covenant by strings of wampum, and, long afterward, in their cabins, would count over the shells on a clean piece of bark and recall to their own memory and repeat to their children or to the stranger the words of William Penn. New England had just terminated a disastrous war of extermination. The Dutch were scarcely ever at peace with the Algonkins. The laws of Maryland refer to Indian hostilities and massacres, which extended as far as Richmond. Penn came without arms; he declared his purpose to abstain from violence; he had no message but peace, and not a drop of Quaker blood was shed in his time by an Indian.

"Was there not progress from Melendez to Roger Williams? from Cortez and Pizarro to William Penn? The Quakers, ignorant of the homage which their virtues would receive from Voltaire and Raynal, men so unlike themselves, exulted in the consciousness of their humanity. 'We have done better,' said they truly, 'than if, with the proud Spaniards, we had gained the mines of Potosi. We may make the ambitious heroes, whom the world admires, blush for their shameful vic-

3

tories.   To the poor, dark souls around about us we teach their rights as men.'"

After the treaty, Penn again journeyed through New Jersey to New York and Long Island, visiting friends and preaching with his usual fervor and earnestness.   Then he returned to the Delaware, and, on the seventh day of November, he went to Uplands (now Chester), where he met the first provincial assembly of his province.   There he made known his benevolent designs toward all men, civilized and savage, and excited the love and reverence of all hearers.   The assembly tendered their grateful acknowledgment to him, and the Swedes authorized one of their number to say to him in their name that they "would live, serve and obey him with all they had," declaring that it was "the best day they ever saw."   He informed the assembly of the union of the "territories" (as Delaware was called) with his province, and received their congratulations.   Then and there was laid the foundation for the great commonwealth of Pennsylvania.

One matter still remained to be adjusted, and that was some satisfactory arrangement with the third Lord Baltimore, concerning the boundary lines.   This at last having been amicably adjusted, Penn went up the Delaware in an open boat to Wicaco, to attend the founding of a city, to which allusion had been made in his concessions in 1681. Before his arrival in America, Penn had thought of this city he was to found, and resolved to give it the name of Philadelphia—a Greek word signifying brotherly love—as a token of the principles in which he intended to govern his province.

Near a block-house constructed by the Swedes, but which had since been converted into a church, he purchased lands extending from the high banks of the Delaware, fringed with pines, to those of the Schuylkill. There his surveyor laid out the city of Philadelphia upon a plan which would embrace about twelve square miles.

The surveyor who aided William Penn in laying out Philadelphia was Thomas Holme. It was at the close of the year 1682, that the town was surveyed, and the boundaries of the streets marked on the trunks of the chestnut, walnut, locust, spruce, pine and other forest trees covering the land. Many of the streets were named for the forest monarchs on which these inscriptions were cut, and still bear the names. The growth of the town was rapid, and, within a year after the surveyor had finished this work, almost a hundred houses had been erected there, and the Indians daily came with the fruits of the chase as presents for "Father Penn," as they delighted to call the proprietor.

In the following March, the new city was honored

by the gathering there of the second assembly of the province, when Penn offered to the people, through their representatives a new charter. The new charter was so liberal in all its provisions, that when he asked the question:

"Shall we accept the new constitution or adhere to the old one?" they voted in a body to accept the new charter, and became at once a representative republican government, with free religious toleration, with justice, for its foundation, and the proprietor, unlike those of other provinces, surrendered to the people his chartered rights in the appointment of officers. From the beginning, the happiness and prosperity of his people appeared to be uppermost in the heart and mind of William Penn. It was this happy relation between the proprietor and the people, and the security against Indian raids, that made Pennsylvania far outstrip her sister colonies in rapidity of settlement and permanent prosperity.

It was late in 1682 that a small house was erected on the site of Philadelphia for the use of Penn, and only a few years ago it was still standing between Front and Second Streets, occupied by Letitia Court.

There he assisted in fashioning those excellent laws which gave a high character to Pennsylvania from the beginning. Among other wise provisions was a board of arbitrators called peace-makers, who were to adjust all difficulties and thus prevent lawsuits. The children were all taught some useful trade. When factors wronged their employees, they were to make satisfaction and one-third over. All causes for irreligion and vulgarity were to be suppressed, and no man was to be molested for his religious opinions. It was also decreed that the days of the week and the months of the year "shall be called as in Scripture, and not by heathen names (as are vulgarly used), as ye First, Second and Third months of ye year, beginning with ye day called Sunday, and ye month called March," thus beginning the year, as of old, with the first spring month. Pennsylvania was first divided into three counties—Bucks, Chester and Philadelphia, and the annexed territories were also divided into three counties—New Castle, Kent and Sussex—known for a long time afterward as the "Three Lower Counties on the Delaware."

Penn returned to England in the summer of 1684, leaving the government of the province during his absence to five members of the council, of which Thomas Lloyd, the president, held the great seal. William Penn's mission in America had been one of success. In 1685, Philadelphia contained six hundred houses; schools were established, and William Bradford had set up a printing press. He printed his "Almanac for the year of the Christian's Account, 1687," a broadside, or single sheet, with twelve compartments, the year beginning with March.

William Penn could look with no little degree of pride upon his work. If ever man was justified in being proud, he was. Looking upon the result of his work, he, with righteous exultation, wrote to Lord Halifax, "I must, without vanity, say I have led the greatest colony into America that ever man did upon private credit, and the most prosperous beginnings that ever were in it are to be found among us."

Penn bade the colonists farewell, with the brightest hopes for the future, saying, "My love and my life are to and with you, and no water can quench it, nor distance bring it to an end. I have been with you, cared for you, and served you with unfeigned love, and you are beloved of me and dear to me beyond utterance. I bless you in the name and power of the Lord, and may God bless you with his righteousness, peace and plenty all the land over." Then of Philadelphia, the apple of the noble Quaker's eye, he said, "And thou, Philadelphia, the virgin settlement of this province, my soul prays to God for thee, that thou mayest stand in the day of trial, and that thy children may be blessed."

given. The people of the territories or three lower counties were still restive under the forced union with Pennsylvania, and Penn made provisions for their permanent separation in legislation, in 1702, and the first independent legislature in Delaware was assembled at New Castle in 1703. Although Philadelphia and Delaware ever afterward continued to have separate legislatures, they were under the same government until the Revolution in 1776.

Shortly after Penn's arrival in America, he received tidings that measures were pending before the privy council, for bringing all of the proprietary governments under the crown. Penn located in Philadelphia, declaring it his intention to live and die there. He erected an excellent brick house on the corner of Second Street and Norris Alley.

Disparaging news from his native land determined him to return to England, which he did in 1701, where he succeeded in setting matters to rights. He never returned to America. Harassed and wearied by business connected with his province, he was making arrangements in 1712 to sell it for sixty thousand dollars, when he was prostrated with paralysis. He survived the first shock six years, though he never fully recovered, then he died, leaving his estates in America to his three sons. His family governed Pennsylvania, as proprietors, until the Revolution made it an independent State, in 1776. During that time the great province of Pennsylvania had borne its share of troubles with the French and Indians.

CHAPTER III.

Heaven from all creatures hides the book of fate,
All but the page prescribed, their present state:
From brutes what men, from men what spirits know ;
Or who could suffer being here below?
The lamb thy riot dooms to bleed to-day,
Had he thy reason, would he skip and play?
Pleased to the last, he crops the flowery food,
And licks the hand just raised to shed his blood.

—POPE.

THAT which was most dreaded in New England and all the American colonies came· to pass. Charles II. died, and his brother James, Duke of York, was crowned King of England. On ascending the throne, the very first act of James II. was one of honest but imprudent bigotry. Incapable of reading the signs of the times, or fully prepared to dare the worst that those signs could portend, James immediately sent his agent Caryl to Rome, to apologize to the pope for the long and flagrant heresy of England, and to endeavor to procure the re-admission of the English people into the com-

43

munion of the Catholic Church. The pope was
more politic than the king and returned him a very
cool answer, implying that before he ventured upon
so arduous an enterprise as that of changing the
professed faith of nearly his entire people, he would
do well to sit down and calculate the cost.

The foolish king, who stopped at nothing, not
even the mild rebuke of the holy father, would
not open his eyes, and as a natural result he was
soon cordially hated by nearly all his subjects.
His brother had left an illegitimate son called the
Duke of Monmouth, who was encouraged to attempt
to seize the throne of his uncle. At first the cause
of the duke seemed prosperous. His army swelled
from hundreds to thousands; but, owing to his lack
of energy and fondness for pleasure, he delayed
and gave the royal armies time to recruit. He was
attacked at Sedgemore, near Bridgewater, and,
owing to the perfidity or cowardice of Gray, his
cavalry general, the rebels were defeated. Monmouth was captured, and his uncle ordered him
beheaded, which was done.

Then commenced the most barbarous punishment
of rebels ever known. An officer named Kirk
was sent by the king to hunt down the Monmouth
rebels, or those sympathizing with them. His
atrocious deeds would fill a volume, and are so
revolting as to seem incredible. Another brutal

ruffian of the time was Judge Jeffries. The judicial ermine has often been disgraced by prejudiced judges; but Jeffries was the worst monster that ever sat on the bench. He hung men with as much relish as did Berkeley of Virginia. His term was called the "bloody assizes," and to this day the name of Judge Jeffries is applied in reproach to the scandalous ruling of a partial judiciary.

The accession of James II. made fewer changes in the American colonies than was anticipated. Perhaps, had his reign been longer, the changes would have been greater. The suppression of Monmouth's rebellion gave to the colonies many useful citizens. Men connect themselves, in the eyes of posterity, with the objects in which they take delight. James II. was inexorable toward his brother's favorites. Monmouth was beheaded, and the triumph of legitimacy was commemorated by a medal, representing the heads of Monmouth and Argyle on an altar, their bleeding bodies beneath, with the following: "Sic aras et sceptra tuemur." ("Thus we defend our altars and our throne.")

"Lord chief justice is making his campaign in the west," wrote James II. to one in Europe, referring to Jeffries' circuit for punishing the insurgents. "He has already condemned several hundreds, some of whom we are already executed,

more are to be, and the others sent to the plantations." The prisoners condemned to transportation
were a salable commodity. Such was the demand
for labor in America that convicts and laborers
were regularly purchased and shipped to the colonies
where they were sold as indented servants. The
courtiers round James II. exulted in the rich harvest which the rebellion promised, and begged of
the monarch frequent gifts of their condemned
countrymen. Jeffries heard of the scramble, and
indignantly addressed the king:

"I beseech your majesty, that I inform you, that
each prisoner will be worth ten pound, if not fifteen
pound, apiece, and, sir, if your majesty orders
these as you have already designed, persons that
have not suffered in the service will run away with
the booty." Under this appeal of the lord chief
justice the spoils were divided and his honor was
in part gratified. Many of the convicts were persons of family and education, and were accustomed
to ease and elegance.

"Take all care," wrote the monarch, under the
countersign of Sunderland, to the government in
Virginia, "take all care that they continue to serve
for ten years at least, and that they be not permitted in any manner to redeem themselves by
money or otherwise, until that term be fully expired. Prepare a bill for the assembly of our

colony, with such clauses as shall be requisite for this purpose."

No legislature in any of the American colonies seconded such malice, for the colonies were never in full accord with James II. Tyranny and injustice peopled America with men nurtured to suffering and adversity. The history of our colonization is the history of the crimes of Europe, and some of the best families in America are descended from the indented servants of the Old World.

In Bristol, kidnapping had become common, and not only felons, but young persons of birth and education were hurried across the Atlantic and sold for money.

Never did a king prove a greater tyrant or more inhuman and cruel than James II. After the insurrection of Monmouth had been suppressed, all the sanguinary excesses of despotic revenge were revived. Gibbets were erected in villages to intimidate the people, and soldiers were intrusted with the execution of the laws. Scarce a Presbyterian family in Scotland, but was involved in proscription or penalties. The jails were overflowed, and their tenants were sent as slaves to the colonies. Maddened by the succession of murders; driven from their homes to caves, from caves to morasses and mountains; death brought to the inmates of a house that should shelter them; death to the bene-

factor that should throw them food; death to the
friend that listened to their complaint; death to
the wife or parent that still dared to solace husband
or son; ferreted out by spies; hunted with dogs;—
the fanatics turned upon their pursuers, and threatened to retaliate on the men who should still continue to imbrue their hands in blood. The council
retorted by ordering a massacre. He that would
not take the oath should be executed, though un-
armed, and the recusants were shot on the roads,
or as they labored in the field, or stood at prayer.
To fly was admission of guilt; to excite suspicion
was sentence of death; to own the covenant was
treason.

Sometimes the lot of an indented slave was a
happy one. Hundreds and thousands of fugitives
flying from persecution came to the New World,
while thousands of others were sent as convicts.

Virginia received her share of the latter.

One bright spring morning a ship from England
entered the James River with a number of these indented slaves to be sold to the planters. Notice had
been given of the intended sale and many planters
came to look at the poor wretches huddled together
like so many beasts in an old shed, and guarded by
soldiers. Mr. Thomas Hull, a planter of considerable means, and a man noted for his iron will, was
among those who came to make purchases.

"Well, Thomas, have you looked over the lot?" asked another planter.

"No, Bradley, have you?"

"Yes, though I am shortened in money, and unable to purchase to-day."

"Well, Bradley, what have you seen among them?"

"There are many fine, lusty fellows; but I was most interested and grieved in one."

"Why?"

"He is a man who has known refinement and ease, is perchance thirty-five and has with him a child."

"A child?"

"Yes, a maid not to exceed ten years, but very beautiful with her golden hair and soft blue eyes."

"Is the child a slave?"

"No."

"Then wherefore is it here?" asked Hull.

"His is truly a pathetic story as I have heard it. It seems he was a widower with his child wandering about the country, when he fell in with some of the Duke of Monmouth's people and enlisted. He was captured at Sedgemore, and condemned by Jeffries. The child was left to wander at will; but by some means she accompanied her father, managed to smuggle herself on shipboard, and was not discovered until the vessel was well out to sea. Then

4

the captain, who was a humane man, permitted them to remain together to the end of the voyage. She is with her father now, and a prettier little maid I never saw."

"By the mass! I will go and see her," cried Hull. "If she be all you say, I will buy them both."

"But she is not for sale."

"Wherefore not?"

"She was not adjudged by the court."

With the cold, heartless laugh of a natural tyrant, Hull answered:

"It will be all the same. He who purchases the father will have the maid also."

He went to the place where the slaves were confined and gazed on the lot, very much as a cattle dealer might look upon a herd he contemplated purchasing. His gaze soon fastened on a fine, manly person in whose proud eye the sullen fires were but half subdued. He stood with his arms folded across his broad chest and his eye fixed upon a beautiful girl at his side.

The captive spoke not. A pair of handcuffs were on his wrists, and the chains came almost to the ground; but slavery and chains could not subdue the proud captive.

Hull delighted in punishing those whom he disliked. He was a papist at heart and consequently in sympathy with James II., so for this indented slave he incurred from the very first a most bitter dislike. When the slave was brought forth to be sold, he bid twelve pounds for him. This was two pounds more than the required price, and he became the purchaser.

"You are mine," cried Hull to the servant. "Come with me." The father turned his great brown eyes dim with moisture upon his child, and Hull, interpreting the look, added, "Hold, I will buy the maid also."

"She cannot be sold," the officer in charge of the slaves answered, "unless the master of the ship sees fit to sell her for passage money."

The master of the ship was present and declared he would do nothing of the kind.

"I will take her back to England, if she wishes to return," he added.

The child was speechless, her great blue eyes fixed on her father.

"What will you do with the maid?" asked Hull, who, having the father, felt sure the child would follow.

"I will return her to England free of charge, if she wills it."

"Who will care for her there?" asked Hull. "Do you know her relatives?"

"No; all are strangers to me."

The father, with his proud breast heaving with tumultuous emotion, stood silently gazing on the scene. He was a slave and he remembered that a slave must not speak unless permission be granted him by his master; but it was his child, the only link that bound him to earth, whose fate they were to decide, and, had he been unfettered, he might have clasped her to his bosom.

"Speak with the maid," suggested a by-stander, "and see if she has a friend in England who will care for her."

The master of the ship went to the bewildered child and, taking her little hand in his broad palm, said:

"Sweet little maid, you are not afraid to trust me?"

She turned her great blue eyes up to him and, in a whisper, answered:

"I am not."

"Have you a mother?"

"No."

"Have you any friends in England?"

"None, since my father came away."

"Where did you live before your father enlisted in the army of Monmouth?"

"We travelled; we lived at no one place."

"Have you no friends or relatives in England?"

"None."

The captain then asked permission to talk with
the father. The permission was given by Hull,
for he saw that his slave had the sympathy of all
present, and it would not be safe to refuse him
some privileges. The master of the vessel and the
magistrate who had superintended the selling of
the slaves for the crown found the slave a very intelligent gentleman. He said he had but one relative living so far as he knew. He had a brother
who had come to America two or three years before; but he had not heard from him, and he might
be dead.

"Do you know any one in England to whom
your child could be sent?"

"I do not."

"What were you doing before you entered the
duke's army?"

"I was a strolling player," the man answered,
his fine tragic eyes fixed firmly on the officers.
"My company had reached a town one day, in
which we were to play at night, and just as I was
getting ready to go to the theatre, the Duke of
Monmouth entered. He was on his way to Sedgemore, and I was forced to join him. My child
followed on foot and watched the battle as it raged.
When it was over I could have escaped, had I not
come upon Cora, who was seeking me. I took
her up in my arms and was hurrying away, when

the cavalry of the enemy overtook me and I was
made a prisoner."

The simple story made an impression on all who
heard it save the obdurate master. The magistrate
asked the slave what he would have done with his
child.

"Let her stay in the colony until my term of
service is ended, then I will labor to remunerate
any who would keep her."

At this Hull said he would take the maid, and
she might always be near the father. All who
knew Hull looked with suspicion on the proposition.

A new-comer had arrived on the scene. This
was a young man of about the same age as the
prisoner. He was a wealthy Virginian named
Robert Stevens, noted for his kindness of heart and
charity. He did not arrive on the scene until after
the indented slave had been sold; but he soon heard
the story of the captive from Sedgemore and his
child. Robert Stevens' heart at once went out to
these unfortunates, and he resolved on a scheme to
make the father practically free.

"Has the slave been sold?" he asked.

"He has, and I am the purchaser," answered
Hull.

"How much did you give for him?"

"Twelve pounds."

"I will give fifty."

"He is already sold," repeated Hull exultingly. He despised Robert Stevens for his wealth and popularity. To have purchased a slave whom Robert Stevens wanted, was great glory for Hull.

"Fear not, good man," said Robert to the unfortunate slave. "I have money enough to purchase your freedom."

Unfortunately those words fell on the ears of Thomas Hull, and he answered:

"It is the order of the king that all serve their term out, and none be allowed to purchase their freedom."

"I will give you one hundred pounds for the slave," cried Robert.

"No."

"A thousand!"

"Robert Stevens, for some reason you want this slave restored to liberty."

"No. Sell him to me, and he shall serve out his term."

"I understand your plan. You would make his servitude a luxury. You cannot have the slave for a hundred times the sum you offer. By law, the convict is fairly mine until he hath fully served his term. I am not so heartless as you deem me. His child can go to my house, where she will be cared for."

"No, no, no!" cried the captive, his eyes turned

appealingly to Robert Stevens. "You take her; you take her. Go with him, Cora."

The child sprang to the side of Robert Stevens, for already she had come to dread the man who was her father's master. Hull's face was black with rage. He bit his lips, but said nothing. With his slave, he hurried home.

The name of the slave was George Waters, and he was soon to learn the weight of a master's hand.

Thomas Hull was the owner of negro slaves, as well as white indented servants, and he made no distinction between them. George Waters, proud, noble as he was, was set to work with the filthy negroes in the tobacco fields. The half-savage barbarians, with their ignorance and naturally low instincts, were intended to humiliate the refined gentleman.

"You is one of us," said a negro. "What am your name?"

"George Waters."

"George—George, dat am my name, too," said the negro, leaning on his hoe. "D'ye suppose we is brudders?"

"No."

"Well, why is we bofe called George?"

"I don't know."

The overseer came along at this moment and threatened them with the lash, if they did not cease talking and attend to their work. Again and again was the proud George Waters subjected to indignities, until he could scarcely restrain himself from knocking Martin, his overseer, down, and selling his life in the defence of his liberty; but he remembered Cora, and resolved to bear taunts and indignities for her sake, until his term of service was ended. His only comfort was that his child was well cared for.

He had been a year and a half on the upper plantation of Thomas Hull, and though he had demeaned himself well, and had done the labor of two ordinary men—though he had never uttered a word of complaint, no matter what burdens were laid upon him, his natural pride and nobility of character won the hatred of the overseer. The fellow had a violent temper and hated George Waters.

One day, from no provocation at all, he threatened to beat Waters. The servant snatched the whip from his hand and said:

"I would do you no harm, sir. I have always performed my tasks to the best of my ability, and never have I complained; but if you so much as give me one stroke, I will kill you."

There was fire in his eye and an earnestness in his voice, which awed the cowardly overseer; but at the same time they increased his hatred. He

resolved to be revenged, and reported to Hull that
the slave was rebellious.   Hull permitted George
Waters to be tied to a tree by four stout negroes,
whose barbarous natures delighted in such work,
and the overseer laid a whip a dozen times about
his bare shoulders.   No groan escaped his lips.
For three days he lay about his miserable lodge
waiting for his wounds to heal, and meanwhile
made up his mind to fly from the colony.

He had heard that a society of Friends, or
Quakers, had formed a colony to the north, which
was called Pennsylvania; and he knew that they
would succor a slave.   As soon as he was well
enough, he stole from a cabin a gun, a knife and
some ammunition, and set out in the night to find
the plantation of Robert Stevens, where Cora was.
His escape was discovered and the overseer, with
Thomas Hull, set out in hot pursuit of the fugitive.
At dawn of day they came in sight of him in the
forest on the Lower James River and, being on
horseback, gave chase. ·

"Keep away! keep back!" cried the fugitive,
"or I will not answer for the consequences," and
he brandished his gun in the air.   The overseer
was armed with pistols and, drawing one, galloped
up to within a hundred paces of the fugitive and
fired, but missed.   Quick as thought, George
Waters raised his gun and, taking aim at the breast

of his would-be slayer, shot him dead from the
saddle.

The body fell to the ground, and the frightened
horse wheeled about and ran away. Thomas Hull,
who was a coward, awed by the fate of his overseer, turned and fled as rapidly as his horse could
go.

Horrified at what he had done, and knowing
that death, sure and swift, would follow his cap-
ture, George Waters turned and fled down the
James River. Some guardian angel guided his
footsteps, for he found himself one night, almost
starved, faint and weak, at the plantation of Robert
Stevens. George was driven to desperate straits
when he accosted the wealthy planter and asked
for food. Robert recognized him as the father of
the little maid whom he had taken to his home
as one of his family.

"I have heard all; you must not be seen," said
Robert. Then he conducted him to an apartment
of his large manor house. "Are you hungry?"

"I am starving."

Robert brought him food with his own hands
and, as he ate, asked:

"Do you want to see Cora?"

"May I?"

"Yes."

"I am a slave and a—a——"

"I know what you would say.   Do not say it, for you slew only in self-defence."

"But I will be hanged if found."

"You shall not be found.   Heaven help me, if I shield a real criminal from justice; but he who strikes a blow for liberty is worthy of aid."

After the fugitive had in a measure satisfied his hunger, Robert said:

"You will need sleep and rest, after which you must prepare for a long journey."

"Whither shall I go?"

"To Massachusetts.   I have relatives in Salem, where you will be safe."

"Safe!"

He repeated the word as if it were a glorious dream—a vision never to be realized.

"Yes, you will be safe; but as you must make the journey through a vast forest, you will need to be refreshed by rest and food."

The wild-eyed fugitive, with his face haggard as death, seized the arm of his benefactor and said:

"They will come and slay me as I sleep."

"Fear not, my unfortunate brother, for I will put you in a chamber where none save myself shall know of you."

"And my child?"

"She shall accompany you to Salem."

The fugitive said no more.   He entrusted everything to the man who had promised to save him. He was led up two flights of stairs, when they came to a ladder reaching to an attic, and they went up this attic ladder to a chamber, where there was a narrow bed, with soft, clean sheets and pillows, the first the prisoner had seen in the New World.

"You can sleep here in perfect security," said Robert. "I will see that you are not molested by any one."

The wayworn traveller threw himself on the bed and fell asleep.

Stevens went below and told his wife of the fugitive. Ester Stevens was the daughter of General Goffe, the regicide, who had been hunted for years by Charles II., for signing the death warrant of the king's father and serving in the army of Oliver Cromwell, and Mrs. Stevens could sympathize with a political fugitive. They ran some risk in keeping him in their house; but as a majority of the colonists had been in sympathy with the Duke of Monmouth, for James II. had few friends in Virginia and Thomas Hull none, their risk was not as great as it might seem.

The fugitive late next day awoke, and Robert carried his breakfast to him. The colony was wild with excitement over the escape of an indented slave and the killing of the overseer. Thomas

Hull represented the crime to be as heinous as possible, to arouse a sympathy for himself and a hatred for the escaped slave. Some people were outspoken in the belief that the escaped slave should be killed; others were in sympathy with him. They reasoned that Hull had been a hard master, and that this poor fellow was no criminal, but a patriot, for which he had been adjudged to ten years' penal servitude.

Many of the searchers came to the mansion house of Stevens; but he managed to put them off the track.

For five days and nights George Waters remained in the attic. On the sixth night Robert Stevens came to him and said:

"You must now set out on your journey."

"But Cora—can I see her?"

"She will accompany you. Here is a suit of clothes more befitting one of your rank and station, than the garb of an indented slave." He placed a riding suit with top boots and hat in the apartment. When he had attired himself, Robert next brought him some arms, a splendid gun and a brace of pistols of the best make.

"You may have need of these," said the planter. "You will also find holsters in the saddle."

"And does Cora know of this?"

"I have told her all."

The father shuddered. In the pride of his soul, he remembered that he was a slave, had felt the lash, and was humiliated.

Under a wide-spreading chestnut near the planter's mansion, stood three horses ready saddled. A faithful negro slave was holding them, and the little maid, clothed for a long journey, awaited her father's arrival. A fourth horse was near on which were a pack of provisions and a small camping outfit.

The father and child met and embraced in silence, and, had she not felt a tear on her face, she would hardly have known that he was so greatly agitated.

"We will mount and be far on the journey before the day dawns," said Robert.

"Do you go with us?" asked George Waters.

"Certainly. I know the country and will guide you beyond danger."

They mounted and travelled all night long. At early dawn, they halted only to refresh themselves with a cold breakfast, and pushed on.

Three days Robert journeyed with them, and then, on the border of Maryland, he halted and told them of a land now within their reach, where the Quakers dwelt. There they might rest until they were able to go to Massachusetts. He gave a purse of gold to the father, saying:

"Take it, and may God be as good to you as he has been to me."

The fugitive murmured out some words of thanks; but his benefactor wheeled his steed about and galloped away, lest the words of gratitude might fall on his ears.

"Let us go on, father," said Cora.

For days, Cora Waters could never tell how long, they journeyed, until at last, on the banks of the Delaware, they came upon a small town where dwelt a people at peace with all the world—the Quakers, and the tired child and her father were taken in, given food and shelter, Christian sympathy, and assured of safety.

CHAPTER IV.

And false the light on glory's plume,
    As fading hues of even,
And Love and Hope, and Beauty's bloom,
Are blossoms gathered for the tomb,—
    There's nothing bright but Heaven.
                                —MOORE.

THE last expiring throe of a mighty superstition
was about to convulse the little society at Salem,
and, as usual in such cases, ignorance and prejudice went hand in hand for the destruction of reason
and humanity. The last of the great religious persecutions was to begin, when eminent divines were
to stand and point with pride to the swaying bodies
of their victims, hanging from the gibbet, and call
them "fire-brands of hell."

In the village of Salem, there was a strife between
Samuel Parris the minister and a part of his people;
a strife so bitter, that it had even attracted the attention of a general court. We all know, even in
these modern days, what a furor can be created in
a church, when a part of the organization is ar-

5   65

rayed against the pastor. Sometimes the divine
shepherd loses his temper and says ugly things
against his flock, and thinks many which he does
not utter.

Parris was a man filled with ambition and prejudice. He was a fanatic and easily driven to frenzy
by opposition. An unfavorable criticism upset his
highly nervous organism, and he set out to find
some proof in the Scriptures for condemning his
enemies. It never entered into his mind to love
those who hated him.

Mr. Parris had lived in the West Indies for several years before going to Salem, and had brought
with him some slaves purchased from the Spaniards.
Among them were two famous in history as John
and Tituba his wife. Historians disagree as to the
nationality of these slaves. Some aver they were
Indians, others call them negroes, while some state
they were half and half. Whatever may have
been their nationality, their practices were the
fetichism of western Africa, and there can be no
doubt that negro blood predominated in their veins.
All their training, their low cunning and beastly
worship, their deception and treachery were utterly
unlike the characteristics of the early aborigines of
America, and were purely African.

John and Tituba were full of the gross superstitions of their people, and were of the frame and

temperament best adapted to the practice of demonology.

In the family of Samuel Parris, his daughter, a child of nine years, and his niece, a girl of less than twelve, began to have strange caprices. During such a state of affairs the pastor actually permitted to be formed, with his own knowledge, a society of young girls between the ages of eight and eighteen to meet at the parsonage, strangely resembling those "circles" of our own time called séances, for spiritualistic revelations. There can be no doubt that the young girls were laboring under a strong nervous and mental excitement, which was encouraged rather than repressed by the means employed by their spiritual director. Instead of treating them as subjects of morbid delusion, Mr. Parris regarded them as victims of external and diabolical influence, and strangely enough this influence, on the evidence of the children themselves, was supposed to be exercised by some of the most pious and respectable people of the community. As it was those who opposed Mr. Parris, who fell under the ban of suspicion, there is room to suspect the reverent Mr. Parris with making a strong effort to gratify his revenge.

Many a child has had its early life blighted and its nerves shattered by a ghost-believing and ghost-story-telling nurse.

No class of people is more superstitious in regard to ghosts and witches than negroes. Whatever fetich ideas may have been among the Indians of the New World, many more were imbibed from the Africans with whom they early came in contact.

Old Tituba was a horrid-looking creature. If ever there was a witch on earth, she was one, and as she crouched in one corner, smoking her clay pipe, her eyes closed, telling her weird stories to the girls, no one can wonder that they were strangely affected.

"Now, chillun, lem me tell ye, dat ef ebber a witch catches ye, and pinches ye, and sticks pins in ye, ye won't see 'em, ye won't see nobody, ye won't see nuffin," said old Tituba.

"What should we do if a witch were to catch us, Tituba?" asked Abigail Williams, the niece of Mr. Parris.

"Dar but one thing to do, chile. Dat am to burn de witch or hang 'em."

"Are there witches now?"

"Yes, dar be plenty. I see 'em ob night. Doan ye nebber see a black man in de night?"

The children were all silent, until one little girl, whose imagination was very vivid, thought she had seen a black man, once.

"When was it?" asked Abigail Williams.

"One night, when I waked out of my sleep, I saw a great black something by my side."

The little blue eyes opened so wide and looked with such earnestness on the assembled children, that there could be no doubting her sincerity.

"Can we catch witches?" Abigail asked Tituba.

"Yes."

"How?"

"Many ways."

Then she proceeded to tell of the various charms by which a witch might be detected, such as drawing the picture of the person accused and stabbing it with a knife of silver, or shooting it with a silver bullet.

"Once, when a witch was in a churn, " continued Tituba, "and no butter would come, den de man, he take some hot water an' pour it in de churn, an' jist den dar come a loud noise like er gun, an' dey see er cloud erbove de churn. Bye um bye, dat cloud turned ter er woman's head an' et war an ole woman wat lib in der neighborhood and war called a witch."

"Is that true, Tituba?" asked one of the little girls.

"It am so, fur er sartin sure fact, chile."

Nothing is more susceptible than a young imagination. It can see whatever it wills, hear whatever is desired, and like wax is ready to receive any impression one chooses to put on it. A child can be made to believe it sees the most unnatural things, and in a few days Tituba and John had thoroughly convinced the children that they saw spirits and witches in the air all about them.

One evening, a pretty young woman, not over twenty-one or two, came to the parsonage, where the witches and ghosts had been holding high revel. She was a brunette with a dark keen eye and hair of jet. Her face was lovely, save when distorted by passion, and her form was faultless.

"Sarah Williams, where have you been, that we have seen nothing of you for a fortnight?" asked Mrs. Parris as the visitor entered the house.

"I have been to Boston, and but just came back yesterday. What strange things have been transpiring since I left?"

At this moment a door opened and Mr. Parris, a tall, pale man, entered from his study. The newcomer, without waiting for the pastor's wife to answer her question, rose and, grasping the hand of her spiritual adviser, cried:

"Mr. Parris, how pale you are! but then I cannot wonder at it, when I consider all I have heard."

"What have you heard, Sarah?" he asked.

"I have heard you are having trouble in your congregation."

"Who told you?"

"The rumor has gone all over the country, even reaching Boston. And they do say that the evil spirits have visited Salem to defame you."

Mr. Parris pressed his thin lips so firmly that the blood seemed to have utterly forsaken them, and his cold gray eye was kindled with a subdued fire, as he answered:

"I am far from insensible that at this extraordinary time of the devil coming down in great wrath upon us, there are too many tongues and hearts thereby set on fire of hell."

"To whom can you trace your troubles?"

"To Goodwife Nurse," answered the pastor. "It is that firebrand of hell who seeks to ruin me."

"I saw Goody Nurse," cried one of the smaller children.

"When?" asked Mr. Parris.

"Last night."

The pastor, the visitor, and the wife exchanged significant glances, and the father asked:

"Where did you see her?"

"She came with the black man to my bed."

"What did she do?"

"She asked me to sign the book."

"What book?"

"I don't know; but it was a red book."

The anxious mother, in a fit of hysterics, seized her child in her arms and cried:

"No, no, no! don't you sign the book and sell
your immortal soul, child!" and she gave way to a
fit of weeping, which unnerved all the children,
who began to howl, as if they were beset by demons.
When the hubbub was at its height, the door to an
adjoining room opened, and Tituba and John stuck
their heads into the room.

"She am dar! she am dar!" cried old Tituba.
"I see her! I see dem bofe!"

"Yes, I see um—see um bofe, Tituba," repeated
John.

"Who do you see?" asked the pastor.

"See de black man and Goody Nurse."

"Where?"

"Dar."

They pointed along the floor, then up the wall
to the ceiling, where they both avowed that they
saw Goodwife Nurse and the black man, or demon, dancing with their heels up and heads down.

The negro clapped his hands, patted his foot on
the floor and cried aloud:

"Doan yer see um, Marster? doan yer see um,
chillun?"

One little girl, who fixed her eyes on a certain
dark corner of the room, thought she could see a
shadow moving on the wall, but was not quite certain.   The pastor was overcome by the presence of
the prince of darkness in his own house, and, fall-

ing on his knees, began to pray. As a natural result, when all minds were directed to one channel, as they were by prayer, the superstitious feeling which possessed them passed away, and the household, which a few moments ago was on the verge of hysteria, became more calm, and when all rose from their knees, Mrs. Parris asked her visitor to spend the evening with them.

"I fain would stay; but I dread the long walk home."

"Samuel will accompany you, unless Charles Stevens comes, as he promised. In case he should, he can go with you."

At the mention of Charles Stevens, the young woman's eyes grew brighter, and her face became crimson.

"Sarah, have you not heard from your husband?" asked the minister.

"No; he is dead."

"Did you never hear of the pinnace?"

"No; but it was no doubt lost."

"How long since he left?"

"A year. He went to New York, was seen to leave that port, and has never been heard from."

"It is sad."

"Verily, it is," and Sarah tried hard to call up a tear, and wiped her eyes with the corner of her apron.

· John and Tituba had retired to their domain, the kitchen, to conjure up more demons and plan further mischief.

Mr. Parris could not keep his mind long from the rebellious members of his flock. "I will be avenged on them," he thought. "Verily, I will be avenged for every pang they have made me suffer."

He had forgotten the command, "Vengeance is mine, I will repay, saith the Lord."

Sarah Williams proceeded to further delve into the trouble with Mr. Parris and his church.

"Is Rebecca Nurse your enemy?" she asked.

"Verily, she is; so is her sister Goodwife Corey."

"Why are they your enemies?"

"They want another pastor, and have done all in their power to ruin me."

"Why do you endure it?" asked Sarah.

"How can I help myself? I retain my charge and shall retain it, despite Goody Nurse."

At this the youngest child said:

"Goody Nurse was at church last Lord's day with a yellow bird."

"A yellow bird?" cried all.

"Yes; I saw a yellow bird fly into the church and light on her shoulder."

Tituba had told the poor deluded child that if

Goodwife Nurse were a witch, she would be accompanied by a yellow bird.

"Surely you saw no yellow bird last Lord's day."

"Verily, I did, and it came first and sat on her shoulder, and then on her knee, and, while father was preaching, it whispered in her ear."

"Could you hear what it said?" asked the pastor.

"No, for I was not near enough."

Then the pastor and his wife and visitor exchanged glances. Foolishly credulous and blindly superstitious, as well as prejudiced, their minds were like the fallow ground ready to receive any impression, however silly.

Before more could be said, there came a rap at the door, and Charles Stevens, the lad who succored the wounded stranger that had so mysteriously disappeared, entered. Charles was almost a man, and bid fair to make a fine-looking fellow. He was tall and muscular, with bold gray eyes and a face open and manly. He had lost none of his mirth, and his merry whistle still shocked some of the staid old Puritans.

As soon as Charles entered, the young widow rose, all blushing, to greet him. She was not more than one or two years his senior, and, being still beautiful, there was a possibility of her entrapping the youth.

· The pastor greeted him warmly and assured him that his visit was most opportune; but he regretted very much that he had not come an hour sooner.

"Wherefore would you have had me come an hour sooner?" asked the merry Charles.

"That you might, with your own eyes, behold some of the wonderful manifestations of the prince of darkness."

With a laugh, Charles answered that such manifestations were too common to merit much comment; but as a matter of course he asked what the manifestations were.

"An example of witchcraft."

At this Charles laughed, and Mr. Parris was shocked at his scepticism.

"Wherefore do you laugh, unregenerated youth?" cried the pastor.

"A witch! I believe there are no witches," he answered.

"Would you believe your eyes, young sceptic?"

"I might even doubt my own eyes."

"Wherefore would you?"

"Nothing is more deceptive than sight; optical delusions are common. Did you see a witch?"

"Not myself; but others did."

"Who?"

"John, Tituba and Ann Parris saw the witches

dancing on the ceiling, with their feet up and their heads down."

At this Charles Stevens again laughed and answered:

"Verily you are mad, Mr. Parris, to believe what those lying negroes say. They have persuaded the child into the belief that she sees strange sights."

Mr. Parris became greatly excited and cried:

"The maid sees the shape of Goody Nurse and the black man at night. They come and choke her, to make her sign the book."

"What book?"

"The devil's book. Do you not remember some time ago a stranger was at your house, who mysteriously disappeared?" Of course Charles remembered. He had never forgotten that mysterious stranger, and often wondered what had been his fate.

"The same shape appeared before John Louder in the forest, where he had gone to stalk deer, and asked him to sign the red book in which is recorded the souls of the damned."

This was the frightful story told by Louder on his return from the night's hunt, and many of the credulous New Englanders believed him. Mr. Parris, having become warmed up on his subject, resumed:

"Charles, Charles, shake off the hard yoke of the devil. Where 'tis said, 'the whole world lies in wickedness,' 'tis by some of the ancients rendered, 'the whole world lies in the devil.' The devil is a prince, yea, the devil is a god unto all the unregenerate, and, alas, there is a whole world of them. Desolate sinner, consider what a horrid lord it is you are enslaved unto, and oh, shake off the slavery of such a lord."

Charles was unprepared for such a sermon, and had no desire to be bored with it, yet he was left without choice in the matter.

The young widow came to his relief and took him off under her protection and soon made him forget that he had ever been rebuked by the parson. Certainly, he had never met a more agreeable person than Sarah Williams. Her husband was a brother of Mrs. Parris, and she wielded a great influence in the minister's family. Gradually she absorbed more and more of Charles Stevens' society, telling him of her recent visit to Boston, and of the latest news from England, inquiring about his mother, and talking only on the subjects which most interested him. He thought her a charming woman.

The hour was late ere they knew it, and Puritanic New England was an enemy to late hours. Sarah declared she must go home.

"Come again, Sarah," said Mrs. Parris.

"I will. Verily, I must go; but see, the moon is down, how dark it is."

Charles was not slower to take the hint than a young man of our own day. Humanity has been the same since Eve first evinced her power over Adam in the garden. Ever since, men have been led by a pretty face often to their ruin. Charles, in a bashful, awkward way, informed the young widow that he was going the same road, and it would not be much out of his way to accompany her to her very door. Of course she was pleased, and Charles and the young widow went away together.

"Have you never learned the fate of your husband, Sarah?" he asked.

"No; poor Samuel is dead," she answered.

"It is sad that you know not his fate. Was he drowned at sea, killed by the Indians, or murdered by the pirates?"

"I know not. I am very lonely now, Charles."

"I pity you."

"Do you?"

"Verily, I do."

"Thank you, Charles."

"Your parents are in Boston, are they not?"

"Yes."

"Do you intend to live always thus alone?"

"Oh, I trust not," and the darkness concealed the sly glance which Sarah cast from her great dark eyes on the unsuspecting youth at her side. The conversation was next changed to Mr. Parris, his quarrel with his flock, and the strange phenomenon developing at his house.

"What think you of it, Charles?"

"It is a sham."

"Oh, no, no! John, the negro man, is bewitched, and has fits."

"A good flogging would very quickly bring him out of his fits."

By this time they had reached the door of Sarah Williams' house. She turned upon the youth and, seizing his arm, in a voice trembling with emotion, said:

"Charles, I beseech of you, as you love life and happiness, do not say aught against Mr. Parris or witchcraft. We stand on the brink of something terrible, and no one knows what the end may be."

As Charles wended his way homeward, he pondered over the strange words of Sarah Williams, and asked himself:

"What does she mean?"

CHAPTER V.

A NIGHT WITH WITCHES.*

As bees bizz out wi' angry fyke
When plundering herds assail their byke,
As open pussies mortal foes,
When, pop! she starts before their nose,
As eager runs the market crowd,
When, "Catch the thief!" resounds aloud,
So Maggie runs, the witches follow,
Wi' monie an eldritch skreech and hollow.
                              —BURNS.

MOST people are. superstitious. In fact, we might put it stronger and say, all people are superstitious. Superstition is natural, and so long as there are great mysteries unrevealed to man, there will be superstition. So long as the great mysteries of life and death and a future existence are shrouded in the unknown, there will be believers in the supernatural. So long as there are powers and forces not understood, they will be attributed to unknown

---

* The incidents narrated in this chapter were gathered from Cotton Mather's "Invisible World," and legends current at the time. Strange as it may seem, these narratives were believed, and some are from sworn testimony in court.

or unnatural causes. Most people are unwilling to
admit, even to themselves, that they are superstitious, yet somewhere in their nature will be found
a belief in some odd and ludicrous superstition.
Many have a dread of the unlucky number; some
will not commence a journey on Friday; they feel
better when they have seen the new moon over
their right shoulder, and when the matter is well
sifted, we find lurking about all a strange, inexplicable superstition.

Two hundred years ago, superstition was far
more prevalent than at present, and some of the
wisest and best of that day possessed the oddest
and most unreasonable opinions.

A few evenings after the incidents narrated in
the foregoing chapter, Charles Stevens, who had
been all day on a hunt, at night found himself near
an old deserted house, four or five miles from town.
The house had been built by some Puritans, years
before, and the family which had lived in it were
murdered by Indians. The house was currently
reported at the village to be haunted; but Charles,
who was not a believer in ghosts, resolved to pass
the night there, in preference to braving a threatening thunderstorm.

His negro man Pete was with him, and when
he told Pete to gather up some dry wood, the
darkey, with eyes protruding from his head, asked:

"Massa Charles, am yc gwine to stay heah all night?"

"Certainly, Pete, why not? A storm is coming, and we could not reach home in such a tempest."

"But dis house am haunted."

"Oh, nonsense, Pete. Get the wood, and don't let such foolish notions as ghosts enter your mind."

Pete reluctantly obeyed, and Charles went into the house where was an old lamp which had been left there by hunters. It was nearly full of oil, and he lighted it by aid of his flint and steel.

Some rude benches and three-legged stools con-stituted the furniture. Pete, finding that nothing could induce his master to go on, gathered a quantity of dry wood before the rain began to fall, and started a fire.

The single lamp, burning dimly on the mantel, gave a weird ghost-like gleam, and Pete shuddered as he glanced into the dark corners and the black attic above, from whence his fervid imagination conjured up lost spirits, ghosts and goblins ready to seize him by the hair.

Just as the first great rain-drops began to fall on the old weather-beaten roof of the deserted house, they heard the rapid tramp of feet without. Pete uttered a horrified yell and sprang into the chimney, where he was trying to start a fire. Charles

told him to refrain from his silly conduct and went
to the door to see who their visitors were.

"Charles, Charles, is it you?" cried a voice
which he recognized as John Louder. "We saw
the light within and determined to seek shelter."

Louder was accompanied by his neighbors Bly
and Gray, all carrying guns and some small game
in their hands.

"You have been in the forest to-day?"

"Yes, with ill luck, too. Marry! I trow,
neighbors, we will have a tempest," cried Louder,
as he and his companions entered the old house.
A burst of thunder shook the earth; the wild winds
raged about the house, making the rickety old
structure creak and groan, while the air about
seemed on fire. For a moment all were awed to
silence; then Charles said:

"It will soon pass. The rain will soon drown
it."

"Have you but just come?" asked Louder.

"Just arrived."

"I would not, under other circumstances, put up
in such a place as this; but it is better than the
storm raging without."

The hunters, thankful for even such poor shelter,
skinned some squirrels, and toasted them before
the glowing fire, which Pete had built. Supper
over, they drew the benches close about the fire,

and while they listened to the raging storm without, conversed on the mysteries of that invisible world, which has always formed an interesting theme for the children of Adam.

"Charles Stevens, only a few years ago, you harbored at your house a wizard," said Louder.

Charles Stevens was half amused and half indignant. He began to expostulate with Louder, when the latter said:

"Nay, nay; I charge you not with bartering with the devil; but list to me. On the self-same day you found the stranger wounded at the roadside near the spring, we three had been hunting among the hills for deer. Some one had bewitched my gun. I know it, for when I fired, the bullet, which never failed on other occasions to go straight to the mark, went astray. All day long that mysterious stranger had followed us, grievously tormenting us and leading astray our shots, until I loaded my piece with a sixpence and fired at a large fat buck which strutted temptingly before me. Had you probed his wound I trow you would have found my sixpence buried in his side."

At this, the negro, who was crouched in a corner, groaned in agony, while Charles was inclined to treat the matter lightly. Louder related how, while at the lake in the wood, he had been visited by this msyterious apparition, who offered him a book to sign, adding that he knew at once that his tormentor was a wizard or the Devil, that his eyes were in an instant changed to fire, and sulphurous smoke issued from his nostrils.

"Can you ask me if I believe my own eyes and my own ears?" concluded Louder. "Those are truths, and had I signed his book, I would have been tormented by fiends and my soul forever lost."

"They do say the people are ready to cry out on Goody Nurse," put in Bly.

"Goody Nurse! surely not," answered Charles. "She is one of the best women I know. She is kind, good and gentle with all."

"Verily, so is Satan, until he has his clutches upon you. Goody Nurse is a witch."

"Beware, John Louder, how you malign such as she," said Charles, growing serious. . "Have the proof before you assert."

"I know whereof I speak," declared John Louder. "About five or six months ago, one morning about sunrise, I was in my chamber assaulted by the shape of Goody Nurse, which looked on me, grinned at me, and very much hurt me with a blow on the side of my head. That selfsame day, about noon, the same shape walked in the room where I was, and an apple strangely flew out of my hand, into the lap of my wife, six or eight feet from me. Can you deny such evidences as this?"

"I have seen her," put in John Bly, "and once when her shape did assail me, I struck at her with my cane, and she cried out that I had torn her coat."

Samuel Gray stated that he had been tormented with spectres and spirits. All this was agony to the horrified negro, who, crouching in one corner, shivered with dread, while his eyes wildly rolled in agony.

"Once a shape appeared to me and did tempt me to sign a book which I refused to do, and the shape whipped me with iron rods to compel me thereunto."

"Did you know the witch?" asked Charles.

"Verily, I did."

"Who was it?"

"One Bridget Bishop. I afterward saw her at a general meeting of witches in a field, where they all partook of a diabolical sacrament, not of bread and wine, but of the flesh and blood of murdered people."

At this the negro groaned and crouched closer to the chimney jamb. The storm roared without, and the rain fell with a steady pouring sound, as the superstitious hunters filled their pipes and gathered closer about the fire.

"There is no need to deny longer that witches exist," said John Louder. "I have seen enough

of them to convince me beyond question that there
are witches. Ann Durent one day left her infant,
William Durent with Amy Dunny, a woman who
has since been known to be a witch. Though
Dunny was an old woman, she afterward confessed
she had given suck to the child, whereat Durent
was displeased and Dunny went away with discontent and menaces.

"The night after, the child fell into strange and
sad fits, wherein it continued for divers weeks.
One doctor Jacob, who knew something of witches,
advised her to hang up the child's blanket in the
chimney corner all day, and at night, when she
went to put the child into it, if she found anything
in it, then to throw it without fear into the fire.
Accordingly at night when she took down the
blanket, there fell out of it a great toad, which
hopped up and down the hearth, uttering strange
cries. A boy caught it, and held it in the fire with
the tongs, where it made a horrible noise, and
flashed like gunpowder, with a report like that of
a pistol. Whereupon the toad was seen no more.
The next day a kinswoman of Dunny said she was
grievously scorched with the fire, and on going to
the house it was found to be even so. After the
burning of the toad, the child recovered."

"I did not believe in witchcraft at first," remarked Samuel Gray, by way of preface to some

weird account of his own; "but I cannot doubt my senses. I had been to Boston on business for the parson and, being belated, was riding along the road homeward. I had just reached the old Plaistowe field, when I suddenly discovered a long black something, like a monster cat or panther, running along the fence at my side. I was seized of some strange power and despite my will was forced to wink my eyes. If I closed my eyes but for a second, the black object was back at the point where it started from and ran along again, until I closed my eyes, when it appeared where I had first seen it. My horse became affrighted and ran away with me."

John Bly knocked the ashes from his pipe and began:

"I have an uncle in Virginia, who was sorely tried by witches. One witch in the neighborhood, especially, did grievously torment him. He would go to his door and see his field full of cattle; but on entering the field itself, no cattle were to be seen. Knowing full well that he was bewitched, he loaded his gun with a silver bullet, and one day fired at a large white cow. Instantly every beast disappeared, and he saw an old woman over the hill limping as if in pain. It was the suspected witch, whom he had shot in the leg. She did not bother him any more; but another witch used to come at night and ride him. She would shake a witch bridle over his head, utter some incantation and my uncle would be turned into a horse, and she would ride him hard until morning. Then she would bring him home, remove the spell, and he would be asleep in bed at dawn. One night he was thus ridden to a witch ball and tied to a tree. He rubbed his head against the tree until he got the bridle off, the spell was broken and he was once more a man. He took the enchanted bridle and laid in wait for the witch. As she emerged from the door, he seized her, shook the bridle over her head, repeated the words she had used, and instantly she was changed into a fine gray mare. He mounted her and rode her furiously, out of revenge, for many miles to a blacksmith, where he alighted and, awaking the smith, had him shoe the mare at once. Then he rode her nearly home, when he turned her loose.

"Next morning he went to the home of his neighbor, whose wife he suspected of being the witch, and inquired after the health of the family.

"'My wife is ill,' answered the head of the house.

"'What ails her?'

"'Alas, I know not.'

"My uncle went into the room where the woman lay in bed suffering greatly.

"'Are you very ill?' my uncle asked.

"'I am sick almost unto death,' the woman answered.

"'Let me hold your hand and see if you have a fever.'

"'No, no, no!' and she sought to hide her hands under the cover; but my uncle was a resolute man, and he seized her hand and drew it from beneath the cover, and behold, a horseshoe was nailed unto it. On each hand and each foot there was nailed a shoe which the smith at the trial swore he had put on the gray mare the night before."

The negro groaned at the conclusion of the narrative, and his face was so expressive of agony, that it formed a comical picture, exciting the laughter of Charles Stevens, and Bly supposing that he was skeptical of the story he had told said:

"Do you doubt the truth of my narrative, my merry fellow? Perchance you may some day feel the clutches of a witch upon you, then, pray God, beware."

"These are matters of too serious moment to excite one to laughter," put in Mr. Gray, solemnly. "Since the devil is come down in great wrath upon us, let us not in our great wrath against one another provide a lodging for him."

Charles, the reckless, merry youth, treated the matter as it would be treated at the present day.

"You need not deride the idea of witches changing people to horses," said John Louder, who, according to accounts given of him, by Cotton Mather, was either an accomplished liar or a man possessing a vivid imagination.

"Have you ever had any personal experience?" asked Charles.

"Indeed I have."

"What was it?"

"Goody Nurse does such things; but she has ever been too shrewd to be caught as was the witch in Virginia."

"Goody Nurse! For shame on you, Mr. Louder, to accuse that good, righteous woman with offences as heinous as having familiar spirits."

With a solemnity so earnest that sincerity could scarcely be doubted, John Louder remarked:

"Glad should I be, if I had never known the name of this woman, or never had this occasion to mention so much as her name. Goody Nurse is the most base of all God's creatures, for she takes unto herself a seeming holiness."

"What hath she done?"

"Listen and I will tell you. She hath grievously afflicted my children. At night her shape appears to them accompanied by a black man. She hath power to change her own form into an animal, a bird or insect at will. Once my little girl was attacked by a large black cat, which she recognized as Goody Nurse.

"Not only does she afflict my children; but my cattle, my gun and myself have been bewitched by her."

John Louder here paused and, refilling his pipe, lighted it, took a few whiffs to get it going and resumed:

"If you will listen to what I say, I will tell you of a certain incident which befell me last summer. One night I had retired early to rest, for, having been in the fields all day, I was somewhat weary. I fell asleep and was dreaming of pleasant forests, running brooks, green meadows, thrift and plenty, when suddenly methought I heard a voice calling unto me.

"'John Louder! John Louder!' it seemed to say.

"I started up from my pillow and sat on the side of my bed. The day had been very hot, the night was still warm, and the window had been left open, that the good south breeze might refresh my heated face. Suddenly in through that window came a great black object. I could see the eyes like blue flames, the face with a hideous grin, great sharp ears and short horns on top. He had bat-like wings, a tail, and on one foot was a cloven hoof.

"I was too much affrighted to speak; but the

shape motioned me to rise. I did so. An instant later, lo, a second shape appeared, and this was Rebecca Nurse. They did not ask me to sign the book, this time, for I had declined so often to do so, that they thought it little need.

"'Come!' said Goody Nurse. I rose and followed, I own, for I was under some strange spell.

"We got out of the house, I know not how, and I saw a great many people waiting. Some were on the ground, and some were in the air. All were on broomsticks.

"'Come, John Louder, mount behind me,' said Rebecca Nurse, and I was compelled to get behind her."

"What was she riding?" Charles asked.

"A broomstick."

Charles, by an effort, restrained the laughter, which the answer had so nearly created, and John Louder resumed:

"She uttered a strange, terrible cry, and we all rose in the air on the broomsticks and away we sped like birds. I was in constant fear lest I should fall and be dashed to death on the ground. I clung to her, and she, uttering strange screeches and cries, sped on like a bird through the air. Her broomstick rose and fell at her command.

"At last we descended to a valley, and all the witches save Goody Nurse disappeared. Here I soon learned that, intsead of riding, I was to be ridden. By a few magic words, my face became elongated, my body grew, my hands and feet became hoofs, my body was covered with hair, I had a mane and tail, and I was a horse, with a saddle on my back, and a bit in my mouth. Mounting me, the old witch cried:

"'Be going, Johnnie, I will give you sore bones ere the cock crows.'

"I was goaded to desperation. I ran, I leaped, I sprang from precipices so high, that, had I not been held up by the spirits of the air, I must have been dashed to death on the rocks below. I was agonized, and I wanted to die.

"WE ALL ROSE IN THE AIR ON BROOMSTICKS."

"At last we came to a valley and a house, which

I recognized as the old Ames Meeting House.   Here
a number of poor wretches like myself who had
been changed to beasts and ridden almost to death,
were tied up.   Some of them were horses, some
were bulls, and one had been changed to a ram,
another to an ostrich.   I was tied to a tree so near
to the door of the house, that I could see within.

"Verily, it was such a sight as I pray God I may
never witness again.   There were the witches at
their infernal feast.   The liver and lungs, torn warm
and bleeding from some helpless wretch, lay on the
table.   They partook of the food, also the diabolical sacrament, and then commenced their dance.   I
saw them dancing with their feet up to the ceiling
and their heads hanging down.

"In my agony of spirit, I seized the tree nearest
me in my mouth, and bit it so hard that I broke
out the tooth," and here the narrator exhibited his
teeth, one of the front ones being gone.   "You
see the tooth is missing.   A week later I went to
the Ames Meeting House and found the tooth stick-
ing in the tree.

"After they had kept up their infernal dance
for an hour, Goody Nurse again appeared and,
mounting on my back, did ride me most grievously
hard over the hills and plains, until we came to my
home.   Then she suddenly slipped from my back
and hurled me head first through the window,

where I fell in my own shape by the side of the bed."

Charles Stevens, feeling assured that he had a solution to the marvellous story, said:

"It was no doubt a frightful dream, which to you seemed real."

"Dream, was it?" cried Louder. "I sprang to my feet, ran to the window, and, sure as I am a white man, there was Goody Nurse soaring away through the air on a broomstick."

When he had finished his story, the horrified group shuddered and gathered closer about the fire which had burned low on the hearth. Pete tried to lay on a stick with his trembling hand, but was not equal to the task. The lamp-wick burned low in its socket, flickered and threatened to go out, while the storm without howled with increasing fury, the rain beat against the side of the house, and the thunder crashed overhead.

A shuddering silence seemed to have seized upon the group, and they sat watching the flickering lamp and smouldering fire, when suddenly all were roused by a loud rapping at the door. The entire group started up in alarm, the negro howled, and Bly gasped:

"God save us!"

"The whole armor of God shield us against the witches," groaned John Louder.

7•

"Heaven help us now!" whispered Gray.

Charles Stevens, though scarcely more than a youth, was the most self-possessed of all. He rose and opened the door. A blinding flash revealed a pair of horses with drooping heads in the rain and storm, while a man and young girl, the late riders of the horses, stood at the door holding the reins.

As soon as the door was opened, the man, holding the little maiden's hand in his own, stepped into the house to be out of the gust of wind and rain.

"We are belated travellers, kind sir, and seek shelter from the storm," the stranger began.

At sound of his voice, John Louder sprang to his feet, and, seizing the lamp, held it close to the man's face. Starting back with a yell, he cried:

"Away! wizard, devil, away! You are he who offered the book to me. Away! away! or I will slay you!"

The startled stranger answered:

"I never saw you before."

John Louder insisted that he was the evil one who had met him at the lake while he was stalking the deer, and had offered him the book to sign.

"I never saw you before in my life," the stranger answered, his theatrical tones making a strange impression on the superstitious Louder.

He read in his face the look of a demon, and continued to cry:

"You must, you shall go away! Prince of darkness, back into the storm which your powers created!"

Charles Stevens was too much amazed to speak for some moments, for, by the combined aid of the lamp and firelight, he saw before him the very features of the man whom he had found wounded and almost dying at the spring. The wanderer turned his sad and handsome face to the youth and asked:

"Can you take us to shelter?"

"I did once, and will again."

"You did once? Truly you mistake, for I never saw you before. My child will perish in this storm."

"It is five miles to my house; but if you will come with me I will show you the way."

They tried to dissuade Charles from going out into the driving storm; but he was not moved by their entreaties. He only saw the young maiden's pale, sweet face and appealing blue eyes, and he set off with the two through the storm, which beat about them so that they were quite wet to the skin when the house of widow Stevens was reached. The man and the maid were given beds and dry clothing.

Next morning, Charles asked the stranger:
"Are you not the man who came here in 1684, wounded?"

"I am not. I was never here before. What is your name?"

"Charles Stevens."

"Have you relatives in Boston?"

"Yes, my grandfather, Mathew Stevens, who was a Spaniard by birth and called Mattheo Estevan, died in Boston twenty years ago, and I have uncles, aunts and cousins living there."

"Have you relatives in Virginia?"

"I have cousins."

"Is one Robert Stevens?"

"He is."

"I know him, he befriended me and sent me here."

Then the stranger told how he had been an indented slave in Virginia, and escaped from a cruel master through the aid of Robert Stevens.

The strangers were George Waters and his daughter Cora.

CHAPTER VI.

THE CHARTER OAK.

When time, who steals our years away
Shall steal our pleasures too,
The memory of the past will stay,
And half our joys renew.
—MOORE.

THE Stevens family was growing with the colonies. Of the descendants of Mathew Stevens who came to New Plymouth in the *Mayflower*, there were many living in Boston, New York, Salem, Rhode Island and Connecticut. The family, widely scattered as its members were, never lost track of each other. They knew all their relatives in Virginia, Maryland and Carolinia.

Charles Stevens, but a youth, was on a visit to Connecticut, when an event transpired, which has since become historical. An aunt of Charles Stevens was the wife of a certain Captain Wadsworth, and Charles was visiting at this aunt's house when the incident happened.

As the student of American history doubtless knows, the tyrannical Governor Andros of New

York, claimed dominion over all that scope of
country denominated as the New Netherland, a
very indefinite term applied to a great scope of
country extending from Maryland to the Connecticut River, to which point Andros claimed jurisdiction.

As early as 1675, he went to the mouth of the
Connecticut River with a small naval force, to assert his authority. Captain Bull, the commander
of a small garrison at Saybrook, permitted him to
land; but when the governor began to read his commission, Bull ordered him to be silent. Andros
was compelled to yield to the bold spirit and superior military power of Captain Bull, and in a
towering passion he returned to New York, fling-
ing curses and threats behind him at the people of
Connecticut in general and Captain Bull in particular.

More than a dozen years had passed since Andros had been humiliated by Connecticut, and,
despite his anathemas, the colony quietly pursued
the even tenor of its way. At the end of that
period, a most exciting incident occurred at Hartford, during the visit of Charles Stevens to that city.
This historical incident has about it all the rosy
hues of romance. On the very day of the arrival
of Charles Stevens at Hartford, while he was talking with Captain Wadsworth, his aunt's husband,

a member of the colonial assembly suddenly entered the house, his face flushed with excitement.

"What has happened, Mr. Prince?" Wadsworth asked, for he could see that the man was greatly excited.

"Governor Andros has come again," gasped Mr. Prince.

"Why should that alarm us? The fellow, though given to boasting, is not dangerous, or liable to put his threats into execution."

"But he has grown dangerous!" declared Mr. Prince. "The liberties of the colony are involved. Andros appears as a usurper of authority—the willing instrument of King James the second, who, it seems, has determined to hold absolute rule over all New England."

Captain Wadsworth became a little uneasy, though he was still inclined to treat the matter lightly. Mr. Prince, to convince him of the danger they were in, continued:

"You remember that on his arrival in New York as governor of New Netherland, he demanded the surrender of all the colonial charters into his hands."

"I remember such an order, and furthermore that all the colonies complied with his infamous demand save Connecticut. We have stubbornly refused to yield our charter voluntarily, for it is the guardian of our political rights."

"That is true, Captain Wadsworth," continued Mr. Prince, "and, to subdue our stubbornness, this viceroy has come to Hartford with sixty armed men, to demand the surrender of the charter in person."

Captain Wadsworth bounded to his feet in a rage and, placing his hand on the hilt of his sword, declared:

"He shall not have it!"

Arriving at Hartford on the 31st of October, 1687, Andros found the general assembly in session in the meeting-house. The members received him with the courtesy due to his rank. Before that body, with armed men at his back, he demanded a formal surrender of the precious charter into his hands.

The members of the assembly were alarmed and amazed at his request.

The day was well nigh spent, when he arrived, and the members were engaged in a heated debate on a subject of the utmost importance.

"Wait until the discussion is ended, and then we will listen to you, governor," the president of the assembly answered to the demand of Andros.

"I have come for the charter, and I will have it!" said Andros, in his haughty, imperious manner.

He consented, however, to await the discussion;

but as soon as it was ended, he declared that he would have the charter.

Captain Wadsworth chanced to be at his house on the arrival of Andros, and, as everybody had the most implicit confidence in the captain's good sense, a member was despatched for him, as has been stated.

After the captain had taken two or three turns across the room, he paused and asked:

- "What is the assembly doing?"

"Engaged in a debate."

"And will he wait until it has ended?"

"He has promised to do so."·

"Hasten back, Mr. Prince, and whisper in the ears of every member to prolong the debate. It will give us time. I am going to do something desperate. Tell them to discuss any side and every side of the question at issue, and have your longest speech-makers do their best—talk on anything and everything whether to the point or against it, so that they kill time until night." *

Mr. Prince fixed his amazed eyes on the captain's face and read there a desperate determination.

"Captain," he began.

"I know what you would say, Mr. Prince; but it is needless to waste words; my resolution is formed, and I am going to save our charter or perish in the attempt."

"I hope you will not endanger your own life——"

"Mr. Prince, our liberties are in danger, and there is no time to think of life. Hasten back to the assembly and I will follow in a few moments."

Mr. Prince bowed and hastily returned to the house where the assembly was in session. As soon as he was gone, Charles Stevens said:

"Uncle, something terrible is going to happen, I know from your look and words. Won't you let me go with you?"

Captain Wadsworth fixed his eyes on the youth and answered:

"Yes, Charles, you will answer."

"What do you mean, uncle?"

"Are you willing to help us?"

"I am."

"Then you can put out the lights."

"What lights?"

"At the proper time, put out the lights in the assembly; but wait; I will go and muster the trainbands, and have them at hand to prevent the governor's soldiers from injuring the members of the general assembly."

Captain Wadsworth went out, and on his way looked into the State-house where everything was going as well as he could have wished. He found the debaters cudgelling their brains for some-

thing to say to the point or against it. Never
did debaters take greater interest in a minor subject.

He summoned his train-bands to assemble at sunset. This done, he went home and found Charles
eagerly waiting.

"Charles, you see the soldiers of Governor Andros at the State-house?"

"Yes."

"They are sent to take our liberties. My train-
bands have their eyes on them."

"What do you intend doing, uncle? Will you
fight them?"

"Not unless they force it. We have no wish to
shed their blood. Listen; the charter is to be
brought to the assembly in the same mahogany box
in which Charles II. sent it to Governor Winthrop.
When it is laid on the table, the lights are to be
snuffed out. Do you understand?"

"Yes."

"Can you do it?"

"Nothing is easier."

"Remember, the work must be done right at the
time, not too soon, nor too late."

"I will do it at the exact moment, uncle. Have
no fear on that score."

The sun was setting, and the captain said:

"Come, Charles, let us hasten to the assembly.

Look well at the setting sun, you may not live to see it rise."

Charles Stevens smiled and answered:

"You do not expect me to be a coward?"

"By no means; but I want you to be fully impressed with the seriousness of your mission."

They went to the general assembly at the meeting-house, where they found everything in the utmost confusion. The debate was at a white heat.

"Take your place, Charles, and be prepared to do your part," whispered Captain Wadsworth.

Charles got as close to the long table used by the secretaries as possible, without attracting special attention.

The discussion went on, darkness came and four lighted candles were placed on the table, and two set on a shelf on the wall. Those two candles on the wall were a great annoyance to Charles until he saw a man stationed near them.

Time passed on, and darkness had enveloped the earth. The debate was drawing to a close, or, in fact, had gone as far as it could, without arousing the suspicion of Governor Andros. When it ended, the governor of New York declared:

"I have waited as long as I will. I demand the charter at once. As governor of New York, this being a part of my dominion, I will have it."

"Wait——" began the president.

CHARLES STEVENS, AT ONE SWEEP, SNUFFED OUT EVERY CANDLE ON THE TABLE.

"No; already I have waited too long. Bring it at once."

There have been so many stories told of the Charter Oak that the author here feels justified in stepping aside from the narrative to quote from the journal for June 15, 1687, the following entry:

"Sundry of the court, desiring that the patent or charter might be brought into the court, the secretary sent for it, and informed the governor and court that he had the charter, and showed it to the court, and the governor bid him put it into the box again, and lay it on the table, and leave the key in the box, which he did, forthwith."

Affairs had proceeded to this point, when Charles Stevens, who had crept quite close to the table, with a long stick, at one sweep, snuffed out every candle on the table.

"Treason! treason!" cried Andros, and at this moment the two remaining candles on the wall were extinguished.

"Lights! lights!" cried a voice, and at the same moment, Andros shouted:

"The boy did it! kill the boy and seize the box!" · His hand was outstretched to take the box from the table, when the same stick which had extinguished the lights gave his knuckles such a rap that he uttered a yell of pain. Though the lights were extinguished, through the windows the faint starlight

dimly illuminated the scene. Charles Stevens saw
the outline of his uncle, who seized the box and
hurried with it from the meeting-house.

He followed him as rapidly as he could. A
terrible uproar and confusion inside attracted the
attention of everybody, so Captain Wadsworth escaped without being noticed, with the precious document under his arm. The youth was close behind
him and, when they were outside, seized his arm.

"Unhand me!" cried Captain Wadsworth,
snatching his sword from its sheath.

"Uncle!"

"Charles, it is you? Marry! boy, have a care
how you approach me. Why! I was about to run
you through."

"Have you got it?"

"Whist! Charles, the governor's soldiers are
near. They may hear you."

"They have enough to do in there," answered
the boy, pointing toward the meeting-house, in
which pandemonium seemed to reign.

The voice of Governor Andros could be heard
loud above the others calling to the troops to come
to his aid. The soldiers began to crowd about the
house, when, at a signal from Captain Wadsworth,
the train-bands came on the scene and prepared to
grapple with the soldiers. A bloody fight seemed
inevitable; but Governor Andros, who was a cow-

ard as well as tyrant, at sign of danger, begged peace.

"Lights! Light the candles!" he cried, "and we will have peace." When the candles were relighted, the members were seen seated about the table in perfect order; but the charter could nowhere be seen. For a few moments, the outwitted governor stood glaring at first one and then the other of the assembly. His passion choked him to silence at first; but as soon as he partially recovered his self-possession, he demanded:

"Where is the charter?" No one answered, and, with bosom swelling with indignation at being cheated by a device of the shrewd members of the assembly, he threatened to have them arrested.

"Governor Andros, we dispute your authority here, and have disputed it before," said a member of the assembly. "You have your soldiers at the door and we have the train-bands of Connecticut ready to defend us against violence."

"Who of you has the charter?"

"I have not," answered one.

"Nor I."

"Nor I," answered each and every one.

"It was the boy," cried the enraged governor. "I saw him; he struck my hand in the dark; yet I knew it was he. Where is he? Whose son is he?"

Every member of the assembly shook their heads. "We do not know him. He does not live in Connecticut."

"Where does he live?"

"He is from Massachusetts and beyond even the claimed bounds of your jurisdiction."

"So this is another trick. You have imported one from a distant colony to steal the charter," the indignant governor cried.

"We resent your insult!" cried an officer of the assembly. "The imputation is false!"

A scene far more stormy than any which had preceded it followed. The governor threatened the colony with the fury of his vengeance, and vowed he would report them to the king as in open rebellion against his authority. The colonists were shrewd and firm, and though some made very sarcastic answers to the governor's charges, they were, in the main, quite respectful.

Meanwhile, Captain Wadsworth and his wife's nephew, having the charter, hurried through the crowd, which opened for them to pass and closed behind them. Once in the street they hastened away at a rapid pace.

"What are you going to do with it?" Charles asked.

"Place it where it cannot be found by the tyrants," said the gallant captain. "There is a

venerable oak with a hollow in it. In this cavity
we will hide the charter, and none but you and
I will know where it is. You can return to Salem,
beyond reach of Governor Andros, and, as for me,
he can flay me alive before I will reveal the hiding-
place."

They had reached the outskirts of the village
and paused beneath the wide-spreading branches of
a great oak tree. The wind, sighing through the
branches, seemed to
the liberty - adoring
Wadsworth to be
whispering of free-
dom.

"Stand a little way
off, Charles," com-
manded the captain.
"And watch to see
that no one is observ-
ing me."

Then, while Charles

THE CHARTER OAK.

stood as sentry, he went to the tree and put the
charter in the hollow. Little did the captain or
his youthful assistant dream that their simple act
would make the old tree historic.

As long as American students shall study the
history of their country, will "The Charter Oak"
be famous.

8

That same night Charles Stevens, fearing the
wrath of Governor Andros, set out for his home at
Salem. The tree in which the document was hidden was ever afterward known as the "Charter Oak."
It remained vigorous, bearing fruit every year until
a little after midnight, August, 1856, when it was
prostrated by a heavy storm of wind. It stood in
a vacant lot on the south side of Charter Street, a
few rods from Main Street, in the city of Hartford.

When, in 1687, Andros demanded the surrender
of the colonial charters, the inhabitants of Rhode
Island instantly yielded. When the order for the
seizure of the charters was first made known, the
assembly of Rhode Island sent a most loyal address to the king saying:

"We humbly prostrate ourselves, our privileges,
our all, at the gracious feet of your majesty, with an
entire resolution to serve you with faithful hearts."

Andros therefore found no opposition in the little
colony. Within a month after his arrival at Boston, he proceeded to Rhode Island, where he was
graciously received. He formally dissolved the
assembly, broke the seal of the colony, which bore
the figure of an anchor, and the word Hope, admitted five of the inhabitants into his legislative
council, and assumed the functions of governor;
but he did not take away the parchment on which
the charter was written. The people of Rhode

Island were restive under the petty tyranny of Andros, and when they heard of the imprisonment of the despot at Boston, in 1689, they assembled at Newport, resumed popular government under the old charter, and began a new independent political career. From that time, until the enforced union of the colonies for mutual defence, at the breaking out of the French and Indian war, the inhabitants of Rhode Island bore their share in the defensive efforts, especially when the hostile savages hung along the frontiers of New York like an ill-omened cloud. The history of that commonwealth is identified with that of all New England, from the beginning of King William's war, soon after, to the expulsion of Andros.

Six years after the charter was hidden in the oak, Andros was succeeded by Governor Fletcher who made an attempt to control Connecticut, but was humbled and prevented and, in fact, driven away by Captain Wadsworth.

In 1689, the charter was brought out from the long place of concealment, a popular assembly was convened, Robert Treat was chosen governor, and Connecticut again assumed the position of an independent colony.

The name of Captain Wadsworth will ever be dear to the people of Connecticut, and so will the venerable oak which concealed their charter.

CHAPTER VII.

I, to the world, am like a drop of water,
That in the ocean seeks another drop,
Who, falling there to find his fellow forth,
Unseen, inquisitive, confounds himself.
So I, to find a mother, and a brother,
In quest of them, unhappy, lose myself.
—SHAKESPEARE.

MR. GEORGE WATERS, the escaped slave from
Virginia, lived very quietly at the home of Mrs.
Stevens. His daughter was constantly with him,
save when he made strange and unknown pilgrim-
ages. During these mysterious visits, she stayed
at the house of Mrs. Stevens.

Cora was a quiet little maid, whose hopes seemed
crushed by some calamity. She never forgot that
her father, the once proud man, had been arrested
and sold as a slave. That long period of servitude,
the flight and the fight were things which never
faded from her mind. In the eyes of Charles
Stevens, there was something singularly attractive
about this child. She was so strange, so silent and

116

melancholy, that he felt for her the keenest sympathy. She lived in the shadow of some dark mystery, which he could not fathom. Her strange father was non-communicative and silent as the grave.

Charles felt an interest in these people. It was a strange interest, one he could not understand himself, and like all good boys, when he wanted wisdom and information, he went to his mother.

"Mother, do you ever talk with Cora?" he asked one day.

"Yes."

"Do you ever talk with her about England?"

"I have; but it seems her father was a roving player, without any fixed abode."

"And her mother?"

Mrs. Stevens, who was busy sewing, answered: "I know nothing of her mother."

"Have you never asked about her?"

"No."

"Has she never mentioned her mother's name?"

"She has not."

The girl was nearly always at the home of Mrs. Stevens, though she sometimes took strolls alone through the town.

The melancholy child attracted the attention of Good-wife Nurse, who asked her to her house and brought her a mug of fresh milk.

"Do you belong here?" asked Goody Nurse.

"I suppose we do," was the answer. "Father is here part of the time."

"And your mother?"

"I have none."

"Did she die in England?"

"Alas, I know not."

"Do you remember seeing her?"

Cora shook her head, and a shadow passed over her face.

"Has your father ever told you about her?" asked Goody Nurse.

"No, madame; I have not heard him speak her name."

Then Goody Nurse, with a curiosity that was natural, sought to question the child about her former life; but all she could gain was that her father had been a strolling player. .

Players were not in good repute in New England at this time. The prejudice against the theatre, growing out of the rupture between the actors and the Roman Catholic Church, was inherited by the Protestants, who, to some extent, still continue their war against the stage. The fact that George Waters had been an actor was sufficient to condemn him in the eyes of the Puritans.

When Mr. Parris learned that a player was in their midst, he elevated his ecclesiastical nose, and seemed to sniff the brimstone of Satan. When he learned that some of the dissenting members of his congregation had been guilty of the heinous sin of speaking kind words to the motherless child of a player, he shook his wise head knowingly and declared, "Truly Satan is kind to his own." He made the player a subject for his next Lord's day sermon, in which he sought to pervert the scriptures to suit his prejudices. The subject of witchcraft was beginning to excite some attention, and he managed in almost every sermon to ring in enough of it to keep up the agitation. In the course of his discourse, he declared:

"The New Englanders are a people of God settled in those, which were the devil's territories, and it may easily be supposed that the devil is exceedingly disturbed, when he perceives such people here, accomplishing the promises of old, made unto our blessed Jesus, that he should have the uttermost parts of the earth for his possessions. There was not a greater uproar among the Ephesians, when the gospel was first brought among them, than there is now among the powers of the air after whom those Ephesians walked, when first the silver trumpets of the gospel made the joyful sound in their dark domain. The devil, thus irritated, hath tried all sorts of methods to overturn this poor plantation."

With this preface he assailed the unfortunate actor and his innocent child as being tools of his Satanic majesty, and denounced those who would lift the wounded, bleeding and beaten wayfarer from the road-side, carry him home, or offer his unfortunate child a cup of cold water as agents of darkness. Mr. Parris had forgotten some of the commands of the divine Master, whom he professed to follow. He assailed "the little maid furiously." That child of sorrow and of tears, whom he had never seen before, and whose young heart ached from the wrongs heaped on her innocent young head, was to him an object of demoniac fury.

She sat in the rear of the church, and, covering her face with her hands as Mr. Parris assailed her father and herself, the tears silently trickled through her small fingers. Goody Nurse, who sat near the child, bent over and whispered some encouraging words in her ear.

"Verily, the Devil's own will be the Devil's own!" declared the pastor, his eyes flashing with fury. "When one of Satan's imps hath been wounded by a shaft of truth, shot from the bow of God, the angels of darkness, verily, will hover over the suffering devil, and seek to undo what God hath done." He called on those suffering from the familiar spirits to behold one even now willing to soothe the offspring of a wicked player.

When Cora left the church that day, she asked
Mrs. Stevens why Mr. Parris hated her and said
such hard things about her. "Surely I never
did him harm, and why doth he assail me so
cruelly?"

Mrs. Stevens strove to comfort the wounded
feelings of the child, by assuring Cora that it was
the mistaken zeal of the minister, who, but for the
scales of prejudice covering his eyes, would by no
means be so cruel with her.

"Oh, would that father would return and take
me from this place!" sobbed Cora.

"Cora, are you tired of me? Have I not been
kind to you?"

"Yes, you have, and I thank you for all your
goodness."

"Are you not happy with me?"

"Yes, I could be very happy, did not Mr. Parris
say such vile things of my father and myself. Do
you think me one of Satan's imps?"

"No, no, sweet child; you are one of God's
angels."

"But I am the child of a player, and he said
none such could enter into the kingdom of the
Lord."

"That is but a display of his prejudice and ignorance, Cora. I have read the good book from beginning to end, and nowhere do I see anything in

God's Holy Bible that excludes even the player from entering into eternal rest."

"But he, the interpreter of God's word, says we are doomed."

"He says more than is narrated in the Book of Life. If the ministers would only keep constantly in their minds these words: 'For I testify unto every man that heareth the words of the prophecy of this book. If any man shall add unto these things, God shall add unto him the plagues that are written in this book,' then there would be less misconstructions put upon the Bible. Men would be more careful not to accuse their brother, while the beam was in their own eye. Why, Cora, you are but a child, and Christ said: 'Suffer little children to come unto me and forbid them not, for of such is the kingdom of Heaven.' Now, instead of following the holy precept of the Master, whom he feigns to serve, he declares you an imp of darkness. His zeal hath made him mad. Where is your father?"

"Alas, I know not."

"When will he return?"

"I know not."

"What are his plans?"

"I am wholly ignorant of them."

Next day Charles Stevens was wandering through the forest near the spring where he rescued the wounded stranger some years before. Often had he thought of that melancholy man and the strange resemblance he bore to Cora's father.

"Where is he now, and what has been his fate?" he thought, as he strolled toward the spring. Suddenly he paused and looked toward the brooklet. Well might he be startled. The negro servants, John and Tituba, were engaged in some of their diabolical incantations in the stream. Kneeling by the water's side, each bent until their foreheads touched the water, then, starting up, they murmured strange fetich words in their diabolical African tongue. John had a whip in his hand, with which he lashed the water furiously, and uttered his eldritch shrieks. Charles paused, spell-bound, hardly knowing what to make of the strange conduct of the negroes, and wishing he could lay the whip about their own bare shoulders.

During a lull in their performance, he heard a rapid tread of feet coming toward the spring, and beheld his mother, followed by Cora. No sooner did the negroes see them, than they left off lashing the water with their whips and, with the most wild, unearthly screams, bounded from the spot and ran off into the woods.

Mrs. Stevens and Cora both screamed, and were about to fly, when Charles emerged from his place of concealment, saying:

"Don't run away, I am here."

"Charles! Charles! what were they doing?" Mrs. Stevens asked.

"It was some of their wild incantations," he answered. "The knaves deserve to have a good whip laid about their bare backs."

"Truly, they do. Why· did they fly at our approach?" asked Mrs. Stevens.

"Perhaps the foolish creatures thought their spell was broken," Charles answered.

"I am so affrighted," said Cora, shuddering. She was growing·dizzy, and Mrs. Stevens said:

"Catch her, or she will fall."

He bore her to the spring and, kneeling by the brook, bathed the fair white brow, until she opened her eyes and murmured:

"Mother!"

Many times afterward, both mother and son, recalling the incident, wondered why she, for the first time, had called for her mother. At all other times and on all other occasions, the maid persistently denied that she knew aught of her mother.

A few days later, her father, who had mysteriously and unceremoniously disappeared, returned. No one asked any questions as to where he had been, or what business had engaged his attention. He gave the widow some golden guineas for her care of his child. That night Charles came accidentally upon the father and daughter in the garden. They were sitting in a green bower, partially screened from view, so he approached to within a few paces without being seen.

"Father, have you heard anything more?" she asked.

"No."

"Nor have you seen any one from there?"

"I have not."

"Do you suppose danger is over?"

"Danger never will be over, until there has been a revolution in the government."

Long did Charles ponder over those mysterious words, and ask himself what they meant. He again conferred with his mother, and when she had heard all he had to tell, she was constrained to ask:

"Who are they?"

Mrs. Stevens, like her son, was too well bred to pry into the secrets of her guests. A few days later Mr. Waters again disappeared and was not seen for two months.

It was at the close of a sultry day in July that Mr. John Louder and his neighbor Bly were returning from Boston in a cart. As usual, their conversation was of the solemn kind, characteristic of the Puritan. The many mysteries in nature and out of nature formed their principal topic. Each had had his long, ardent conflict with sin and Satan.

Each was a firm believer in personal devils and legions of devils. The spirits of the air were thought to be all about them, even at that very moment.

"Neighbor Bly, I believe that she is a witch," said Louder.

"Verily, even so do I."

"If the magistrates would so adjudge her, she would, according to the laws, be hung."

"Truly she would. I saw her shape again last night."

"Did you?"

"Yes, she came to my bed and did grievously torment me, by sitting for fully two hours upon my chest."

"Why did you not call upon the name of God, and she would have gone?"

"Fain would I have done so, had it been possible; but her appearance took from me the power of speech, and I was dumb. She sat upon me, grinning at me, and she said:

"'Would ye speak if ye could?'

"Then at last a yellow bird came in at the window and whispered some words in her ear, and the shape flew away with a black man."

"Verily, neighbor Bly, you have been grievously tormented; yet little worse is your case than my own. My cattle are bewitched and die. The witches hurl balls at them from any distance, which strike them, and they shrink and die at once. The other morn I had salted my cows, when one suddenly showed strange signs of illness and soon fell on her side and did die. Neighbor Towne, who witnessed it, said the poor beast was struck with a witch ball. He says they gather the hair from the back of the afflicted beasts and, making a ball of it from the spittle of their mouths, blow their breath upon it and hurl it any distance to an object. The object so struck will at once wither and die. He said that, should I strip the hair from the spine of the dead brute, a ball made of it would strike down any other beast of the herd, even if thrown by my own hand."

With a sigh, Bly said:

"Truly, we live in the age when the devil is to be loosed for a little season. Would to Heaven, St. John would again chain the dragon."

The sun had almost dipped behind the long line of blue hills. A listless repose, peculiar to New England autumns, seemed to have settled over the hills and valleys about the neighborhood of Salem. A drowsy, dreamy influence overhung land and sea and pervaded the very atmosphere. No wonder that the superstitious Puritans of that day and age believed the place bewitched. Certain it is, that it seemed under the same power, that held strange

spells over the minds of the good people, causing
them to walk in a continual revery. These early
Puritans were given to all kinds of marvellous be-
liefs, as we have seen, subjected to trances and
visions, and frequently saw strange sights, and
heard wonderful noises in the air. All Salem
abounded with local tales, haunted spots and twilight superstitions. Shooting stars and flaming
meteors were more often seen about that enchanted
spot, than in any other part of the country.

The two travellers silently jogged along in the
cart, casting occasional glances down the road.
Just before reaching Salem, the road dipped below
the trees, which concealed some glens and breaks,
above which only the church, standing in the sub-
urb of the village, could be seen. The seques-
tered situation of the meeting-house seemed to have
always made it a favorite resort for troubled spirits.
It stood on a knoll, surrounded by beech trees and
lofty elms, from among which its decent white-
washed walls shone modestly forth, as the only
bright object among so much sombre gloom and
shade. A broad path wound its way down a gentle
slope to the creek, which emptied into the bay,
bordered by tall trees, through which glimpses of
the sea and blue hills might be caught. Between
the travellers and the church extended a wide,
woody dell, along which the brook roved among

broken rocks and trunks of fallen trees. Over a deep, black part of the stream was thrown a bridge. The road which led up to it was thickly shaded, and in places indistinguishable at any great distance by overhanging trees, which cast a gloom about it, even in daytime, but occasioned a fearful darkness at night.' This place was reputed to be a favorite resort for the witches of Salem, for they had frequently been seen dancing upon the bridge.

It was with some degree of nervousness that the travellers drew near to the bridge. The sun had dipped behind the blue hills of the west, and the pale, lambent glow of the evening star shot athwart the sky, ere the bridge was reached. While it was yet twilight in the uplands, it was night here. The hollow sounds of the horse's feet on the bridge chilled the hearts of the occupants of the cart, and when the outline of a horse and rider appeared on the other side, Louder seized Bly by the arm and gasped:

"God save us! Where did they come from? They were not there a moment before."

"They rose up out of the ground."

Their horse, which was very much frightened, would have dashed down the road had not the horseman brought his steed directly across their path.

"Your beast seems affrighted," coolly remarked the horseman.

9

At sound of his voice, Louder gave utterance to a wild yell of dismay. The horse stood trembling and refused to move the cart an inch. Louder rose from the seat and glared through the deepening gloom at the stranger. That white face, those great, sad eyes once seen could never be forgotten. He uttered a yell of horror, crying:

"Begone, wizard! The armor of God be between me and thee! Fiend of the regions of darkness, it was thou who offered me the book to sign. Away! begone! tempt me no more, for, by the grace of Heaven, I defy you! I will not sign!"

At this moment, the horse at the cart, seeing an opening in the road, dashed on to the village, leaving the horseman gazing in mute wonder after them. His white face wore a puzzled and pained look. He turned his horse's head into another path, saying:

"It has been some years since I was here, and yet, if I mistake not, this is surely the path that leads to her house."

Thirty minutes later, the same horseman drew rein in front of the widow Stevens' cottage and, dismounting, tied his horse to a small tree and approached the house. A light was shining through the window, and the whirr of the wheel told that the industrious widow was at her evening work. He rapped at the door and was bidden enter. On entering, he discovered that three persons occupied the cottage—the widow, her son and a beautiful, sunny-haired maiden. The latter started up at his appearance, crying:

"Father! father!" and, leaping forward, threw her arms about his neck. The new-comer looked in amazement upon the girl, but made no answer.

"Father, father, why don't you speak?"

"There is some mistake!" he began.

"Are you not my father?"

"I never saw you before, little maid."

Then Cora started back and gave the stranger a curious glance. He looked exactly like her father, save that he was dressed almost wholly in buckskin, and had a wild, forest-like appearance. Then, as she scrutinized him more closely, she perceived a slight scar on his left cheek. This was not on her father's face.

"You are not my father; but you are very like him," she said.

"I am not your father, little maid. I came to thank these people for their kindness to me a few years ago."

"Are you he whom I found by the brook, wounded and dying?" asked Charles.

"I am."

"Your mysterious disappearance occasioned much comment."

Before the stranger could frame an answer, the door was again thrown open, and this time it was Cora's father, in reality, who entered the house. She sprang to him, saying:

"Father, I see now there is a difference between you and him!"

For the first time, George Waters saw the stranger. As their eyes met, each started, gazed at the other a moment, as if to be assured he was right, and then George Waters cried:

"Harry!"

"George!"

. A dramatic episode, such as is so often acted upon the stage, or described in novels, followed, and, by degrees, the small audience caught from words dropped by the men, that they were brothers, who had long been separated, and had been searching for each other.

When the excitement attending the discovery had in a measure subsided, the brothers walked down toward the spring, where, seating themselves on a moss-grown stone, George Waters told his brother of joining Monmouth's army, of being arrested and sold as a slave in Virginia, and of his escape and long perilous flight to New England.

"Where have you been since you were here, Harry?"

"I was a captive among the Indians for a few

months, was liberated by some French Jesuits and
went to France and thence to England, hoping to
see you. I was several weeks at our old home near
Stockton. Then I came back to America and have
been in New York trading in furs."

A silence of several moments followed. George,
whose soul seemed stirred with some deep emotions,
asked:

"Harry, while in England, in Stockton, did you
see her?"

Harry knew to whom he referred, and he answered:

"No."

"Where is she?"

"I know not."

"Do you know whether she be living or dead?"

"I do not."

"God grant that she be dead!"

At this moment, Cora, who had followed behind
them and overheard their strange words, came forward and asked:

"Father, what do you mean?"

"Nothing, child. There, let us return to the
house, for it is growing late."

Then, as they walked up the gentle slope to the
cabin of the widow, the maiden repeated to herself:

"But he does mean something!"

CHAPTER VIII.

Laws formed to harmonize contrarious creeds,
And heal the wounds through which a nation bleeds ;
Laws mild, impartial, tolerant and fixed,
A bond of union for a people mixed ;
Such as good Calvert framed for Baltimore,
And Penn the Numa of th' Atlantic shore.

THE Stevens family were so intimately related to their country, that the history of one is the history of the other. Philip Stevens, or Estevan, had located in the south and left behind a numerous progeny, while his brother Mathew, who came over in the *Mayflower*, had left an equally large family in New England. Their descendants began to push out into the frontier colonies, those in the south going as far north as Pennsylvania, and those in the east pushing out westward to New York and New Jersey.

The family were lovers of freedom, and, wherever a struggle has been made on American soil for liberty, one of these descendants of the youth who landed on American soil with Columbus, in 1492,

134

has been found. They disliked Andros, and the members of this now extensive and widely scattered family were in sackcloth and ashes, so to speak, when King James, in 1688, gave Andros a vice-regal commission to rule New York and all New England.

When the viceroy journeyed from Boston to New York City, early in August the same year, George Stevens, a cousin of Charles, accompanied him, and saw Andros received by Colonel Bayard's regiment of foot and horse, who was entertained by the loyal aristocrat. In the midst of the rejoicings, the news came that the queen, the second wife of James, had been blessed with a son, who became heir to the throne. The event was celebrated the same evening by bonfires in the streets and a feast at the city hall. At the latter, Major Van Cortlandt became so hilarious, that he made a burnt sacrifice to his loyalty of his hat and periwig, waving the burning victims over the banquet table on the point of his straight sword.

Princess Mary, the eldest daughter of King James, had married the Prince of Orange, and this new birth in the royal family was a disappointment to the Dutch inhabitants of New York, as well as the Protestant republicans, who had begun to hope that William and Mary would succeed James to the throne of England. This event intensified the general discontent, because of the consolidation of New York with New England and the abridgment of their rights, and the people were ready to rebel at almost any moment, especially as Andros had rendered himself particularly obnoxious.

Like the other colonies, Maryland was shaken by the revolution in England, in 1688, and, for a while, experienced deep sorrows. The democratic ideas, which, for several years, had been spreading over the provinces, could not reconcile the rule of a lord proprietor with the true principles of republicanism. Even when Charles Calvert went to England after the death of his father, signs of political discontent were conspicuous in Maryland. In 1678, the general assembly, influenced by the popular feeling, established the right of suffrage— "casting of a vote for rulers"—on a broad basis. On the return of Charles, in 1681, he annulled this act and, by an arbitrary ordinance, resisted the right of freemen owning fifty acres of land, or personal property of the value of forty pounds sterling. This produced great disquietude, and Ex-Governor Fendall planned an insurrection for the purpose of abolishing the proprietorship and establishing an independent republican government. The king was induced to issue orders that all the offices of the government in Maryland should be filled by

Protestants alone; and so, again, the Roman Catholics were deprived of their political rights.

Lord Baltimore went to England again, in 1684, leaving the government of his province in charge of several deputies under the nominal governorship of his infant son. There he found his rights in great peril; but before the matter could be brought to a direct issue by the operation of a writ of *quo warranto*, King James was driven from the throne, and Protestant William and Mary ascended it. Lord Baltimore immediately acquiesced in the political change. On account of his instructions to his deputies to proclaim the new monarchs being delayed in their transmission, he was charged with hesitancy; and a restless spirit named Coode, an associate of Fendall in his insurrectionary movements—"a man of loose morals and blasphemous speech"—excited the people by the cry of "a popish plot!" He was the author of a false story put in circulation, that the local magistrates in Maryland and the Roman Catholics there had engaged with the Indians in a plot for the destruction of the Protestants in the province. An actual league at that time between the French and the Jesuit missionaries with the savages on the New England frontiers for the destruction of the English colonies in the east seemed to give color to the story; which created great excitement. The old feud burned in-

tensely. The Protestants formed an armed associa-
tion led by Coode. They marched to the Maryland
capital, took possession of the records and assumed
the functions of a provisional government, in May,
1689. In the following August they met in convention, when they prepared and sent to the new
sovereigns a report of their proceedings, and a
series of absurd and false accusations against Lord
Baltimore. In conclusion, they requested the
monarchs to depose Lord Baltimore by making
Maryland a royal province and taking it under the
protection of the crown.

William and Mary listened favorably to the request and, moved by the false representations, complied with it. Coode was ordered to administer
the government in the name of the king. He
ruled with the spirit of a petty tyrant, until the
people of every religious and political creed were
heartily disgusted with him, and, in 1692, he was
supplanted by Sir Lionel Copley, whom the king
sent to be governor of Maryland. On the arrival
of the new governor, in the spring of 1692, he
summoned a general assembly, to meet at St.
Mary's in May. New laws abolishing religious
toleration were instituted. The church of England
was made the state church for Maryland, to be supported by a tax on the whole people.

"Thus," says McMahan, "was introduced, for

the first time in Maryland, a church establishment, sustained by law and fed by general taxation." Other laws oppressive in their bearings upon those opposed in religious views to the dominant party were enacted, some of which remained in force until the glorious emancipation day, in the summer of 1776, gave freedom to our nation.

Partly in order to better accommodate the people of Maryland, but more for the purpose of punishing the adherents of Lord Baltimore, who constituted a greater proportion of the population of St. Mary's, the seat of government was moved from there to Anne Arundel, a town on the shore of the Chesapeake, early in 1694, and there a general assembly was convened in February. The following year, the name of the place was changed by authority to Annapolis, and the naval station of the province was established there. Annapolis has, ever since, continued to be the capital of Maryland, while St. Mary's, dependent for its existence upon its being the capital of the province, speedily sunk into ruins.

Lord Baltimore never recovered his proprietary rights. Neither did he return to America, but died in England in the year 1714, at the age of eighty-five years. He was succeeded by his son Benedict Leonard Calvert. That son had abandoned the faith of his father and, in the spring of 1715, died,

when his title to the province devolved upon his
infant son Charles, who, with his brothers and
sisters, had been educated as Protestants. Charles
Calvert, Lord Baltimore and William Penn were
contemporaries, and were equally conspicuous for
their beneficent disposition. They are regarded as
the best of all the proprietors, who owned charted
domains in America.

Rufus Stevens, an uncle of Charles Stevens, the
youth of Salem, was living in New Jersey, when
Lord Berkeley, disgusted by the losses and annoy-
ances which the ownership of the colony brought
upon him, sold his interests in the province to John
Fenwick and Edward Byllinge, English Friends,
or Quakers, for the sum of five thousand dollars.
The tract thus disposed of was in the western part
of the province. With some emigrants, mostly of
the society of Friends, Fenwick sailed for his new
possessions. They entered at a spot not far from
the Delaware River, which they named Salem, on
account of the peaceful aspect of the country and
the surrounding Indians. There, with the peculiar
gravity of the sect, Fenwick and his two daughters,
thirteen men (most of them heads of families) and
one woman, the wife of one of the emigrants, sat
in silent worship, according to their custom, under
the shadow of a great tree, with covered heads
and quiet bodies, on the ensuing " First Day" after

their arrival. Then they built log cabins for shelter, and so began a new life in the wilds of New Jersey. The principal proprietor was Byllinge; but soon after the departure of Fenwick, heavy losses in trade made him a bankrupt, and his interest in New Jersey was first assigned to William Penn and others for the benefit of his creditors, and was afterward sold to them. These purchasers and others who became associated with them, unwilling to maintain a political union with other parties, bargained with Carteret for a division of the province. This was done in July, 1676, Carteret retaining the eastern part of the province, and the new purchasers holding the western part. From that time, until they were united and became a royal-province in 1702, these divisions were known as East and West Jersey. Even to this day, we frequently hear the expression, "The Jerseys," used.

Most of the settlers of West Jersey were Friends, and the proprietors gave them a remarkably liberal constitution of government, entitled: "The concessions and agreements of the proprietors, freeholders and inhabitants of the province of West Jersey in America." The following year (1677), more than four hundred Friends came from England and settled below the Raritan. Andros required them to acknowledge his authority as the representative of the Duke of York. This they refused to do, and the matter was referred to the eminent crown-lawyer and oriental scholar, Sir William Jones, for adjudication. Sir William decided against the claims of the duke, who submitted to the decision, released both provinces from allegiance to him, and the Jerseys became independent of foreign control. The first popular assembly in West Jersey met at Salem, in November, 1681, and adopted a code of laws for the government of the people. One of these laws provided that in all criminal cases, excepting treason, murder and theft, the aggrieved party should have power to pardon the offender.

In the year 1679, Carteret died, and the trustees of his American estates offered East Jersey for sale. It was bought, in 1682, by William Penn and others, among them the earl of Perth, the friend of Robert Barclay, whom the proprietors appointed governor for life. Barclay was an eminent young Friend, whose writings were held in high estimation by his own sect, especially his "Apology for the true Christian Divinity, as the same is held forth and practised by the people called in scorn Quakers," and his "Treatise on Christian Discipline." The purchase of these lands was not made in the interest of either religion or liberty, but as a speculation. Barclay governed the province by deputies until 1690.

England and Scotland contributed a large number of Friends to East Jersey, and other immigrants
flocked from Long Island, to find repose and peace;
but repose is not to be found by lovers of freedom,
under royal rule, and they were forcibly impressed
with the significance of the injunction, "Put not
your trust in princes," for James the king failed to
keep the rosy promises of James the duke, and
they were forced to submit to the tyranny of Andros. When that detested viceroy was expelled
from the country, in 1689, the Jerseys were left
without a regular civil government, and so they
remained for several years. Wearied with con-
tentions, with the people of the provinces and with
the government at home, and annoyed by losses in
unprofitable speculations, the proprietors of the
Jerseys surrendered them to the crown, in 1702,
when Queen Anne was the reigning British monarch. The government of that domain was then
confided to Sir Edward Hyde (Lord Cornbury),
whose instructions constituted the supreme law of
the land. He was then governor of New York and
possessed almost absolute legislative and executive
control within the jurisdiction of his authority.
In New Jersey the people had no voice in the
judiciary or the making and executing of laws other
than recommendatory. All but Roman Catholics
were granted liberty of conscience; but the bigoted

governor always showed conspicuous favors to the members of the Church of England. The governor was dishonest and a libertine, and under his rule the people of New Jersey were little better than slaves. Printing, except by royal permission, was prohibited in the province, and the traffic in negro slaves was especially encouraged.

New Jersey remained a dependency of New York, yet with a distinct legislative assembly of its own, until the year 1738, when it was made an independent colony, and it so remained until the Revolutionary War, when it became a separate State. After the province gained its freedom from New York, Mr. Morris was commissioned its governor. He was the son of an officer in Cromwell's army, who, about the year 1672, settled on a farm of three thousand acres on the Harlem River, New York, which was named Morrisania.

Last of the royal governors of New Jersey was William Franklin, son of Dr. Benjamin Franklin, who was appointed in 1763, and closed his official career in the summer of 1776, when he was deposed by the continental congress and sent under guard to Connecticut. There he was released on parole and went to England, where he died in 1813.

One of the Stevens family having served as governor of North Carolinia, it was only natural that other members of the southern branch of that rapidly increasing family in the south should push out into the Carolinias and take part in the early settlement of these colonies.

After the failure of the schemes of Loche and Cooper to form "Fundamental Constitutions," a splendid government, in 1669, was completed. The "constitutions" were signed in March, 1670, and were highly lauded in England, as forming the wisest scheme for human government ever devised. Monk, Duke of Albemarle, was created palatine or viceroy for the new empire, who was to display the state parade of his office, with land-graves, barons, lords of manor and heraldry, among the scattered settlers in pine forests, living in log cabins with the Indians. Never was a more ludicrous idea entertained with any degree of seriousness; yet, so far as the proprietors were concerned, this splendid government was established; but the simple settlers had something to say; and when the governor of the Albemarle county colony attempted to introduce the new government, they said, "No." They had a form of government of their own, far better adapted to their social circumstances than the one sent from England, and they resolved to adhere to it.

All attempts to enforce obedience to the new form of government, all oppressive taxation im-

10

posed upon the people, and especially the com-
mercial restrictions authorized by the English navigation laws, produced wide-spread discontent.
Most particularly was this fostered by refugees
from Virginia, who had been engaged in Bacon's
rebellion, and who sought personal safety among
the people below the Roanoke. These refugees,
smarting under the lash of tyranny, scattered
broadcast over the generous soil the germinal ideas
of popular freedom, and successful oppression was
made difficult, if not impossible.

At this period, North Carolinia did not contain
four thousand inhabitants. They carried on a
small trade in tobacco, maize and fat cattle with
the merchants of New England. This sort of
smuggling was perhaps excusable, when we consider the grinding navigation laws of the monopo-
lists. The little vessels, trading between North
Carolinia and New England, brought many articles
to the southern colonies, which they were incapable
of producing. English cupidity envied them their
small prosperity, and the navigation laws of 1672
were put in force. An agent of the government
appeared, who demanded a penny for every pound
of tobacco sent to New England. The colonists resisted the levy and the tax-gatherer became rude
and had frequent collisions with the people. On
one occasion, he went to the home of Francisco

THE STURDY WIFE ASSAILED HIM WITH HER MOP-STICK AND DROVE HIM AWAY.

Stevens, a planter, who had shipped some tobacco to a relative in Boston, and demanded a steer in payment for the shipment. The tax-gatherer attempted to drive away the ox, when the sturdy wife assailed him with her mop-stick and drove him from the premises.

The exasperated people finally, in December, 1677, seized the public funds and imprisoned the governor and six of his councillors, called a new representative assembly and appointed a chief magistrate and judge. Then, for two years, the colonists were permitted to conduct the affairs of their government without any foreign control. Meanwhile, John Culpepper, their leader, whom the royalists denounced as an "ill man, who merited hanging for endeavoring to set the people to plunder the rich," conscious of his integrity, went boldly to England to plead the cause of the colony. While in the act of re-embarking for America, he was arrested, tried for treason and honorably acquitted. Returning to North Carolinia, he was appointed surveyor-general of the province, and, in 1680, laid out the city of Charleston in South Carolinia.

Until the arrival of Seth Sothel as governor, North Carolinia enjoyed a period of repose. He had purchased a share in the provinces of Clarendon, and was sent to administer the government.

On his voyage, he was captured by Algerine
pirates, but, escaping them, reached North Carolinia, in 1683.

It has been said of this avaricious, extortionate
and cruel statesman, that "the dark shades of his
character were not relieved by a single virtue."
His advent disturbed the public tranquillity. He
plundered the people, cheated the proprietors, and
on all occasions seems to have prostituted his del-
egated power to purposes of private gain. About
six weeks of his misrule were all the independent
colonists could stand. Then the people rose in rebellion, seized the governor, and were about to
send him to England to answer their accusations
before the proprietors, when he asked to be tried
by the colonial assembly. It is asserted by historians of note, that that body was more merciful
than his associates in England would have been,
for they found him guilty and sentenced him to
only one year's punishment and perpetual dis-
qualification for the office of governor.

Sothel withdrew to the southern colony, and was
succeeded by Philip Ludwell, an energetic, honest
man, whose wisdom and sense of justice soon restored order and good feeling in the colony. He
was succeeded by John Archdale, a Quaker, who,
in 1695, came as governor of the two colonies. His
administration was a blessing. The people over

whom he ruled were as free in their opinions and actions as the air they breathed. Legal or moral restraints were few; yet the gentle-minded people were enemies to violence or crime. They were widely scattered, with not a city or town and scarce a hamlet within their sylvan domain. The only roads were bridle paths from house to house, and these were indicated by notches cut in trees— "blazed roads." There was not a settled minister in the colony until 1703.

The southern, or Carteret County Colony was, meanwhile, steadily moving along in population and wealth. The settlers, perceiving the fatal objections to the "Fundamental Constitutions" as a plan of government for their colony, did not attempt conforming thereto, but established a more simple government adapted to their conditions. Under it, the first legislative assembly of South Carolinia convened, in the spring of 1672, at the place on the Ashley River where the colony was first seated. In that body, jarring political, social and theological interests and opinions produced passionate debates and violent discord. South Carolinia has ever been a seething political caldron, and, even in that early date, there was a proprietary party and a people's party, a high church party and a dissenters' party, each bigoted and resolute. At times, the debates were so heated and earnest, that they seemed on the eve of plunging the colony into civil war.

The savages had commenced plundering the frontier, and all factions of the whites were forced to unite against this common enemy. The bold frontiersman, with his trusty rifle, was often unable to defend his home. His cattle were run away or slaughtered before his very eyes. Old Town was the first point selected for the capital; but Charleston was finally laid out on Oyster Point, and the seat of government was removed to this city, where the second assembly met, in 1682. Immigrants flowed in with a full and continuous stream. Families came from Ireland, Scotland and Holland, and when the edict at Nantes, which secured toleration to Protestants in France, was revoked, a large number of Huguenots fled from their country, and many sought an asylum in the Carolinias. The traditionary hatred of the English for the French was shown at this time. For fully ten years these French refugees were deprived the privilege of citizenship in the land of their adoption.

A colony of Scotch Presbyterians, numbering ten families, was located at Port Royal, South Carolinia, in 1682, and four years later was attacked and dispersed by the Spaniards, who claimed Port Royal as a dependency of St. Augustine.

The persecution of the Huguenots in France

drove many to seek homes in the colonies, despite English hatred to them.

The struggles of South Carolinia with the Indians, and the attempted oppression of the home government is but a repetition of the experience of the other colonies, until the good John Archdale came as governor of the Carolinias. His administration was short, but highly beneficial. He healed dissensions, established equitable laws, in the spirit of a true Christian example of toleration and humanity. He cultivated friendly intercourse with the Indians and the Spaniards at St. Augustine, so that his administration was marked as a season of peace, prosperity and happiness.

CHAPTER IX.

CHARLES AND CORA.

We wandered to the pine forest,
That skirts the ocean foam.
The lightest wind was in its nest,
The tempest in its home.
The whispering waves were half asleep
The clouds were gone to play,
And on the bosom of the deep
The smile of heaven lay.
—SHELLEY.

IN a thousand artless ways, Cora, despite the strange mystery which seemed to envelop her, won her way to the hearts of all who knew her. Goody Nurse, who was a frequent caller at the home of the widow Stevens, was loud in her praises of the maiden, who had budded into womanhood. Charles found her growing more shy, as she became more mature and more beautiful; but as she grew more reserved, her power over him became greater, until, though unconscious of it, she had made him her slave.

One day he met her in one of her short rambles about the wood near the house. Her eyes were on

the ground, and her face was so sad that it seemed
to touch his heart. He went toward her, and she
started from her painful reverie and looked as if
she would fly.

"Cora, it is I, are you afraid of me?" he asked.
"No."

Then he went to her side and asked:

"Why are you so sad to-day?"

"Do I seem sad?"

"You look it."

"It is because of the good pastor's hatred of me.
You were not at Church last Lord's day?"

"No; I was in Boston."

"Hath not your mother told you of it?"

"She told me nothing."

Her sad eyes seemed to swim in tears, and
Charles entreated her to tell him what Mr. Parris
had said of her. Without answering his question,
she asked:

"What do you think of Goody Nurse and her
sisters, Goody Cloyse and Goody Easty?"

"They are very excellent women," Charles answered, "I would that we had more like them."

"Is it wrong for a young maid such as I to keep
their company?"

"Assuredly not."

Charles saw that Cora had something to tell,
and he begged her to come to a large moss-covered

log, on which they seated themselves, and then he asked:

"Cora, who said it was wrong?"

"Mr. Parris."

"When?"

"On last Lord's day he did upbraid us as the emissaries of the Devil, and Goody Nurse avowed if the minister did not cease to upbraid her in church, she would absent herself."

"That would be a violation of law. All are compelled to attend worship on Lord's day."

She was silent for several moments and then remarked:

"Can a law compel one to go where she is maligned and all the calumnies hate can invent heaped upon her head?"

"By the laws of the colony, all must attend church on Lord's day."

The laws of the Puritans were exacting, and ministers of the character of Mr. Parris took advantage of them.

"It is sad," sighed Cora.

"What did Mr. Parris say of you on last Lord's day, Cora?"

"I cannot recall all that he said. Even his text I have forgotten, for, as he was announcing it, Abigail Williams was seized with a grievous fit, and did cry out that Goody Nurse was pinching

her. When she became quiet, and the pastor
again announced his text, Abigail interrupted him
with: 'It is not a doctrinal text, and it is too
long.' He said that when the children of God
went to worship, Satan came also. Then he declared that the Devil was in the church at that moment, and he looked at Goody Nurse and me, who
sat near each other in the church. 'Do any of
you doubt that the imps of darkness are in your
presence? Behold how they associate the one with
the other. Those who afflict and persecute the
children of the righteous, and the unholy offspring
of a player!' He grew in a towering passion and
cried out so against me, that all eyes were turned
upon me, and I bowed my head. No sooner had
I done so, than he called on all to witness how
Satan rebuked dared not show his face in the house
of God. If I but looked on him to deny his
charges he called it the brazen impudence of a
child of darkness. All through his sermon, I sat
listening to reproof for what I cannot help, or the
frequent allusions to the familiar spirits of Goody
Nurse."

Tears quietly stole from the sad eyes and trickled
down the cheeks of the maiden. He sought to
console her and, to change her mind to a more
cheerful subject, asked:

"Where is your father?"

"Alas, I know not, save that he has gone with his brother Harry Waters to Canada to procure furs."

"Cora, what strange mystery surrounds your life?"

"I know not."

"Don't you remember aught of your mother?"

"No; I never saw her. My earliest recollections are of the theatre, where a nurse cared for me in the greenroom, while my father performed on the stage."

"Does he never talk of her?"

"My mother?"

"Yes."

"He never mentions her name."

"Have you never asked him about her?"

"Yes."

"What answer does he make?"

"He says I may learn all in due time."

To Charles Stevens, it was quite evident that Cora's father was purposely putting off some important revelation. He gazed upon her fair young face and in it could see little or no resemblance to her father. Then a suspicion entered his mind, that she might not after all be the child of George Waters. Though mysterious, Cora tried to conceal nothing; her manner and conversation were frank and open.

"Your father was captured at the battle of Sedgemore, was he not?"

"Yes; he was impressed into the army of Monmouth. My father had no interest in either army.
What were their quarrels to him? Part of the
time he was in the Netherlands, and a part of the
time in France, Scotland or Wales. I don't think
at any time he knew much of England's trouble.
We were roving all the time and thought little of
political questions. When he was arrested and
forced into Monmouth's army, at Bridgewater, he
asked whose army it was."

"And you followed him?"

"I followed at a distance and from a lofty hill
watched the long, hard struggle. Oh, such a scene
as it was! Ranks of cavalry and ranks of infantry
dashing at each other. Through the great volumes
of smoke and dust, I watched the regiment to
which my father had been attached. I saw it in
the thickest of the fight and, kneeling by a stone
fence, prayed God to spare him. God answered
my prayer, for he was spared. When I saw Monmouth's army retreating and the ruthless butchers
of the king in pursuit, I ran down the lane, weeping and wringing my hands, expecting to find his
dead body. I was very young then; but the scene
has been indelibly stamped on my memory.

"As I was running down the hill, I met him,

so covered with dust and blackened with gunpowder,
that at first I knew him not. He knew me, and,
as I swooned at his feet, he carried me across a
field to a road-side inn, where I recovered, and we
were about to resume our flight, when the king's
soldiers surrounded the house. One of the officers
cocked his pistol to shoot my father and would have
done so, had I not clung to his neck and presented
my body as a shield between him and the trooper's
bullet.

"'Spare him for the hangman,' suggested another.

"He was spared, and at the trial it appeared that
he held no commission in the rebel's army, so he
was condemned to ten years' penal servitude in the
colonies, and was sent to Virginia, whither I went,
also. Of our escape, through the kindness and
courage of your relative in Virginia, you already
know."

"Is your father going to take you away?"

"Yes; he says that my persecution at Salem
will cease as soon as he can prepare a home for me."

"Where?"

"In Maine."

"Do you want to go away, Cora?"

She was silent for a long while, in fact, so long
was she silent that he asked the question again before she answered. Then, fixing her beautiful

eyes, with a startled expression, on him, she answered:

"No, no! I would not go away, if I could remain
in peace; but our persecutions seem endless. My
father is a good man. Although he was a player,
he was ever the kindest of fathers, and taught me
only the purest religious sentiments, yet Mr. Parris
calls him the agent of the devil."

Charles shudderingly responded:

"Cora, I fear we are on the verge of a fearful
upheaval of ignorance and superstition. Religion,
our greatest blessing, perverted, will become our
greatest curse. I cannot understand it, Cora; but
we are on the brink of some terrible volcano, which
will destroy many, I fear."

That Charles Stevens was no false prophet, sub-
sequent history has fully proven. Coming events
seemed to cast their dark shadows before. In New
England, there had been a preparation for this
stage in the temper with which the adventurers had
arrived in the country, and the influences which at
once operated upon them. Their politics and religion were gloomy and severe. Those who were
not soured with the world were sad, and, it should
be remembered, they fully believed that Satan and
his powers were abroad and must be contended
with daily and hourly and in every transaction of
life. There was little in their new home to cheer

them; for the gloomy and unexplored forests shrouded the entire land beyond the barren seashore. Their special enemy, the Indian, always on the alert in some mysterious glade to take advantage of them, was not, in their view, a simple savage. Their clergy, ignorant and fanatic as they were zealous, assured them that the Indians were worshippers and agents of Satan; and it is difficult to estimate the effect of this belief on the minds and tempers of those who were thinking of the Indians at every turn of daily life. Indian hatred has ever been mingled with ferocity and fanaticism quite inconsistent with mild precepts of Jesus Christ. This passion, kindled by the first demonstration of hostility on the part of the Massachusetts red man, grew and spread incessantly under the painful early experience of colonial life, and has been only intensified by time. In turn, every man had to be scout by day and night, in the swamp and in the forest, and every woman had to be on the watch in her husband's absence to save her babes from murderers and kidnappers. Whatever else their desires might be, even to supply their commonest needs, the citizens had first to station themselves within hail of each other all day, and at night to drive in their cattle among the dwellings and keep watch by turns. Even on Sundays, patrols were appointed to look to the public safety while the citizens were at church. Mothers carried their babes to the meeting-house in preference to remaining at home in the absence of husbands and neighbors. The Sabbath patrol was not only for the purpose of looking for Indians, but to mark the absentees from worship, note what they were doing, and give information accordingly to the authorities. These patrols were chosen from the leading men of the community—the most active, vigilant and sensible—and one can easily perceive that much ill-will might have accumulated in the hearts of those whom they saw fit to report. Such ill-will had its day of triumph when the Salem tragedy reached its climax.

Levity, mirth and joy were condemned by the Puritans, and nearly all amusements were discarded. The merry whistle of the lad was ungodly in their eyes, and Charles Stevens had come in for his share of the reproof because God had given him a light heart. Life to them was sombre, and, usually, sombre lives lead to bloodshed, crime and fanaticism.

Charles sought to instil some of his joy into the sad life of the unfortunate maid. To him the sun shone brightly, the flowers bloomed radiantly, and the birds sang sweetly for the pleasure of man. Life was earnest, but not austere, and religion did not demand gloom.

11

"Have no care for what Mr. Parris may say," he said. "His congregation is divided against him, and he cannot harm you."

"Only a little longer, just a little longer, and I will be gone where they can torment me no more," answered Cora. "In the forests of Maine, I will be hidden from the eyes of my enemies and be alone with God."

They rose and wandered down the path on either side of which the densest of thickets grew. Both were lost in thought. A shadow had come over the face of Charles Stevens the moment Cora spoke of going away. He had never admitted even to himself that he loved her; yet, ever since that stormy night when he volunteered to brave the tempest and conducted her home, he had been strangely impressed with Cora.

The mystery of her early life was somewhat repugnant to one of his plain, outspoken nature; yet, with all that, he was forcibly impressed by her sweet, pure and sad disposition.

They were wandering pensively hand in hand toward his mother's home, when a voice called to them from across the brook. The sound of the voice broke the spell, and, looking up, he saw Sarah Williams coming toward them.

"Hold, will you, Charles Stevens, until I speak to the one who accompanies you."

The young widow was greatly excited, and her voice trembled with emotion.

"Who is that woman?" asked Cora, trembling with agitation.

"Sarah Williams."

"I have seen her."

"Where?"

"At church. She was the one who upbraided Goody Nurse for being a witch."

Cora was greatly agitated, as she saw Sarah Williams, with demoniacal fury, hastening toward her. Surely she would do her no injury, for Cora was not conscious of ever having given her offence.

"Have no fears, Cora, she will not harm you. I trow it is some commonplace matter of which she would speak."

Thus assured, she had almost ceased to dread the approach of the woman, when Sarah Williams suddenly cried, in a voice trembling with fury:

"Cora Waters, have you no sense of shame? Are you wholly given up to the evil one?"

"What mean you?" Cora asked.

"Why do you torment me?"

"I do not, knowingly."

"False tool of Satan! Did not your shape come at me last night?"

"Assuredly not."

"Oh woman, woman! why will you speak so falsely? I saw you."

"When?"

"Last night, as I lay in my bed, you came and choked me, because I would not sign the little red book which you carried in your hand."

Filled with wonder, Charles Stevens turned his eyes upon Cora, whose face expressed blank amazement, and asked:

"What does this mean?"

"I take God to be my witness, that I know nothing of it, no more than the child unborn," she answered.

"Woe is the evil one, who speaks falsely when accused!" cried the enraged Sarah Williams. Then she closed her fist and made an effort to strike Cora, who, with a scream, shrunk from her.

"Hold, Sarah Williams! Don't judge hastily, or you may judge wrongly."

"Go to! hold your peace, Charles Stevens, for, verily, I know whereof I speak, when I charge that the shape of Cora Waters does grievously torment me."

"Are you mad?"

"No."

"Then of what do you accuse her?"

"She is a witch."

At this awful accusation both Charles and Cora

shrunk back in dismay, and for a moment neither could speak; but Sarah Williams was not silent. She continued upbraiding the unfortunate girl, heaping charge upon charge on her innocent head, until Cora felt as if she needs must sink beneath the load.

"You have bewitched my cows; my sheep and swine die mysteriously. Your form is seen oft at night riding through the air. My poultry die strangely and mysteriously, and my dog has fits. Even my poor cat hath fallen under the evil spell which you cast on all about me. Alas, Cora Waters, you are bold and bad. Charles Stevens, beware how you are seen about her, lest the wrath that will fall upon her head involve you in ruin."

Cora Waters, leaning against a tree, covered her face with her hands and murmured:

"Oh, God! wilt thou save me from the wrath of these misguided people?"

"See how she blasphemes! For a witch to call on the name of God is blasphemy of the very worst kind. Away, witch!" and Sarah stamped her foot in violence upon the ground.

"Stay, Cora!" Charles interposed, very calmly. Then he turned upon Sarah Williams, and added:

"You accuse her falsely, Sarah. Beware how you charge her of what the law makes a crime, or you may have to answer in a court for slander."

"Charles Stevens, beware how you defend the being at your side. She is an imp of darkness, and a day is coming when such will not be permitted to run at large. Beware! *beware!* BEWARE!" and with the last command amounting almost to a shriek, she turned about and ran away.

Long Charles Stevens stood gazing after the retreating woman. The gentle breeze, stirring the leaves of the sweet-scented forest, bore pleasant odors to them, the birds sang their sweet peaceful songs, while a squirrel, with a nut in its paws, skipped nimbly over the leaves near and, pausing, reared upon its hind legs and looked at them from its bright little eyes, while the flowers nodded their gaudy little heads as if to invite every one to be glad; but Charles and Cora saw not all these beauties of nature. She stood leaning against the friendly trunk of a giant oak, and turned her eyes on him with a look of helpless appeal and agony. He was so dazed by the bold accusation, that he could not speak for several seconds. She was first to regain her speech.

"She, too, is my enemy."

"Yes," he answered.

"I have no friend——" she began.

"Don't say that, Cora. While mother and I live, you have two friends," he interrupted.

"Yes—yes; I had not forgotten you; but you

may be powerless to aid me. I learned that they were going to arrest and try some of the accused people for witches. It is terrible," she added with a shudder. "In England they burn witches at the stake. My father saw one thus roasted. He said it did touch him with tenderness to see the gallant way she met her fate—cursing and reviling the hooting mob gathered about her, whilst the angry flames, leaping upward, licked her face, caught her locks, crackling about her old gray head. I trow it was a sorry sight, and God be praised, I never saw such a one!"

"You never will, Cora, for those days are passed. We live in a more enlightened and humane age. People are not burned to death now, as they used to be. We are safe under the shelter of humane and wise laws."

Charles was mistaken. Human laws have never been perfect or just, and mankind will never be safe while laws are interpreted by partial magistrates. Laws are never perfect, for, were they, continual amendments would be unnecessary.

On their way home, Charles and Cora were compelled to pass the Salem church. As they did so, they met Mr. Parris face to face, as he was coming out of the sanctuary whither he had gone to pray. He paused near the door and, fixing his large gray eyes on the unfortunate maid, glared at her much as an angry lion might gaze on the object of its hatred; then he turned away on his heel with something about the children of darkness profaning the house of the Lord.

Cora shuddered as long as he was in sight, and when he had disappeared, she said:

"Surely, he is a bad man!"

They resumed their walk to the house. Though neither spoke, they went slowly, each buried in thought. The gentle zephyrs, the frisking squirrels, the nodding flowers, the singing birds, were all unheeded by them. When the home was reached, he found his mother standing in the door, her face almost deathly white.

Though she said nothing, he knew she was greatly disturbed. Her wheel stood idle, the great heap of wool rolls lying unspun at the side of it. She smiled faintly and, as Cora passed into the little room set apart for her, turned her eyes anxiously to her son.

"Mother, has any one been here since we left?" he asked.

"Yes."

"Was it Mr. Parris?"

"It was."

"We saw him come out of the church as we passed."

"He was here but a moment since."

Then Charles felt that something had been said to his mother to occasion alarm, and he asked her what it was.

"He advised me to warn you to flee from the wrath to come. He said you would be involved in ruin ere you knew it, if you continued in your present course."

" What did he mean? "

" He referred to her," and Mrs. Stevens significantly nodded toward the apartment in which Cora was. Charles had expected this answer. He went slowly to the door and looked down the road to see if the pastor was still in sight; but he was not. Only the broad, well-beaten thoroughfare, with the great, old trees standing on either side, and the blue sea beyond the hill, with the village in the valley were visible. The youth's heart was full of bitterness, and the manner in which his mother's words were spoken was not calculated to allay the storm within his breast. Though her words did not say so, her manner indicated that she shared the opinions of Mr. Parris. Turning from the door, Charles went toward her and said:

"Mother, whatever he said of her is false. I know he hates Cora, that he would make her one of the emissaries of Satan; but his charges are false. You know—you must know that she is a pure, good girl."

"I do know it," she answered, her face still anxious and pale. "The accusation is false. I know it is false; yet he threatens."

"Whom does he threaten?"

"You."

Charles laughed, as only a brave lad can laugh at danger. Why need he fear Mr. Parris? Charles was young and inexperienced. He knew not the age in which he lived, and little did he dream of the power which Mr. Parris, as pastor of the church, could wield over the public. The pulpit controlled judges and juries, law-makers and governors in that day, and when an evil-disposed person like Mr. Parris became pastor of a congregation, he could wield a terrible influence.

"Mother, how can he injure me?" Charles asked.

"In more ways than one."

"What are they?"

"I don't know, Charles; but I know—I feel that something terrible is about to happen. Our people will suffer from Mr. Parris—especially all who oppose his ministry."

"I oppose his ministry, and I have no fear of him. All he can do is to wound the feelings of that poor girl; but she will go away soon, beyond reach of his calumny."

"Heaven grant she may, and right soon, too." As Charles was about to leave the house, his mother asked: "Have you heard that Adelpha Leisler from New York is coming?"

"Adelpha Leisler! No——" He started, half in joy and half in regret.

"She is. Surely, you have not forgotten her."

"No, mother. I will never forget the pretty maid."

"Who, you said in your boyhood, was one day to be your wife."

"Truly, I did. I have heard that Adelpha hath kept the promise of early childhood to make a beautiful woman. When will she come?"

"It is said she will be here before next Lord's Day."

The expression of joy uttered in words, as well as the glow which lighted up his countenance, was seen by the white-faced young woman in the next apartment. Cora was not an intentional eaves-dropper. Her door had been left accidentally ajar, and when she heard the name Adelpha Leisler spoken, she started to her feet, moved by a strange impulse quite inexplicable to her. She had never heard the name Adelpha Leisler before, and yet she intuitively felt that the name had some terrible bearing on her destiny. With loud beating heart, lips parted and her whole being expressing pain, she crouched close to the door and listened.

CHAPTER X.

Night is the time for rest,
 How sweet when labors close,
To gather round an aching breast
 The curtain of repose,
Stretch the tired limbs, and lay the head
Upon our own delightful bed.
                    —MONTGOMERY.

JEALOUSY, for the first time, entered the heart of Cora Waters. Blessed is the being free from this curse. The green-eyed monster, unbidden, enters the heart and enthrones himself as ruler of the happiness of the individual over whom it assumes sway. She heard all that mother and son said, and then watched him as he went out. Then she closed the door of her apartment and retired to her bedroom.

It was almost evening, and when Mrs. Stevens informed her that tea was ready, she feigned headache and asked to be excused. It was the heart rather than the head that ached.

Charles Stevens was gathering in the herds as
172

was the custom for the night, when he came rather suddenly upon John Louder, returning from the forest.

"Ho, Charles Stevens, where were you last Lord's Day?" asked Louder.

"Was I missed?"

"You were, and I trow the patrol could not find you."

"I was in Boston."

"Do you know that Mr. Parris hath begun to cry out against some of the people?"

"I have heard as much, and I think the pastor should be more careful, lest he will do an injustice."

Louder shook his head and, seating himself on the green bank of a brooklet, answered:

"Goody Nurse is a witch. She hath grievously tormented me on divers occasions and in divers ways. Fain would I believe her other but I cannot."

"John Louder, you are a deceived and deluded man."

"Nay, nay, Charles, you mock me. I have had her come and sit upon my chest and oppress me greatly with her torments. Have I not been turned into a beast and ridden through thorns and briars at night and awoke to find myself in bed?"

Charles, laughing, answered:

"It was the troubled dream from which you awoke."

"Nay; I found the thorns and briars pricking my hands and legs."

"Perchance you walked in your sleep."

"Charles, why seek to deceive me in that way, when I know full well that what I tell you is surely truth? I see with my eyes, I hear with my ears, and I feel with my senses. Only night before last, I was ridden into a field where they partook of a witches' sacrament."

"And what was it, pray?" asked Charles with a smile of incredulity.

"The flesh and blood of a murdered victim."

Charles laughed outright.

"Nay, nay, Charles, you need not laugh," cried Louder, angrily. "She was there, too."

"Who?"

"The maid who hath lived at your house. The offspring of a vile player. Behold, I saw her partake of the sacrament."

Charles Stevens' face alternately paled and flushed as he answered:

"John Louder, you are the prince of liars, and beware how you repeat your falsehoods, or I shall crack your skull."

Louder, who was a coward, as well as superstitious, had a wholesome dread of the stout youth.

He sprung back a few paces and stammered:

"No, no, I don't mean any harm. I—I am not saying anything against you."

"John Louder, you are a notorious liar, and I warn you to be careful in the future how your vile tongue breathes calumny against innocent people. Begone!"

Louder slowly rose and slunk away, and Charles Stevens returned home. The evening air fanned his heated brow, and he sought to cool his angry temper before he reached home. The silent stars watched the sullen youth who, pausing at the gate, gazed in his helpless misery on the broad-faced moon and murmured:

"How will all this end?"

It was his usual bedtime when Charles Stevens entered the house, and his face was calm as a summer sky over which a storm had never swept. His mother was still plying her wheel, and the heap of wool rolls had grown less and continued to diminish. She asked her son no questions. He sat down near the table, took up a book of psalms and proceeded to read.

There was one in the next apartment who heard him enter. It was Cora, and, rising, she crouched near the door to listen. Perhaps they would say something more of Adelpha Leisler; but he did not mention her name again, and she almost hoped he

cared nothing for her now, although he had confessed that in his boyhood he had looked upon her
as his future wife. Almost every man selects his
wife in his early boyhood; but the child lover seldom becomes the husband. The love of a play-
mate, tender as it may be, is not the love of maturity.
Cora strove to console herself with these thoughts;
but there was another danger that would obtrude
itself in her way. That was the knowledge that
he had not seen Adelpha for years, and she had
developed from a child to a beautiful woman.
Long she sat near the door, feeling decidedly guilty
at playing the part of an eavesdropper; but when
Charles rose, closed his book and went to his room,
and the mother put away her work, Cora rose and
went to her bed. Despite her sorrow and mental
worry, she had sweet dreams. Somebody, who
was Charles, appeared to her in light, and she rose
with the sun in her eyes, which at first produced
the effect of a continuation of her dream. Her
first thought on coming out of the dream was of a
smiling nature, and she felt quite reassured. The
dream had been so pleasant and sweet; life seemed
so peaceful and full of hope; nature smiled so
brightly on this holy morn, that she almost forgot
the hot words of the pastor and her jealousy of the
night before. She began hoping with all her
strength, without knowing why, and suffered from

a contraction of the heart. It was a bright day; but the sunbeam was still nearly horizontal, so she reasoned that it was quite early; but she thought she ought to rise in order to assist Charles' mother in her household duties. She would see Charles himself, feel the warmth of his glance and hear the music of his voice. No objection was admissible; all was certain. It was monstrous enough to have suffered the pangs of jealousy on the night before; but now that the bright dreams and glorious dawn had dispelled these, she felt sure that good news had come at last. Youth is so constituted, that it quickly wipes its tears away, for it is natural for youth to be happy, while its breath is made up of hope.

Cora could not have recalled a single instance in which Charles Stevens had uttered a word of hope or encouragement to her. Her thoughts seemed to play at hide and seek in her brain, and she was so strangely, peculiarly happy this morning, that she preferred to enjoy the revels of day-dreams to the realities of life. Leaving her bed, she bathed her face and said her prayers.

Voices were heard without, and she listened. One was the well beloved voice of Charles Stevens. He was speaking with some one, whom she rightly guessed had just arrived. The voice of the new-comer was too far distant for her to recognize it at

12

first: but her eye, glancing through the lattice, de-
scried the form of a man coming toward the house.
That tall form, with thin, cadaverous features
and stern, unbending eye, was the man who had
publicly condemned her and held her up to the
scorn of the whole congregation, because she was
the child of a player. Cora did not hate him, for
she was too pure, too good, too heavenly to hate
even the man who had declared her to be a firebrand of perdition. What was his object this
lovely morn? His appearance dispelled all the rosy
dreams and once more plunged her into that horrible, oppressive gloom, which seemed heavier than
lead upon her heart.

"You are abroad early, this morning, Mr. Parris," Charles answered to the minister's morning
greeting.

"Not too soon, however," the reverend gentleman answered. "The devil does not sleep. He
is abroad continually, and, verily, one needs must
rise early to be before him and his minions."

"Where are you going, Mr. Parris?" asked the
youth.

"I am coming here."

"Your call is early."

"Not earlier than Satan's. I trow he is here
even already and hath abided with you, before I
came."

Charles made no answer to this, for there is no wrath like the wrath of an angry preacher, whose zeal warps his judgment and makes a fanatic of him. Bigoted, tyrannical, haughty and cruel, Parris swooped down on his enemies with the fury of an eagle.

Charles Stevens was a little amazed at the manner of the minister and asked:

"Is your business with me?"

"It is."

"What is it?"

"It seems best that we converse where there is no danger of being overheard, Charles, as what I have to say is of a very grave and serious nature and concerns your soul's welfare."

When a bigoted, ambitious zealot becomes interested in the welfare of a person, that person is in danger.

The anxious girl, whose face was pressed close to the window lattice watching the men, heard all and turned so pale, that even the warm rays of the sun failed to give the tint and glow of life to the cheek. She saw them walk away down the path and go across the brook among the trees and over the distant hill.

To Charles, it was like making a pilgrimage to some place of evil, the end of which he dreaded. Across the hill, hidden from the town by trees and intervening slope, they paused near the corner of a stone fence, and Mr. Parris leaned against the wall and gazed on Charles in silence.

"What have you to say, Mr. Parris?" the young man asked, as the cold, gray eye, like a gleam of steel fell upon him. Mr. Parris, in slow and measured tones, answered:

"No man knows until the time comes what depths are within him. To some men it never comes. Let them rest and be thankful. To me it was brought—it was forced upon me. I am despised, misused and abused by the world for the fact that I stand in the hand of God to do his holy will."

"You talk strangely, Mr. Parris," said Charles, when the wild-eyed fanatic had finished and turned his haggard face up toward heaven. "I think your earnestness and zeal are mistaken."

"Yes, mistaken by all; but I know the Lord ordains me for this good and holy work, and I will serve my Master, hard as the task may be."

"Mr. Parris, may we not be mistaken in what constitutes the service of the Master?"

"Aye! Is not the way so plain that a wayfaring man, though a fool, cannot err therein?"

"Yet, 'they shall put you out of the synagogues; yea, the time cometh that whosoever killeth you will think that he doeth God service.' The great question to decide is which is right. 'Not every one that saith Lord, Lord, shall enter into the kingdom of heaven.'"

"I am right!" cried Mr. Parris, his face flaming with passion.

"So Melendez believed, when he drenched the soil of Fort Carolinia with the blood of innocent women and children."

"Young man, I am the preacher, not you. It is for me to speak and you to listen. Satan has been unchained, and the air is full of evil spirits."

"Mr. Parris, I have heard enough. Let me stop you here. It will be better for you and better for me. Let me go home."

"Not yet. The Lord commands, and it must and shall be spoken. I have been in torments ever since I stopped short of it before. Look not amazed nor alarmed when I tell you that the day of the wrath of the Lord is coming, and the minions of hell that torment this accursed land will be gathered into the fires of destruction. Charles, forgive this earnestness, it is for your sake. It is another of my miseries. I cannot speak on that subject nor of that subject without stumbling at every syllable, unless I let go my check and run mad;" and as Charles Stevens gazed into those wild eyes and hollow cheeks, he thought the man must already be mad.

"Let us return home, Mr. Parris. Take an-

other day to think, before you give expression to
what you would say."

"No, no; you must hear me now! Here is a
man driving his cows forth to graze. He will be
gone directly. I entreat you let us walk down the
road and return, for what I would say, Charles,
must be for your ears alone."

He yielded to the entreaty. How could he do
otherwise, for there could be no harm in walking
with the pastor? Mr. Parris, among his other ac-
complishments, had the power of dissembling. He
could assume a smiling exterior while a devil raged
in his heart. After they had gone aside some distance, and the farmer had passed on with his cows,
they returned to the old stone wall, and Charles
waited, very much as a criminal might, who stood
to receive his sentence.

"You know what I am going to say," the pastor began, his austere face once more assuming its
terrible expression. "You don't like me, your
mother don't like me, and the congregation is divided, doing all in their power to dispossess me;
but I am right. What other men may mean when
they use that expression, I cannot tell. What I
mean is that I am under the influence of some tre-
mendous power, which I know is God Almighty,
Himself, and resist that power I dare not. I may
be called a fanatic, cruel, mad; but the great and

good God who made me ordains me in all things. This power—this spirit—this will, whatever it may be, is the chief motive that moves me. It could draw me to fire; it could draw me to water; it could draw me to the rack, as it did martyrs of old; it could draw me to any death—to anything pleasing, or repulsive; but I am mistaken, misunderstood by people, and the future as well as the present generation may condemn me in their narrow views as being dishonest, as being revengeful, as being even bloodthirsty; but, Charles, when God did command Peter to slay, did he refuse? No. If my God commands me to slay, I will do it, though rivers of blood shall flow——"

The face of the wild fanatic was terrible to look upon. Charles Stevens, bold as he was, gazing on him in the full light of day, could not repress a shudder. His thin, cadaverous face, smooth shaven and of an ashen hue, was upturned to heaven, and those great, awful eyes seemed gazing on things unlawful for man to see. The long right arm was raised toward the sky, and again that deep voice called out:

"O thou great Jehovah, do but command me, and rivers of blood shall flow——"

"Mr. Parris!" began Charles, alarmed.

"Stop! I implore you do not interrupt me, Charles. Wait until, by fasting and prayer and

long, solemn meditation on these mysterious subjects, the Lord has opened your eyes to the invisible
world, then you may judge. If you become
weary with long standing, sit down, and I will
pour into your ears such proofs that you can no
longer deny the existence of witchcraft."

Charles felt the strange spell of the fanatic's
presence, and he merely bowed his head as a signal for him to proceed. Mr. Parris, in his deep
sepulchral voice, continued: *

"Mr. John Higginson, that reverend and excellent person, says that the Indians, which came
from far to settle about Mexico, were, in their progress to that settlement, under a conduct of a Devil,
very strangely emulating the blessed covenant
which God gave Israel in the wilderness. Acosta
says that the Devil, in their idol Vitzlipultzli, governed that mighty nation. He commanded them
to leave their country, promising to make them
lords over all the provinces possessed by six other
nations of Indians, and give them a land abounding
with all precious things. They went forth, carrying their idol with them in a coffer of reeds, supported by four of their principal priests, with whom
he still discoursed in secret, revealing to them the
successes and accidents of their way. He advised

---

* Like argument is used by Cotton Mather in his "Invisible World."

them when to march and where to stay, and, without his command, they moved not. The first thing they did wherever they came, was to erect a tabernacle for their false god, which they always set in the midst of their camp, and they placed the ark upon an altar. When, wearied with the pains and fatigues of travel, they talked of proceeding no further in their journey than a certain pleasant stage, whereto they were arrived, the Devil, in one night, horribly killed the ones who had started this talk by pulling out their hearts, and so they passed on till they came to Mexico.

"The same Devil, which then thus imitated what was in the church of the Old Testament, now among us, would imitate the affairs of the church in the New. The witches do say that they form themselves after the manner of Congregational Churches, and that they have baptism and a supper and officers among them, abominably resembling those of our Lord. What is their striking down with a fierce look? What is their making of the afflicted rise with a touch of their hand? What is their transportation through the air? What is their travelling in spirit, while their body is cast into a trance? What is their causing cattle to run mad and perish? What is their entering their names in a book, their coming together from all parts at the sound of a trumpet, their appearing sometimes

clothed with light and fire upon them, then covering themselves and their instruments with invisi-
bility? Are not all these but a blasphemous imita-
tion of certain things recorded about our Saviour,
or his prophets, or the saints in the kingdom of
God?"

"Mr. Parris," said Charles, when the fanatic had
paused in his wild harangue for want of breath,
"you seem in earnest; but you must bear in mind
that there is a mistaken zeal——"

"Hold, Charles, I know what you would say;
but God has opened my eyes to the abominations
of witchcraft."

"So Bishop Mendoza thought, when he ordered
the innocent slain. Beware of false prophets, Mr.
Parris. They are more to be dreaded than the
protean devil of which you speak. Be sure that
you remove the beam from your own eye, before
you try to see the mote in the eye of your brother."

The sallow face of the fanatic grew more ghastly
than before. His teeth gnashed, and his great
eyes seemed starting in hatred from his head.
Seizing the wrist of Charles with his hand, he
clutched it so tightly as to almost make him cry
out in pain.

"Charles, Charles, why persecutest thou me?
Have not the scales of infidelity fallen from your
eyes? Would you deny the power of God?"

Charles Stevens, by an effort, freed his hand and, with a boldness which increased as he spoke, answered:

"It is not God whom I deny, but man. God is good and just and kind. He who, in the name of the Lord, would pervert His holy word is an impostor and blasphemer more base than a thief or an infidel."

"Charles, beware!"

"I have listened patiently to you, Mr. Parris. Now listen to me. Where do you find in Scripture justification for the charges you lay at the doors of innocent people such as Goody Nurse, Goody Easty, Goody Cloyse and the poor little maid Cora Waters? What harm have they ever done you, that you, as a Christian man, might not forgive them?"

"Charles——" interrupted Mr. Parris.

"Hold, sir; you shall hear me through. Mr. Parris, you must be a man of singular shamelessness, craft, ruthlessness and impudence, withal. You began your operations with sharp bargaining about your stipend and sharp practice in appropriating the house. and land assigned for the use of successive pastors. You wrought so diligently, under the stimulus of your ambition, that you have got the meeting-house sanctioned as a true church and yourself ordained as the first pastor of

Salem Village. Because you were opposed by Goody Nurse, her sisters and others, you seek to charge them with offences made punishable under our laws with death."

The sallow face of the pastor grew almost white; but, in a voice of forced calmness, he said:

"Go on—go on!"

"No; it is for you to tell, without further discussion, why you brought me here. Rather let me guess it. You have brought me to say something to me about Cora Waters. You have come to tell me she is a witch, and I tell you it is false."

The passionate minister glared at the youth for a moment and said:

"Charles, do you deny that she is the child of a player?"

"I do not; but what sin follows being the child of a player, or being even a player? Nowhere does the Bible condemn the actor for his profession; and, if the player be godly, his calling is unobjectionable. Oh, Mr. Parris, eradicate from your heart the deadly poison of prejudice, and there will appear no harm in that fair, innocent and much-abused young maid. She has ever been a child of sorrow and of tears, one who never in thought wronged any one. Tell me that child is a witch? Mr. Parris, it is false!"

"Then," cried the pastor, suddenly changing his tone, turning to Charles, and bringing his clenched hand down upon the stone fence with a force that laid the knuckles raw and bleeding; "then you may both go down — down to the infernal regions together!"

"THEN YOU MAY BOTH GO DOWN—DOWN TO THE INFERNAL REGIONS TOGETHER!"

The dark look of hatred and revenge with which the words broke from his livid lips, and with which he stood holding out his bruised and bleeding hand, made Charles shudder and turn to go home; but the pastor caught his arm.

"Mr. Parris, let me go. I have heard quite enough. We understand each other thoroughly."

"And you will not give her up?"

"Never."

"Verily, she hath bewitched you."

"I do not believe in witchcraft."

"What! Do you deny the word of God? Have a care! You are going too far in this. And your mother?"

"She does not believe in it, either."

"Charles, why have you and your mother grievously opposed me?" he demanded, his eyes glaring with hatred and his breath coming hard, while a white froth, tinged with blood, exuded from his lips.

"Because you are a bad man, Mr. Parris," cried Charles. "You are a saintly fraud."

The rage of the pastor knew no bounds. Pointing his wounded and bleeding hand at Charles, he cried:

"Go! and may the curse of an outraged God go with you!"

Charles went home.

CHAPTER XI.

ADELPHA LEISLER.

Oh, my luve's like a red, red rose,
. That's newly sprung in June ;
Oh, my luve's like the melodie,
   That's sweetly played in tune.
As fair art thou, my bonnie lass,
   So deep in luve am I ;
And I will luve thee still, my dear,
   Till a' the seas gang dry.
                        —BURNS.

THERE are moments in every life when the soul hovers on some dark brink. It may be the brink of atheism, of despair, of crime, or superstition. Outside influences go far toward impelling life's voyager on his course. If the current takes a sudden turn, it bears him in a different direction from which he had intended. The human mind is inexplicable. It is not a machine that can be taken apart and analyzed. It is not material that can be grasped and comprehended. It is that mysterious knowing, feeling and willing, independent of circumstances; that immortal, indestructible portion of man called soul. It is governed by no known laws, and at times seems to assume all the caprices of chance.

Charles Stevens was a youth of good strong, common sense; yet he could but feel strangely impressed by the words and the awful look of Mr. Parris. The man was surely more than mortal. His voice, hollow and sepulchral, seemed to issue from the tomb. His thin, cadaverous face was sufficient in itself to inspire wonder. Those great, blazing eyes had within them all the fires of lunacy, fanaticism and cunning. Mr. Parris was nothing more than an unscrupulous bigot. He was ambitious, as is proven by his machinations in getting himself declared the pastor of Salem. He was greedy, as is shown by his taking the parsonage and lands as well as demanding an increase in his stipend. He was revengeful, as is shown by the way in which he persecuted those who opposed him. He was unscrupulous in his methods, as is proven in the means he employed. He was filled with prejudice, as is shown in his assailing Cora Waters, because her father was an actor; yet Mr. Parris believed himself a righteous and holy man, walking in the path of the just.

Charles Stevens failed to tell his mother of the strange interview with the pastor, somehow he could not. He unaccountably shuddered when he thought of it, and, despite the fact that he had little superstition in his composition, he felt at times a strange instinctive dread at the awful warning of the pastor.

Since the evening on which the name of Adelpha Leisler had been mentioned, Cora Waters had been strangely shy and reticent, so that Charles Stevens could not tell her of the interview with Mr. Parris, even if he would. Cora was a remarkable girl. She united in the highest perfection the rarest of earthly gifts—genius and beauty. No one possesses superior intellectual qualities without knowing it. The alliteration of modesty and merit is pretty enough; but where merit is great, the veil of that modesty never disguises its extent from its possessor. It is the proud consciousness of rare qualities, not to be revealed to the every-day world, that gives to genius that shy, reserved and troubled air, which puzzles and flatters you, when you encounter it. Cora realized her beauty and genius; but, with that charming versatility, that of right belongs to woman, she had the faculty of bending and modelling her graceful intellect to all whom she met.

Her rare genius, however, could not brook the cold reproofs of the bigoted Parris. The flower which might have ornamented his chapel and filled the little church with sweetest perfume was withered by the chilling frosts of bigotry and prejudice.

13

A player could yield no perfume for Christ, and the sweet, musical voice was stilled, and the heart so full of love, emotion and religion was chilled and driven into exile; but she lived and hoped in her own little world. The sunlight of love was on her heart, until the name of Adelpha Leisler shut out that sunlight and left all in darkness and despair.

Though Cora was excommunicated for being the child of a player, she never let go her hold on Christ. Her father, strolling actor as he was, had taught her to look to God for everything, and in her hour of trial, she knelt in the seclusion of her own room and prayed that this cup might pass from her lips, if it be the Lord's will; but if not, she asked God to give her strength to bear her suffering and trials. She freely forgave Mr. Parris, for she believed his persecution of herself and others was through mistaken zeal.

With Charles Stevens, she was more shy than she used to be. She kept aloof from him for two or three days, until her conduct became noticeable, and Charles one day sought her in the garden for an explanation.

"Have I offended you, Cora?" he asked.

She turned her frightened eyes to his for a moment and answered:

"No."

"Then why do you avoid me? I have scarcely seen you for three days."

She was overwhelmed with hope and confusion for some moments; then, with a faltering voice, she asked:

"Did you wish to see me?"

"I did, Cora. I would not give offence to you for the world, and I feared I had in some way wounded your feelings."

"Charles, was not Mr. Parris here the other morning?"

"Yes."

"You went away with him; I saw you through my window."

"I did."

"Why did he come?"

"Don't ask me about that man. He is one whom I would to God I had never known."

"Don't speak so of him, Charles."

"Cora, he is a bad man."

"He is the pastor."

"For all that, he is cruel and bloodthirsty. I know it. I feel it."

Cora shuddered and made a feeble effort to defend the pastor who had persecuted her; but Charles, who had the retaliating spirit of humanity in his soul, declared he was a pious fraud and a disgrace to his cloth.

On their return to the house, Mrs. Stevens met them at the door with a glad smile on her face, and cried:

"She has come, Charles."

"Who?" he asked.

"Adelpha Leisler."

Mrs. Stevens saw an immediate change in the face of Cora. The features which had begun to glow with happiness suddenly grew sad and clouded, and the eyes drooped. Charles did not perceive that sudden change so apparent to his 'mother, for, at the announcement of the arrival of one whom he had known in his happy childhood days, his heart bounded with joy.

"Where is she, mother?"

"With Goody Nurse."

He hastily took leave of Cora, who, with an oppressive weight on her heart, which seemed to almost suffocate her, went to the little room in which she had known so much joy and misery. All was dark now. Her heart vibrated painfully in her breast. Hope and joy seemed forever banished. He was gone. She could hear his footsteps moving away from the house, and, throwing herself on the couch, she gave way to a fit of weeping. Never did Cora Waters so feel her utter insignificance and loneliness. She was a child of an indented slave, utterly dependent

on the one whom she had had the audacity to
love.

When she realized how unworthy she was, the
unfortunate girl sobbed, half aloud:

"Oh, God, why didst thou create me with desires and ambitions above my sphere? Why didst
thou cast me into this place, where I would meet
him, only to suffer? Father, father, come and
take me hence!"

Meanwhile, Charles Stevens, unconscious of her
suffering, was hurrying as rapidly as he could to
the home of Goody Nurse, where he was to meet
Adelpha Leisler. He reached the house and was
greeted by a tall, beautiful young woman, with
great, black eyes and hair.

The greeting she gave him was warm, almost
ardent, for, although Adelpha was an accomplished
young lady, she had all of the genial warmth of
youth. They were soon talking pleasantly of those
happy days of long ago.

Glorious past, gone like a golden dream to return no more! The very memory of such pleasure
produces pain, because it is forever gone. Great
changes had come since last they met. His father
was living then, a handsome, strong man, noted
for his kindness of heart. Many friends, who
now existed only in pleasant remembrance, then
lived, breathed and moved upon the earth.

Then he loved Adelpha, and she loved him, and he half hoped that this meeting in mature life would reproduce the pleasant sensations of childhood; but there is a love which is not the love of the thoughtless and the young—a love which sees not with the eyes and hears not with the ears, but in which soul is enamoured of soul. The cave-nursed Plato dreamed of such a love. His follow-ers sought to imitate it; but it is a love that is not for the multitude to echo. It is a love which only high and noble natures can conceive, and it has nothing in common with the sympathies and ties of coarse affections. Wrinkles do not revolt it. Homeliness of features do not deter it. It demands youth only in the freshness of emotions. It re-quires only the beauty of thought and spirit.

Such a love steals on when one least suspects and takes possession of the soul. Such a love cannot be uprooted by admiration or fancy. . Charles Stevens found Adelpha grown so beautiful, so witty and accomplished, that he was awed in her presence at first; but her freedom of manner re-moved all restraint, and in an hour they seemed transported back to childhood's happy hours.

Next day they wandered as they had done in earlier years by purling streams and mossy banks, under cool shadows of friendly trees. Every old playground and hallowed spot was visited once more, and they lived over those joyous scenes of childhood.

"I sometimes wish that childhood would last forever," said Charles.

"Childhood brings its joys, but its sorrows as well," Adelpha answered, as she sat on the mossy bank at his side, her bright eyes on his face. "One would grow weary of never advancing. Don't you remember how, in your boyhood, you looked forward with pleasure to the time when you would be a man?"

"I do."

"And how you planned for a glorious future?"

"I remember it all."

"To doom you to perpetual childhood, to constantly have those hopes of being a man blasted would eventually bring you to endless misery. No, Charles, childhood, to be happy and joyous, must be brief. The youth with ambition longs to enter man's estate. He sees life only in its rosiest hues, and his hopes and anticipations form half his happiness."

"Your words, Adelpha, teach me how foolish and idle was my remark. Let us change the subject to something more practical. Will your father, as governor of New York, be disturbed?"

Her face grew sad.

"I have great fears."

"For what?"

"Father and Jacob Milborne may be declared usurpers."

"But it was on the accession of William and Mary to the throne of England that your father became governor."

"True. It was not until Andros had been seized in Boston, imprisoned and sent to England, that my father suggested the seizure of Fort James. He was made commander and afterward governor, and so holds his office to this day. I don't know how William and Mary, our dread sovereigns, will be affected by this seizure of the government of New York."

"It was in their interest."

"It was so intended; but we have all learned not to put our trust in princes. It is quite dangerous to do so, and I sometimes fear that trouble will come of it."

"Surely, Adelpha, one of your happy turn of mind would not borrow trouble. It will come quite soon enough without, and a philosopher would wait until it comes rather than seek it."

"You are right, Charles; let us be young again, romp in the wood, chase butterflies and forget the dark clouds that may be hovering over us." She started to her feet and asked: "Charles, who is that lovely, but shy young girl, whom I see hurrying along the path?"

He looked in the direction indicated by Adelpha's jeweled finger, and said:

"She is Cora Waters."

"And who is Cora Waters?"

"A very sweet and amiable girl tarrying here for the present. Her father was a player, and he became involved in the rebellion in England."

Charles did not care to tell all, for Cora was a disagreeable subject to discuss with Adelpha; but the companion of his childhood was not to be so easily put off.

"Charles, she is very pretty. Why have you not told me of her before?"

"I did not suppose you would be interested in her," the young man answered.

"Not interested in her, with all the romance attached to her. A child reared in old England, of which I have heard so much, the daughter of a player, perchance an actress herself. Oh, Charles, I am very anxious to see her and talk with her."

"Adelpha, do you forget that she is a player?"

"Oh, no; we descendants of the Netherlands look on such things in a far different light from the fanatical Puritans of New England. I must know this Cora Waters."

"You shall."

As Charles strolled away from the spring with Adelpha, the face of Sarah Williams appeared from behind some bushes. Her jet black eyes flashed with fire, and her teeth gnashed until they threatened to crack between her angry jaws.

"He hath another! Which of the two doth he love most? I will know, and then—woe betide her!"

Sarah Williams was cunning and utterly unscrupulous. As she glared after Charles and Adelpha, her fertile brain was forming a desperate, wicked scheme. She watched them until they disappeared over the hill, and then, turning about, walked hurriedly to the parsonage.

Adelpha, who was a merry, light-hearted girl, in love with all the world, insisted on forming the acquaintance of Cora, until Charles, to gratify her, granted her request, and the maids met. Cora was distant and conventional, while Adelpha was warmhearted and genial. They came to like each other, despite the fact that each looked on the other as a rival.

Cora had given up Charles Stevens, realizing that she was inferior and unworthy in every sense, and certainly not capable of competing with the daughter of the governor of New York. On the other hand, Adelpha saw a dangerous rival in this mysterious maid with eyes of blue and hair of gold;

but Adelpha was honest and true, as were the old Knickerbockers who followed her. She realized the maid's power and, in her frank and open manner, loved her rival. Despite the fact that they were rivals, the girls became friends, and as Adelpha had learned more of Cora's trials, she gave her the full sympathy of her warm, loving heart.

Sarah Williams, who watched them with no little interest, asked herself:

"I know he loves both. Can a man wed two? No; he must choose between the two, so I will stand between."

Charles, on account of his superior education, was regarded as an extraordinary personage. He was gloomy and sad of late, for Sarah Williams, with her keen woman's instinct, had probed his secret. He was troubled to know which maid he loved most.

Cora, with her melancholy beauty, appealed to his strong emotions; but Adelpha, with her fine figure, her great, dark, lustrous eyes and charming manner, seemed equally attractive. If Cora were the stream that ran deepest, Adelpha was the one that sparkled brightest. At one moment he was ready to avow his love for one, and the next moment he was willing to swear eternal fealty to the other.

Late one afternoon, he wandered with Cora at his side across the flowery meadow to a point of land presenting a grand and picturesque view of green fields, blue hills and the distant sea. They had come to watch the sunset, and Charles wished to be alone with Cora, that he might sound the depths of his heart and ask himself if he really loved her.

Her father was to come in a few days and take her away to the far-off wilderness, so, if he spoke the promptings of his soul, he must do it now. Long they sat on the grassy knoll and watched the declining sun.

"How long have you known Adelpha?" Cora asked.

"We were children together."

"Has she always lived in New York?"

"Yes; but our grandparents knew each other. Matthew Stevens had a Dutch friend, Hans Van Brunt, whom he met in Holland. When Van Brunt emigrated to New Amsterdam and Matthew Stevens to New Plymouth they renewed their friendship. Their descendants have always kept up the friendship. Matthew Stevens was my grandfather, and Hans Van Brunt was Adelpha Leisler's great-grandfather. When quite a child, Adelpha's mother, the wife of a prosperous New York merchant, spent a year in Boston where I lived. It was then Adelpha and I first became acquainted."

Cora's eyes were on the distant blue hills; but her thoughts seemed elsewhere. Charles would have given much to have known what was in her mind. Did she, in her heart, entertain hatred for Adelpha? Her remark a moment later convinced him to the contrary.

"Adelpha is a lovely maid and as good as she is beautiful. Her lot is a happy one."

There was no bitterness, no regret in the remark; yet her words were so sad, that they went to the heart of Charles.

"Cora, there is such a difference in the lots of people, that sometimes I almost believe God is unjust."

"Charles!" she cried, quite shocked.

"Hear me out, before you condemn me, Cora. Here is Adelpha, who has known only sunshine and happiness, health and prosperity. She was born in a wealthy family, and has all the luxuries that riches can buy——"

"She is good and deserves them," interrupted Cora. "God has rewarded her."

"But, on the other hand, you are just as good; yet your life has been one of bitterness. Misery seems to steal some people at their birth; but sometimes there come changes in the lives of peo-

ple.   All may run smoothly for a while, then
storms gather about the head of the child of fortune, while, on the other hand, to one who has
fought and struggled through storms and adversity
a peaceful harbor may open——"

Cora suddenly said:

"God forbid, Charles, that our lots should be
reversed. I would not have Adelpha Leisler drain
the cup of bitterness, as I have done; but we must
change our subject, for, see there, Adelpha and
Alice Corey are coming."

He looked up and saw the two near at hand.

Alice Corey was a bright-eyed girl of fourteen,
a niece of Goody Nurse who had been accused of
witchcraft. She was a girl of a light and happy
disposition, and, as yet, cares sat lightly on her
brow.

"Watching the sunset, are you?" said Adelpha,
breathless with rapid walking.

"We have been," answered Charles.

"Well, it is a pretty thing to see, and I wish he
would always be setting," declared Alice Corey.

"A child's wish," answered Adelpha.   "What
would become of your flowers?"

"I am sure I don't know. I do so love that
red tinge over there, just where it touches the
gray."

"It is somewhat like that queer sea-shell which

Cora showed me yesterday," said Adelpha. " What splendid paints these mermaids must use, down in their deep sea-caves! It is a kind that does not rub off with wetting. The shells are their pink saucers."

" What! Do they really paint?" cried the credulous Alice.

Charles Stevens laughed softly and answered: " No, child. You must not believe such stories. I will tell you a prettier one if you'll listen."

" Oh, I'll listen!" cried Alice, who, like all children, was ever ready to give ears to a story. Charles began:

" Once upon a time, long before Adam and Eve lived, I believe it was, while the earth was young, there lived on it a fair, radiant maiden, sweeter than the breath of fresh-blown roses and more lustrous than the morning star. All the world was her own paradise, and she traversed it as she chose, finding everywhere trees bearing golden fruit, which never turned to ashes, flowers in perpetual bloom, fountains that bubbled and birds that sang in the linden groves, all for her. Nothing was forbidden her. No cares, no fears, or griefs marred her pleasures; for she had no law to consult but her own wishes. When she would eat, the trees bent down their boughs, and whispered, 'Choose my fruit.' When she would listen, the

birds vied with each other in their melodies.
When she would walk, the green sod was proud
to bear her, and, when weary, the gentlest flower-
laden zephyrs soothed her to rest.   Thus she might
have remained always happy; but one day she
chanced to see herself in the water, and she thought
how every thing else was double.   Then she became conscious of a strange pain.   Every thing
now lost its charm.   She sought a companion; but
she could find none.   Nothing was wanting but
the thing she most desired—the sight of her own
kin.   At last, she instinctively felt that the burning gaze of a lover was bent upon her face, and,
looking up, she saw only the sun in the sky, shining as though myriads needed his light.   'Alas!'
she sighed, 'He is as lonely as I, and he shall be
my lover;' but the sun was coy and timid.   He
gazed proudly at her from a great distance, and
veiled himself behind a cloud when she would see
him, that his brightness might not harm her; but
he never came nigh.   At last, when she was worn
out with longing for a closer companionship, she
set out to find her adored sun; and as she sighed,
'Shall I find him never?' some one from a grotto
near by answered, 'Ever?'   'Who are you?' cried
the maid.   'I am a bodiless spirit,' was the answer, 'the voice of one that is gone.   I tell impossible things.   I am the shadow of the past, the

substance of events to come. Man is a mocker.'
'Can you tell me where to find my lover?' asked
the maid. Echo told her not to look up for him,
for he was too high above her, not to seek him in
the east, for then he was hastening away; but to
seek him in the west, where he laid himself
and rested at night, for the night was made for
lovers. Then she hastened joyously, till she
came to the extreme west, to the very edge of the
world."

"How could she get to the edge, when it is
round?" interrupted Alice.

"Probably the world was not round at that
time," explained Adelpha.

Charles went on:

"The maid summoned all the powers of nature
and the air, and bade them build a palace. It
was not like other palaces. There were no jewels
there; but every thing was warm and crimson and
ruddy. The gates were parallel bars of cloud,
with the west wind for warden. Crystals of rain-
drops paved the court-yard. The architecture was
floating mists and delicate vapors, filled with a
silent music, that waited only for the warm touch
of the player to melt it into soul-subduing harmo-
nies; and along the galleries ran a netted fringe of
those tender whispers, which only the favored may
hear. So she built her palace and filled it with

14

all things such as she thought the sun would like,
not forgetting an abundance of fire to warm him,
lest even her love would prove insufficient for one
of so fiery a nature.   Then she dismissed her at-
tendants and sat down alone to wait his coming.
The day seemed long and drear and weary; but
she had seen him watching her, and he was coming
at last.   Down the slope he glided, holding his
fiery steeds in check.   There was joy for the desolate one, for her lover was coming; but the pitiless
sun descended and swept by, scorning the open
gates, and her siren voice, that would have wooed
him thither.   The next day passed, and the next,
and the next, and she was still disappointed; but
she could not believe that all her labor had been
in vain, and still she nursed her sickly, dying
hope.   Though that sun has set thousands of times
since then, she hopes for their union still.   In the
day time the palace is dark like the clouds; but,
as evening approaches, she lights it up for his
coming.   Then we see those glorious tints of crimson and gold and purple and dun, dimming till
they mingle with the white clouds above, and, were
we near enough, we might possibly hear the tones
of the reviving music, as it melts; but as the sun
goes fairly down, the music hushes, the beautiful
tints fade and die, the palace becomes a dark spot
again, and the poor little watcher within sighs

forth her disappointment and composes herself to wait for another sunset."

"I don't believe your story, Charles Stevens," said Alice, at the conclusion, "and I don't see what good it does, anyhow, to make up such a one as that."

"The moral in it is man's faithlessness and woman's constancy," put in Cora Waters, who had, for a long time, been silent.

Adelpha, who had watched the sun sink beneath the distant blue hills, as she listened to Charles, now chanced to glance over her shoulder at the sea behind, with the moon just rising above the watery horizon, and with a merry peal of laughter she added:

"Charles, your heroine is more dull than modern maids, or, when the sun jilted her, she would have wooed the moon."

Alice, rising, said, "It is growing dark. Let us go home."

"Alice, are you afraid of the witches, which seem to disturb Mr. Parris and Cotton Mather?" asked Adelpha.

"There are no witches," Alice Corey answered with a shudder. "Father and mother both deny that there are any witches, and it is wrong to cry out against my aunt, Goody Nurse."

"I dare say it is. The evening grows chill. Let us go home."

As the four wended their way across the fields
and meadows, Charles Stevens, who walked between Cora and Adelpha, cast alternately furtive
glances at each, sorely troubled to decide which
he liked best.

"Both are beautiful," he thought. "Ere long
I must wed, and which of the twain shall it be?
Both are beautiful, and both are good; but, un-
fortunately, they are two, and I am one."

The child, who had lingered behind to pluck a
wild flower, at this moment came running after
them, calling:

"Wait! wait! I implore you, wait for me!"

"What have you seen, Alice?"

"A black woman."

The girls were almost ready to faint; but
Charles, who was above superstition, bade them be
calm and hurried through the deepening shades of
twilight to the trees on the hill where the woman
had been seen. He came in sight of the figure of
a woman clothed in black, sitting at the root of an
oak.

"Who are you?" he asked, advancing toward
her.

"Charles Stevens!" she gasped, raising her head.

"Sarah Williams, what are you doing here?"

"Prythee, what are you doing?" she asked.

"This is unaccountable."

She rose and, turning her white face to him, said:

"Charles Stevens, which of the twain do you

"WHICH OF THE TWAIN SHALL IT BE?"

love best?" and she pointed to Cora and Adelpha. He made no answer. "Which of the twain is it?" she repeated. "Aye, Charles Stevens, you shall never wed either. Do you hear?"

"Woman, what mean you?"

"You cannot decide which you love most. Wed neither, Charles. Wed me!"

"You!" he cried, in astonishment.

"Yes, why not?"

"You already have a husband."

"No; he is dead, he was lost at sea. I am still young and fair, and wherefore not choose me?"

Charles Stevens burst into a laugh, half merriment and half disgust, and turned from the bold, scheming woman. She followed him for a few paces, saying in tones low but deep:

"Verily, Charles Stevens, you scorn me; but I will yet make you repent that you ever treated my love with contempt. You shall rue this day."

He hurried away from the annoyance, treating her threats lightly, and little dreaming that they would be fulfilled.

Winter came and passed, and Adelpha Leisler still lingered at Salem. Rumors of trouble came to her ears from home; but the light-hearted girl gave them little thought. One morning in May, 1691, Charles met her coming to seek him. Her face was deathly white, and her frame trembling.

"What has happened, Adelpha?"

"There is trouble at home, Charles," she cried. "Father and Milborne have been arrested and imprisoned and I fear it will fare hard with them.

I want to set out for New York at once. Will you accompany me?"

"I will."

They found his mother and Cora and told them all. He implored Cora to remain with his mother, until he returned, which she consented to do.

CHAPTER XII.

LEISLER'S FATE.

The boast of heraldry, the pomp of power,
And all that beauty, and all that wealth e'er gave,
Await alike the inevitable hour :——
The paths of glory lead but to the grave.

—GRAY.

IN order to explain the sudden danger which menaced the father of Adelpha Leisler, and which she, like a true, heroic daughter, hastened to brave, we will be compelled to narrate some events in our story of a historical nature. Jacob Leisler was an influential colonist of an old Dutch family, as has been stated, and a Presbyterian.

Under the reign of James II. the Presbyterians had suffered, and no one rejoiced more at the accession of William and Mary than did the Dutch of New York.

Sir Edmond Andros, the weak tool of the Duke of York, had rendered himself decidedly unpopular as governor of New York, Connecticut and Massachusetts. Every one rejoiced when he was

216

finally arrested at Boston and sent to England, and
no one rejoiced more than the New Yorkers themselves.

The accession of William and Mary to the throne
of England was hailed with joy throughout the
American Colonies. In New York, a general dis-
affection to the government prevailed among the
people. Under the smiles of Governor Andros,
papists began to settle in the colony. The collec-
tor of the revenues and several principal officers of
King James threw off the mask and openly avowed
their attachment to the doctrines of Rome. A
Latin school was set up, and the teacher was
strongly suspected of being a Jesuit. The people
of Long Island were disappointed in their expecta-
tions of the favors promised by the governor on his
arrival, and became his personal enemies, and in a
word the whole body of the people had begun to
tremble for the Protestant cause.

Here the leaven of opposition first began to work.
Intelligence from England of the designs there
in favor of Orange elevated the hopes of the dis-
affected; but until after the rupture in Boston, no
man dared to act. Sir Edmond Andros, who was
perfectly devoted to the arbitrary measures of King
James, by his tyranny in New England had drawn
upon himself the universal odium of a people animated with a love of liberty, and in the defense of

it resolute and courageous. Therefore, when unable longer to endure his despotic rule, he was
seized, imprisoned and afterward sent to England as
has been stated. The government was, in the
meantime, vested in a committee of safety, of which
Mr. Bradstreet was chosen president.

Already, information of the popular uprising in
England for the Prince of Orange had reached New
York and was stirring the blood of the progenitors
of the old Knickerbockers, who longed to have their
own beloved prince with them. On receiving news
of the arrest of the detested Andros, several captains of the New York militia convened themselves
to concert measures in favor of the Prince of
Orange. Among them was Jacob Leisler, Adelpha's
father, who was most active of all. He was a
man of wealth and considerable esteem among the
people, but destitute of the qualifications essential
to such an enterprise. His son-in-law, Milborne,
a shrewd Englishman, directed all his councils,
while Leisler as absolutely influenced the other
officers.

The first thing they contrived was to seize the
garrison of New York; and the custom, at that
time, of guarding it every night by militia gave
Leisler a fine opportunity of executing the design.
He entered it with forty-nine men and determined
to hold it till the whole militia should join him.

Colonel Dougan, who was about to leave the province, then lay embarked in the bay, having a little before resigned the government to Francis Nicholson, the lieutenant-governor. The council, civil officers and magistrates of the city were against Leisler, and therefore many of his friends were at first fearful of espousing a cause opposed by so many noted gentlemen. For this reason, Leisler's first declaration in favor of the Prince of Orange was subscribed by only a few among several companies of the train-bands. While the people, for four successive days, were in the utmost perplexity to determine what party to choose, being solicited by Leisler on the one hand and threatened by the lieutenant-governor on the other, the town was alarmed with a report that three ships were coming up with orders from the Prince of Orange. This report, though false, served to further the interests of Leisler; for on that day, June 3d, 1689, his party was augmented by the addition of six captains and four hundred men in New York and a company of seventy men from East Chester, who all subscribed a second declaration, mutually covenanting to hold the fort for that prince. Until this time, Colonel Dougan continued in the harbor, waiting the issues of these commotions, and Nicholson's party, being unable longer to contend with their opponents, were totally dispersed, the lieutenant-governor himself absconding on the very night after the declaration was signed.

Leisler, being in complete possession of the fort, sent home an address to King William and Queen Mary, as soon as he received the news of their accession to the throne. The address was a tedious, incorrect, ill-drawn narrative of the grievances which the people had endured and the methods lately taken to secure themselves, ending with a recognition of the king and queen over the whole English dominion. This address was soon followed by a private letter from Leisler to King William, which, in very broken English, informed his majesty of the state of the garrison, the repairs he had made to it, and the temper of the people, and concluded with a strong protestation of his sincerity, loyalty and zeal.

Jost Stoll, an ensign, on delivering this letter, had the honor to kiss his majesty's hand; but Nicholson, the lieutenant-governor, and one Ennis, an Episcopal clergyman, arrived in England before him, and by falsely representing the late measures in New York, as proceeding rather from their aversion to the Church of England than zeal for the Prince of Orange, Leisler and his party were deprived of the rewards and notice which their activity for the revolution justly warranted. Though the king made Stoll the bearer of his thanks to the people for their fidelity, he so little regarded Leisler's complaints against Nicholson, that the latter was soon after made the governor of Virginia, while Dougan returned to Ireland and became Earl of Limerick.

Leisler's sudden rise to supreme power over the province, with fair prospects of King William's approbation of his conduct, could but excite the envy and jealousy of the late council and magistrates, who had refused to join in aiding the revolution; and hence the cause of all their aversion both to the man and his measures. Colonel Bayard and Courtland, the mayor of the city, headed the opposition to Leisler, and, finding it impossible to raise a party against him in the city, they very early retired to Albany, and there endeavored to foment the opposition. Leisler, fearful of their influence, and to extinguish the jealousy of the people, thought it prudent to admit several trusty persons to a participation in that power which the militia, on the first of July, had committed solely to himself. In conjunction with these, who, after the Boston example, were called the committee of safety, he exercised the government, assuming to himself only the honor of being president of their councils.

This mode of government continued till the

month of December, when a packet arrived with a
letter from the Lords Carmarthen, Halifax and
others, directed to "Francis Nicholson, esq., or,
in his absence, to such as, for the time being, take
care for preserving the peace and administering the
laws, in their majesty's province of New York,
in America." This letter was dated the 29th of
July and was accompanied by another from Lord
Nottingham, dated next day, which empowered
Nicholson to take upon him the chief command,
and to appoint for his assistance as many of the
principal freeholders and inhabitants, as he should
deem necessary, also requiring him "to do every
thing appertaining to the office of lieutenant-governor, according to the laws and customs of New
York, until further orders."

As Nicholson had absconded before the letter
reached New York, Leisler considered the letter
as directed to himself, and from this time issued
all kinds of commissions in his own name, assuming the title and authority of lieutenant-governor.
It was while he was thus acting as governor that
his daughter made a visit to Salem as was stated
in the preceding chapter. On the 11th of December, he summoned the committee of safety and,
agreeably to their advice, swore in the following
persons for his council. "Peter De Lanoy, Samuel
Stoats, Hendrick Jansen and Johannes Vermilie,

for New York; Gerardus Beekman, for King's County; Thomas Williams for West Chester, and William Lawrence, for Orange County.

Except the eastern inhabitants of Long Island, all the southern part of the colony cheerfully acquiesced to Leisler's command. The principal freeholders, however, by respectful letters, gave him hopes of their submission, and thereby prevented his taking up arms against them, while they were privately soliciting the colony of Connecticut to take them under its jurisdiction. It was not so much an aversion to Leisler's authority, as a desire to unite with a people from whom they had originally sprung, which prompted the Long Islanders to desire a union with Connecticut, and when Connecticut declined their offer of annexation, they appeared to openly advocate Leisler's cause.

At Albany, the people were determined to hold the garrison and city for King William, independent of Leisler, and on the 26th of October, before the arrival of the packet from Lord Nottingham, they formed themselves into a convention to resist what they called the usurpation of Leisler. As Leisler's attempt to reduce this country to his command was the original cause of divisions in the province, and in the end brought about the ruin of himself and his son-in-law, it may not be out of place here to give the resolution of the convention at large, a copy of which was sent down to the usurping governor.

"Peter Schuyler, mayor, Dirk Wessels, recorder, Jan Wendal, Jan Jansen Bleeker, Claes Ripse, David Schuyler, Albert Ryckman, aldermen, Killian Van Rensselaer, justice, Captain Marte Gerritse, justice, Captain Gerrit Teunisse, Dirk Teunisse, justices, Lieutenant Robert Saunders, John Cuyler, Gerrit Ryerse, Evert Banker, Rynier Barentse.

"Resolved: since we are informed by persons coming from New York, that Captain Jacob Leisler is designed to send up a company of armed men, upon pretence to assist us in this country, who intend to make themselves master of their majesties' fort and this city, and carry divers persons and chief officers of this city prisoners to New York, and so disquiet and disturb their majesties' liege people; that a letter be written to Alderman Levinus Van Schaic, now at New York, and Lieutenant Jochim Staets, to make narrow inquiry of the business, and to signify to the said Leisler, that we have received such information; and withal acquaint him, that, notwithstanding we have the assistance of ninety-five men from our neighbors of New England, who are now gone for, and one hundred men upon occasion, to command, from the

county of Ulster, which we think will be sufficient
this winter, yet we will willingly accept any such
assistance as they shall be pleased to send for the
defence of their majesties' county of Albany; provided they be obedient to, and obey such orders
and commands as they shall, from time to time,
receive from the convention; and that by no means
they will be admitted to have the command of their
majesties' fort or this city; which we intend, by
God's assistance, to keep and preserve for the be-
hoof of their majesties, William and Mary, King
and Queen of England, as we hitherto have done
since their proclamation; and if you hear that they
persevere with such intentions, so to disturb the inhabitants of this county, that you then, in the
name and behalf of the convention and inhabitants
of the city and county of Albany, protest against
the said Leisler, and all such persons that shall
make attempt for all losses, damages, bloodshed, or
whatsoever mischiefs may insue thereon; which you
are to communicate with all speed, as you perceive
their design."

Taking it for granted that Leisler at New York
and the convention at Albany were equally affected
by the revolution, nothing could be more egre-
giously foolish than the conduct of both parties,
who, by their intestine divisions, threw the province into convulsions, sowing the seeds of mutual

15

hatred and animosity, which, for a long time after, greatly embarrassed the public affairs of the colony. When Albany declared for the Prince of Orange, there was nothing else that Leisler could properly require; and, rather than sacrifice the public peace of the province to the trifling honor of resisting a man who had no civil designs, Albany ought to have delivered the garrison into his hands, until the king's orders were received; but while Leisler was intoxicated with his new-gotten power, Bayard, Courtland and Schuyler, on the other hand could not brook a submission to the authority of a man, mean in his abilities and inferior in his degree. Animated by these feelings both sides prepared for hostilities. Mr. Livingston, a principal agent for the convention, retired into Connecticut to solicit aid for the protection of the frontier against the French. Leisler, suspecting that these forces were to be used against him, endeavored to have Livingston arrested as an aider and abettor of the French and the deposed King James.

The son-in-law of Leisler, Jacob Milborne, was commissioned for the reduction of Albany. Upon his arrival before the city, a great number of the inhabitants armed themselves and repaired to the fort, then commanded by Mr. Schuyler, while many others followed the members of the convention to a conference with him at the city hall. In order

to win the crowd over to his side, Milborne de-
claimed much against King James, popery and arbitrary power; but his oratory was lost upon the
hearers, who, after several meetings, still adhered
to the convention. Milborne drew up a few of his
men in line of battle and advanced to within a
few paces of the fort with bayonets fixed. Mr.
Schuyler had the utmost difficulty to prevent both
his own men and the Mohawks, who were then in
Albany, and perfectly devoted to his service, from
firing upon Milborne's party, which consisted of
an inconsiderable number. Under these circumstances, he thought proper to retreat, and soon after
departed from Albany. A second expedition in the
Spring proved more successful, for he gained possession of the city and fort. No sooner was he in
possession of the garrison, than most of the principal members absconded, upon which, their effects
were arbitrarily seized and confiscated, which so
highly exasperated the sufferers, that their posterity, for a long time, hurled their bitterest invec-
tives against Leisler and his adherents.

It was during these intestine troubles and the
threatened Indian wars, that Governor Leisler's
daughter was in Salem out of the way of danger.
The New Englanders were keeping up a petty warfare with the Owenagungas, Ourages and Peno-
cooks. Between these and the Schakook Indians,

there was a friendly communication, and the same was suspected of the Mohawks, among whom some of the Owenagungas had taken sanctuary. This led to conferences between commissioners from Boston, Plymouth, Connecticut and other places, for it was essential to the peace of the English colonists to preserve peace and general amnesty with the powerful Five Nations, and hold them as allies against the hostile French in Canada and the Indians of the east.

Colonel Henry Sloughter had been commissioned governor of New York, January 4, 1689; but he did not arrive to take possession until 1691, over two years after his commission, when the vessel bearing the new governor, *The Beaver*, arrived in the harbor.

Fair historians have acquitted Mr. Leisler of any blame in what others have been pleased to call his usurpation. He was a man not wholly without ambition, yet he was honest and did what he thought right. He had much of the stubbornness as well as honesty of the Netherlands in his composition, and believing himself in the right, determined to persist in it. Jacob Milborne, his English son-in-law, was the more ambitious of the two, and had guided and directed the affair. Leisler was sitting in his house when informed by Milborne that a vessel called *The Beaver* had arrived, bearing Colonel Sloughter, who purported to have a governor's commission.

"Then we will greet him as our governor," said the honest Leisler.

"Wait until you know he is not an impostor, and that this is not a trick to seize our fort," cautioned Milborne. Then Leisler, reconsidering the matter, decided to wait.

The Beaver brought with it one Ingoldsby, who had a commission as captain. When Ingoldsby appeared, Leisler offered him quarters in the city:

"Possession of his majesty's fort is what I demand," Ingoldsby replied, and he issued a proclamation requiring submission. The aristocratic party, which had long been chafing under the rule of the republican uprising under Leisler, thus obtained as a leader one who held a commission from the new sovereign. Leisler, conforming to the original agreement made with his fellow-insurgents, replied that Ingoldsby had produced no order from the king, or from Sloughter, who, it was known had received a commission as governor, and, promising him aid as a military officer, refused to surrender the fort. The troops as they landed were received with all courtesy and accommodation; yet passions ran high, and a shot was fired at them. The outrage was severely reproved by Leisler, who, on March 10th, the day of the landing of the troops issued proclamations and counter proclamations, promising obedience to Sloughter on his arrival.

It was on the evening of March 19th, that this profligate, needy, and narrow-minded adventurer, who held the royal commission, arrived in New York, and Leisler at once sent messengers to receive his orders. Leisler's messengers were detained, and next morning he sent the new governor a letter asking him to whom he should surrender the fort. His letter was unheeded, and Sloughter, who had already come to hate the republican Leisler, ordered Ingoldsby to arrest him and all the persons called his council.

The prisoners, eight in number, were promptly arraigned before a special court, constituted for the purpose by an ordinance, with inveterate royalists as judges. Six of the inferior insurgents, who made their defence, were convicted of high treason and reprieved. Leisler and Milborne denied to the governor the power to institute a tribunal for judging his predecessor, and appealed to the king. In vain they plead the merit of their zeal for King William, since they had so lately opposed his governor. Leisler in particular attempted to justify his conduct from the standpoint that Lord Nottingham's letter entitled him to act in the capacity of lieutenant-governor; but through ignorance, or sycophancy, the judges, instead of delivering their

EIGHT MEN, BEARING LITTERS, WERE AT THE DOOR. ALL WERE DRIPPING
WITH WATER.

own opinion on this branch of the prisoner's defence, referred it to the governor and council,
praying their opinion, whether that letter, "or any
other letters, or papers, in the packet from White-
hall, can be understood, or interpreted, to be and
contain any power or direction to Captain Leisler,
to take the government of this province upon himself, or that the administration thereupon be holden
good in law."

Of course the decision was against Leisler, and
they were arraigned at the bar of justice for the
crime of high treason. On their refusal to plead,
they were condemned of high treason as mutes,
and sentenced to death. Joseph Dudley of New
England, but at this time chief justice of New
York, gave it as his opinion that Leisler had no
legal authority whatever, while Sloughter wrote:

"Certainly, never greater villains lived; but I
have resolved to wait for the royal pleasure, if, by
any other means than hanging, I can keep the
country quiet."

Jacob Leisler was tried and condemned early in
May, 1691, while Charles Stevens and Adelpha
were hastening to New York. Charles, who had
heard something of the offence of Governor Leisler,
and who, young as he was, had come to realize
that royalty yielded nothing to the republican
ideas, began to fear the worst. The acts of Leisler

had the semblance of popular government, and even the liberal William and Mary had their dread of the people. Charles knew Sloughter by reputation as a narrow-minded, bigoted knave, who would scruple at nothing which tended to elevate him in the eyes of the aristocratic party, of which he was a conspicuous devotee. Charles could offer but little consolation, and, as he contemplated Adelpha's sad future, he asked himself:

"Has the wheel of fortune changed its revolutions, and is the sun which has ever shone bright for Adelpha to be clouded? God forbid!"

Charles Stevens and Adelpha reached New York on the very day the assembly was convened (May 14th, 1691) to determine the fate of Leisler and Milborne.

It was evening, and when they entered the town and the once beautiful home now despoiled, was dark and sad. The weeping mother met her daughter at the door.

The character of the assembly was thoroughly royalist. It passed several resolutions against Leisler, especially declaring his conduct at the fort an act of rebellion, and on the 15th of May, the second day of their session and the next after the arrival of Adelpha, Sloughter, in a moment of excitement, assented to the vote of the council, that Leisler and Milborne should be executed. "The house, according to their opinion given, did approve of what his excellency and council had done."

The families of the doomed were notified that on the next day, the 16th of May, 1691, Leisler and Milborne would be hung. The morning of the 16th dawned gloomy and dark. The rain poured in torrents; but Mrs. Alice Leisler and her family, accompanied by Charles, went to bid the doomed men adieu at the jail. Then Charles hurried the weeping women and children home. Great thunderbolts seemed to rend Manhattan Island. The lightning spread a lurid glare on the sky, and the rain fell in torrents. All of the household knew what was being done, and, falling on their knees, they prayed God for strength. Two hours wore on, and then there came a rap at the door.

Charles went and opened it. Eight men, bearing litters, on which were stretched two lifeless forms, were at the door. All were dripping with water.

"Come in!" said Charles, and he sprang to seize Adelpha, who had fallen to the floor in a convulsion.

CHAPTER XIII.

The weird sisters, hand in hand,
Posters of the sea and land,   .
Thus do go about, about ;
Thrice to thine, and thrice to mine,
·   And thrice again, to make up nine.
                                —SHAKESPEARE.

CHARLES STEVENS was detained in New York until early in 1692. First he became involved in trouble through his sympathy with the unfortunate Leisler family and was thrown into prison; but a few days later he was released on bond. Then he lingered awaiting his trial; but the case was finally dismissed, and then he joined an expedition against the Indians on the frontier. He wrote home regularly and never failed to mention Cora in his letter. All the while, Charles was at a loss to decide whether it was Cora or Adelpha who had won his affections. Adelpha's great misfortune and grief only seemed to endear her to him, for the noblest hearts grow more tender with sorrow.

Early in 1692, he returned to Salem after an
234

absence of ten months. Great changes were soon to come about. Salem was about to enter upon that career of madness known in history as Salem Witchcraft. There are few portions of ancient or modern history which exhibit stranger or more tragical and affecting scenes than that known as Salem Witchcraft, and few matters of authentic history remain so deeply shrouded in mystery at the present day. The delusion has never been satisfactorily explained, and time seems to obscure rather than throw light upon the subject.

At this period, the belief in witchcraft was general throughout Christendom, as is evinced by the existence of laws for the punishment of witches and sorcerers in almost every kingdom, state, province and colony. Persons suspected of being witches, or wizards, were tried, condemned and put to death by the authority of the most enlightened tribunals in Europe. Only a few years before the occurrences in New England, Sir Matthew Hale, a judge highly and justly renowned for the strength of his understanding, the variety of his knowledge and the eminent Christian graces which adorned his character, had, after a long and anxious investigation, adjudged a number of men and women to die for this offence.

Only a few rare minds, such as Charles Stevens, living far in advance of the age, were skeptical on the subject of witchcraft. These bold spirits placed themselves in great danger of being "cried out upon" as witches themselves.

This delusion had its fountain-head in Salem; but it was by no means confined to this locality. It spread all over the American colonies and, like most superstitions, hovered along the frontier, where it was fostered in the shadow of ignorance and grew in the dark halls of superstition. The author will not deny that there are many, to this day, who attribute what they do not in the light of reason understand, to supernatural agencies. In Virginia, in Ohio, Kentucky, Illinois and Missouri there existed, in their early days, strange stories of witchcraft.

If the butter did not form from the milk, some witch was in the churn. If the cattle died of an epidemic, or a disease unknown to the poor science of the day, it was the result of witchcraft. If a child or grown person was afflicted with some strange disease, such as epilepsy, the "jerks," "St. Vitus' dance," "rickets" or other strange nervous complaints, which they could not understand, they as once attributed it to witchcraft.

There sprang up a class of people called "witch-doctors" who, it was claimed, had power to dispel the charm and bring the witch to grief. The only way a witch could relieve herself and reestablish her power was to go to the house of the person bewitched and borrow something. As, in those early days, all articles of domestic use were scarce, and neighbors depended on borrowing, many an old lady was amazed to find herself refused, and was wholly unable to account for the sudden coolness of persons, whom she had always loved.

Mr. Parris, the fanatic, fraud and schemer, perhaps did more to augment witchcraft, than any · other person in the colonies. Parris was ambitious. The circle of young girls, as the reader will remember, first held their seances at his home. Their young nervous systems were so wrought upon, that, at their age in life, they were thrown into spasms resembling epileptic fits. Instead of treating their disease scientifically, as such cases would be treated at present, the parson foolishly declared that they were bewitched. Those children could not have been wholly impostors. They were deceived by the preachers and the zealous, bloodthirsty bigots into actually believing some of the statements they uttered. Their nerves were shattered, their imaginations wrought upon, until they took almost any shape capricious fancy or the evilminded Parris would dictate.

When Charles Stevens arrived in Salem, instead · of finding the dread superstition a thing of the past, to be forgotten or remembered only with a sense

of shuddering shame, he found that the flame had
been fanned to a conflagration.   Mr. Parris and Mr.
Noyes contrived to preach from their pulpits sermons on protean devils and monsters of the air,
until the more credulous of their congregations
were almost driven to insanity.   One evening, as
Parris was passing the home of Goody Vance, she
met him at the door, and, with a face blanched
with fear and annoyance, said:

"Mr. Parris, I am grievously annoyed with a
witch in my churn."

"What does she do?" he asked.

"She prevents the butter from forming, and I
have churned until my arms seem as if they would
drop off."

The parson's face grew grave, and, going to a
certain tree, he broke some switches from it and
entered the house.

"Take the milk from the churn," he said.
"Pour it into a skillet and place the skillet on the
coals before the fire."

This was done, and the astounded housewife,
with her numerous children, stood gazing at the
pastor, who, with his white, cadaverous face, thin
lips and hooked nose, looked as if he might have
power over the spirits of darkness.   He drew a
chair up before the fire and, seating himself, began
whipping the milk, saying:

"I do this in the name of the Lord," which he
repeated with every stroke.

Goody Nurse, who was on the best of terms with

AT EVERY STROKE HE REPEATED, "I DO THIS IN THE NAME OF
THE LORD."

Goody Vance, had unfortunately broken the spindle
of her wheel and, knowing that her neighbor had
an extra one, came to borrow it. She was astonished to see their pastor seated before a skillet of

milk whipping it with switches. No sooner was her errand made known, than Parris, leaping to his feet, cried:

"No! no! lend her nothing, or you will break the spell! Avaunt, vile witch, or I will scourge you until your shoulders are bare and bleeding."

Goody Nurse, astonished and terrified, retired, and next Lord's day the incident formed a theme for Mr. Parris' sermon. This was the first sermon Charles had heard since his return.

"Mother, I will go no more to hear Mr. Parris," Charles declared, on reaching home.

"You must, my son. The laws of the colony compel the attendance on divine worship."

"Such laws should be repealed as foolish. Compel one to go to church, to listen to such nonsense!" and Charles hurried away in disgust.

Cora had been watching him during his conversation with his mother. He had scarcely been able to speak with her at all since his return. Charles turned toward her as he ceased speaking, and Cora, seeming to dread meeting his eyes, was about to disappear into her room, when he called her:

"Cora, don't go away. I must talk with you."

"What would you say?" she asked, her heart fluttering in her bosom like a captive bird.

"There is much. Let us go down to the brook and sit on the green banks as we used to do."

She trembled, hesitated a moment and acquiesced. They went slowly down the path, neither saying a word until the brook was reached. When they were seated on the bank, Charles asked:

"Cora, are you still persecuted by Mr. Parris? Does he continue to denounce you?"

"He does."

"That is an evidence that he is a man of low qualities. And he still assails Goody Nurse?"

"Yes, sir. Goody Nurse, Goody Corey, Bishop and Casty have all been cried out upon, and it is not known when they will stop."

"This craze has assumed dangerous proportions, Cora."

"It has. They are going to law," she answered. "Some are already in jail."

"I have heard of it, and, with prejudiced judges and juries and false witnesses, life will be in great peril."

"I know it."

Then Charles was silent for a moment, listening to the song of a bird in its leafy bower. When the feathered songster had warbled forth his lay and flown to a distant tree on which to try its notes, Charles asked:

"Have you seen your father recently?"

16

"He was here two months ago."

"Did he want to take you away with him?"

"He did; but I could not go. I promised to remain until your return."

"Cora, may it not be dangerous so far on the frontier?"

"There is danger; but he has secured me a home with the family of Mr. Dustin, where he thinks I will be safe."

"Is your father's brother with him?"

"He is."

"Did they come here together?"

"Yes; they are inseparable."

"Cora, don't you think there is some mystery about those brothers, which you do not understand?"

"I know there is."

"Were they both players?"

"I believe they once were."

"Have you told your father of the persecutions of Mr. Parris?"

"Not all."

"Why not?"

"It would have done no good, and would have caused him unnecessary annoyance," she answered meekly.

"Just like you, Cora, always afraid of making some one trouble."

Her eyes were on the brooklet and filled with tears, as she remembered how happy Adelpha Leisler had been when at Salem, and how heavily the hand of affliction had fallen upon her.

"Charles, were you with her when it happened?" she asked.

"I was."

"Did you comfort her?"

"Such poor words of comfort as one can offer on such occasions, I gave her," he answered.

"It was so sad, and she is so good, so kind and so noble. Did she bear up well under her great afflictions?"

"As well as one could."

"Alas, the fires of affliction are to try the faithful. God gave her strength to bear up under her trials and sufferings."

"Her troubles are over, Cora, and ours are but just begun."

"What do you mean?"

"This cloud of superstition which is settling about us may engulf us in ruin."

She made no answer. Cora was very pretty as she sat on the embankment, her eyes upon the crystal stream, gliding onward like a gushing, gleesome child, and he could not but declare her the most beautiful being he had ever seen. Charles Stevens was no coquette. He was not trifling with

the heart or happiness of either Cora or Adelpha,
and he had never yet spoken a word of love to
either. Both had won his sympathy, his esteem
and admiration; but, until he had satisfied himself
which had in reality won his heart, he would make
no avowal to either. Seeing that what he said
was calculated to throw a shade of gloom over her,
he changed the subject by saying:

"Let us not anticipate evil, Cora. Wait until
it is upon us."

"Spoken like a ·philosopher," she answered;
"but, Charles, if you see evil in the future, why
not all go away?"

" Where should we go?"

"Far to the north and east. My father has
found a home in the heart of a great, dense forest.
There man is as free as the birds of the air, and
nothing can fetter thought or will. No bigoted
pastor can say, 'You shall worship God in this
fashion;' but all are permitted to worship God as
they choose. There are only the friendly skies,
the grand old forest and God to judge human actions, instead of narrow-minded people, with false
notions of religion."

"I could not go, Cora."

"Why not?"

"This is my home. I know no other. Over
in yonder church-yard, sleeps my sainted father.

He won this pleasant home from the stern, unyielding wilderness, and I will not be driven from it by a set of false fanatics, who accuse, or may accuse us of impossible crimes."

"Charles, if my father builds us a home in the great wilderness, won't you and your mother come and visit with us, until this storm cloud has blown away? I do not ask you to give up your home. I do not ask you to shrink from the defence of it; but a short sojourn abroad cannot be thought to be an abandonment. You should accept our hospitality to afford us an opportunity to repay the debt of gratitude we owe, as well as to secure your mother from an annoyance, which is growing painful."

Her argument was very strong and had its weight with Charles.

"When do you expect your father?" he asked.

"Any time, or no time. He knows not himself when he may come. Poor father; he hath labored arduously to subdue the forest and build us a home. We had nothing,—we were slaves."

"But slaves no longer, Cora."

"Why not? Our term has not expired."

"King William has pardoned all the participators in Monmouth's rebellion."

For a moment, she was overwhelmed with joy and, clapping her hands, gazed toward heaven, murmuring:

"Oh my God, I thank thee!" but, anon, the re-
action came. The pardon for participation in
Monmouth's rebellion was granted; but the sub-
sequent crime—the flight from the master and the
slaying of the overseer—could not be cured by the
king's pardon to the Monmouth rebels. With a
gasping sob, she said:

"But that other—that awful thing?"

"What, Cora?"

"The flight, the pursuit and the death of the
overseer. Oh, Charles, we can never be safe,
while that hangs over us."

Charles Stevens gazed upon the pretty face
bathed in tears, beheld the agony which seemed to
overwhelm her, and his soul went out toward the
poor maid. He had little consolation to offer; but
his fertile brain was not wholly barren of resources.

"Cora, don't give way to despair," he said.
"What your father did was right and justifiable,
though technically the law may take a different
view. I have a relative living in Virginia, wealthy
and influential. I shall write to him to procure a
pardon for your father."

"I know him. The good man, Robert Stevens,
who so kindly gave us a home and aided us to escape. He will do all he can for us."

"He is rich and powerful, and I believe he can
ultimately procure a pardon for Mr. Waters."

Having consoled her, they rose and returned to the house.

That same evening, Charles Stevens met John Bly near the house of his mother.

"How have you been, John?" Charles asked. "This is the first time I have seen you since my return."

"I am as well as one can be who has been ridden twenty leagues," Bly answered.

"Ridden twenty leagues?" cried Charles Stevens in amazement. "Pray what do you mean?"

"I was turned into a horse last night and ridden twenty leagues during the darkness, and I am sore and almost exhausted now."

Charles laughed and passed on.

"I verily believe that all are going mad," he thought. As he went away, he heard Bly say:

"Verily, if you doubt that this one Martin is a witch, fall but once in her power, and you will give ear to what I have said of her."

Next day he met John Kembal, a woodman. Kembal had his axe on his shoulder, and his face was very pale.

"Charles, why did you not tarry in the west?" he asked. "Why came you back to this land most accursed of devils."

"John Kembal, have you, too, gone mad over this delusion of witchcraft?" asked Charles.

"Charles, verily, you have forgotten that the Scriptures say that he that hath eyes let him see, and he that hath ears let him hear. Thank God, I have both eyes and ears, and I have seen and heard, though I would that I had not."

"What have you seen, John Kembal?" Charles asked.

"I will tell you without delay; but I can but pause to thank God with every breath that she can no longer do me injury, seeing she is in prison and chains."

"Whom do you accuse?"

"Susanna Martin."

"What harm has she done you?"

"Listen, and I will tell you all that I know myself. Susanna Martin, the accused, upon a causeless disgust, did threaten me, about a certain cow of mine, that she should never do me any more good, and it came to pass accordingly; for, soon after, the cow was found dead on the dry ground, without any distemper to be discerned upon her; upon which I was followed with a strange death upon more of my cattle, whereof I lost to the value of thirty pounds."

"Perchance, some disease broke out among them," suggested Charles.

"Nay, nay; do not forge that excuse for this creature of darkness. I have more to tell.

Being desirous to furnish myself with a dog, I applied myself to buy one of this Martin, who had a female with whelps in her house; but she not letting me have my choice, I said I would supply myself at one Blezdel's, whereupon I noticed that she was greatly displeased. Having marked a puppy at Blezdel's, I met George Martin, the husband of Susanna Martin, who asked me:

" 'Will you not have one of my wife's puppies?' and I answered:

" 'No; I have got one at Blezdel's, which I like better.'

" The same day one Edmond Eliot, being at Martin's house, heard George Martin relate to his wife that I had been at Blezdel's and 'had bought a puppy. Whereupon Susanna Martin flew into a great rage and answered:

" ' If I live, I'll give him puppies enough!'

" Within a few days after, I was coming out of the woods, when there arose a little black cloud in the northwest, and I immediately felt a force upon me, which made me not able to avoid running upon the stumps of trees that were before me, albeit I had a broad, plain cart-way before me; but though I had my axe on my shoulder, to endanger me in my falls, I could not forbear going out of my way to tumble over the stumps, .where the trees had been cut away. When I came below the meeting-house, there appeared unto me a little thing like a puppy, of a darkish color, and it shot backward and forward between my legs. I had the courage to use all possible endeavors of cutting it with my axe; but I could not hit it. The puppy gave a jump from me and went, as to me it seemed, into the ground.*

"ITS MOTIONS WERE QUICKER THAN THOSE OF MY AXE."

"On going a little further, there appeared unto me a black puppy, somewhat bigger than the first, but as black as a coal. Its motions were quicker than those of my axe; it flew at my belly, and away; then at my throat; so, over my shoulder one way, and then over my shoulder another way. My heart now began to fail me, and I thought the dog would have torn my throat out; but I recovered myself and called upon God in my distress; and, naming

* See Cotton Mather's "Wonders of the Invisible World," p. 144,

the name of Jesus Christ, it vanished away at once."

Charles Stevens tried to argue with Bly that he had had an attack of blind staggers, and that the dog was only an optical delusion; but he could in no way convince him that it was not a reality, and that he was not bewitched.

According to Mr. Bancroft, New England, like Canaan, had been settled by fugitives. Like the Jews, they had fled to a wilderness. Like the Jews, they had looked to heaven for a light to lead them on. Like the Jews, they had heathen for their foes, and they derived their highest legislation from the Jewish code. Cotton Mather said, "New England being a country whose interests are remarkably inwrapped in ecclesiastical circumstances, ministers ought to concern themselves in politics." Cotton Mather and Mr. Parris did concern themselves in politics, and the latter, being unscrupulous and ambitious as well as fanatical, caused hundreds of unfortunate people to mourn.

The circle of children who had been meeting at the house of Mr. Parris began to perform wonders. In the dull life of the country, the excitement of the proceedings of the "circle" was welcome, no doubt, and it was always on the increase. The human mind requires amusement, as the human body requires food, exercise and rest, and when

healthful and innocent amusements are denied, resort is had to the low and vicious. Mr. Parris,
who preached sermons against the evils of the
theatre and excommunicated the child of an actor,
fostered in his own house an amusement as diabolical and dangerous as has ever been known.
Results of that circle were wonderful. Whatever
trickery there might be—and, no doubt, there was
plenty; whatever excitement to hysteria; whatever
actual sharpening of common faculties, it is clear
that there was more; and those who have given
due and dispassionate attention to the process of
mesmerism and its effects can have no difficulty in
understanding the reports handed down of what
these young creatures did and said and saw, under
peculiar conditions of the nervous system. When
the physicians of the district could see no explanation of the ailments of the afflicted children "but
the evil hand," they, with one accord, came to the
conclusion that their afflictions were through the
agencies of Satan.

Convulsions and epilepsy are among the many
mysteries which medical science has not mastered
to this day, and one cannot wonder that the doctors
two centuries ago should declare the afflicted ones
bewitched. Then came the inquiry as to who had
stricken the children, and the readiest means that
occurred was to ask this question of the children

themselves. At first they refused to disclose any
names; but there was soon an end to any such
delicacy. The first prominent symptoms occurred
in November, 1691, and the first public examination of witches took place March 1st, 1692, just
before the return of Charles Stevens from New
York.

One among the first arrested was Sarah Good,
a weak ignorant, poor, despised woman, whose
equally weak and ignorant husband had abandoned
her, leaving her to the mercy of evil tongues.
This ignorant woman was taken to jail, and,
shortly after, her child, little Dorcas, only four
years old, was also arrested and imprisoned in
chains on charge of witchcraft. All this met the
approval of Mr. Parris, whose pale, thin face
glowed with triumph as he declared:

"Now is the coming of the Lord, and the con-
sumption of the fire-brands of hell."

No wonder Charles Stevens was serious. Over
twenty people were in prison on charge of witchcraft, among them an Irish woman, a Roman Catholic, hated more on account of her religion than
any suspicion of evil against her. She was among
the first to hang.

Parris, the wild-eyed fanatic, swinging his arms
about, walked up and down the village, crying
against the evil spirits of the air and longing to

get his clutches on the vile actor, who had dared
enter the consecrated village of Salem.

One evening Mr. Waters returned as mysteriously as he had disappeared. His daughter was
greatly rejoiced to see him and, after the joy of the
first greeting was over, told of all that was transpiring and of the threats of Mr. Parris.

"You must go away," he said.

"When?" she asked.

"On the morrow."

Charles had a short talk with Mr. Waters, and
arrangements were made for the departure of Cora
on the morrow. Mr. Waters retired late that
night to his room. As he was in the act of un-
dressing, he became conscious that a face was
pressed against the window. He stood in the dark
corner where he could scarce be seen. He held a
pistol in his hand until the face disappeared from
the window, and creeping to it, looked out.
There stood a man in the broad glare of the moon.
He had only to glance at his tall form and his
ruffian features to recognize him as the brother of
the overseer whom he had shot in Virginia. For
ten minutes Mr. Waters did not move, but kept
his eyes riveted on the man, who, instinct and
reason told him, was an enemy. At last the man
retired down the path under the hill. Mr. Waters
hurridly wrote a few lines on a scrap of paper, with

only the moon for his candle, and, folding the letter, addressed it to his daughter and laid it on his pillow. Then he opened the window and leaped out to the ground.

He followed the man under the hill, where he found him in conversation with three other men, Mr. Parris, John Bly and Louder. He was near enough to hear what they said and catch their plans; but he did not wait to listen. As he was creeping among the bushes, a man suddenly rose before him. His dark, tawny skin, his blanket and features indicated that he was an aborigine. He had seen the white men under the hill, and he told Mr. Waters that he had ten braves at hand.

"Tell them to do no one harm, Oracus," said Mr. Waters. "I have never harmed mankind, save in defence, and, God willing, I never will. I am going away."

The Indian silently bowed and disappeared into the forest. Mr. Waters paused under a large oak tree and gazed at the house where his daughter was sleeping so peacefully; then he went away to the great north woods.

CHAPTER XIV.

THE FATE OF GOODY NURSE.

Oh! lives there, Heaven, beneath thy dread expanse,
One hopeless, dark idolator of chance,
Content to feed, with pleasures unrefined
The lukewarm passions of a lowly mind?
—CAMPBELL.

CHARLES STEVENS was sleeping soundly, dreaming of Cora and peace, when there came a rap at the outer door. He rose and, but half-dressed, proceeded to open it. Four tall, dark men stood without. By the aid of the moon, he recognized Mr. Parris, Bly and Louder.

"Is Mr. Waters here?" asked Mr. Parris.

"He is asleep in his room," Charles answered.

"Awake him. This good man from Virginia wants to see him."

Charles turned away and went to Mr. Waters' room. The door was ajar, and, entering, he found the apartment vacant. An open window showed by what means Mr. Waters had made his escape. Charles hastened to inform the nocturnal visitors, and a scene ensued that can be as well imagined as described. Charles was upbraided for aiding a criminal to escape. Mr. Joel Martin, the brother of the overseer shot in Virginia, was enraged that his brother's slayer should, after years of search, be discovered only to escape his clutches, while Mr. Parris, with assumed piety declared:

"It is ever thus, when one covenants with the devil. An actor in the theatres taken to the home and family of those claiming to be Christians. Verily, I am not surprised that he is also a murderer. When one lets go his hold on the Lord, there can be no crime to which he will not descend."

The household was roused, and Cora was informed of her father's narrow escape. Mr. Martin from Virginia had a requisition from that colony for his arrest. She wept, but said not a word. When the disappointed officers went away, Charles sought to comfort her; but she answered:

"Cruel fate seems to have doomed me to misery, Charles. Father cannot return; I cannot escape, and I feel that Mr. Parris is drawing a net about me, which will entangle my feet."

"Trust in God, and all is well!" Charles answered. Often, in their darkest hours, her pious father had offered the same advice, for he was a firm believer in divine intervention in human affairs.

17

Next day a daughter of Goody Nurse came to the house, weeping as if her heart would break.

"What is the matter, Sarah?" asked Mrs. Stevens.

"Mother is arrested!" sobbed the young woman.

"Arrested!"

"Yes."

"For what charge?" Charles asked.

"For being a witch. A warrant has been sworn out against her, and she was taken away this morning." Here the unfortunate young woman broke down and sobbed in silence.

"Where was she taken?" asked Mrs. Stevens.

"To jail and put in irons, for a witch must be put in irons. It is charged that she hath bewitched Abigail Williams and the other children of Mr. Parris' circle."

Were Mr. Parris a creation of fiction and not a real character of history, no doubt the critic would say he was overdrawn; but Samuel Parris was a living, breathing man, or a fiend in human form. He had a large following, and was spoken of as our beloved pastor. Mr. George Bancroft, America's greatest historian, says:*

"The delusion, but for Parris, would have languished. Of his own niece, the girl of eleven

---

* Bancroft's "History of the United States", vol. ii., p. 256.

years of age, he demanded the names of the devil's
instruments, who bewitched the band of 'the afflicted,' and then became at once informer and
witness. In those days, there was no prosecuting
officer, and Parris was at hand to question his Indian servants and others, himself prompting their
answers and acting as recorder to the magistrates.
The recollection of the old controversy in the
parish could not be forgotten; and Parris, moved
by personal malice as well as blind zeal, 'stifled
the accusation of some,' such is the testimony of
the people of his own village, and, at the same
time, 'vigilantly promoting the accusation of
others,' was 'the beginning and procurer of the
afflictions of Salem village and country.' Martha
Corey, who, on her examination in the meeting-
house, before a throng, with a firm spirit, alone,
against them all, denied the presence of witchcraft,
was committed to prison. Rebecca Nurse, like-
wise a woman of purest life, an object of special
hatred of Parris, resisted the company of accusers,
and was committed. And Parris, filling his
prayers with the theme, made the pulpit ring with
it. 'Have not I chosen you twelve,'—such was
his text,—'and one of you is a devil?' At this,
Sarah Cloyce, sister to Rebecca Nurse, rose up and
left the meeting-house, and she, too, was cried out
upon and sent to prison.''

Mrs. Stevens, her son and Cora Waters tried to soothe the fears of the poor young maid, who, in her hour of affliction, childlike, had flown to her friends with her tale of woe.

"I will go at once and denounce Mr. Parris for the part he has played in this!" cried Charles, starting from the house.   At the little gate, he was overtaken by Cora, who, laying her hand on his arm, said:

"Don't go, Charles.   Don't leave the house while in this heat of passion."

"Cora, I cannot endure that hypocrite longer. He is a devil, not a man, to carry his malice so far."

"But reflect, Charles.   What you might say in the heat of your anger can do poor Goody Nurse no good."

"It will be a relief to me."

"No; it may engender future trouble.   This is a trying hour; the danger is great; let us take time for deliberation."

He was persuaded by Cora to say nothing at that time and returned to the house.   To the sorrowing daughter had been administered such consolation as faithful, loving friends could offer, and she went home hoping that her unfortunate mother might yet escape the wrath of Mr. Parris.

"It is all the work of Samuel Parris," declared

Mrs. Stevens. "Because Goody Nurse opposed his ministry, he seeks revenge."

"Parris is an unworthy man," Charles declared.

Before he could say more, Cora Waters, who had posted herself as a sentry at the door said:

"Here comes Ann Putnam."

At mention of this woman's name, both Charles and his mother became silent. She was the mother of one of the afflicted children, and was herself of high nervous temperament, undisciplined in mind, and an absolute devotee to her pastor. She was at this time about thirty years of age, with blue eyes, brown hair and face fair and round. As she entered the door, almost out of breath, she cried:

"I come, Goody Stevens, to be the bearer of what I trust will be welcome tidings. Goody Nurse hath been arrested and sent to prison for her grievously tormenting the family of Mr. Parris and myself."

"Can you suspect that such news will be welcome tidings in this home?" cried Mrs. Stevens. "Ann Putnam, truly you must believe that I am unworthy to be called woman, if you think I can rejoice at the downfall of that good woman."

"Good woman!" shrieked Ann Putnam, stamping her foot on the floor with such force as to make the house quiver. "Good woman! She is a witch! She opposed our beloved pastor his stipend;

she wished to remove him, and because she failed, she now assails his household with her witchcraft. Oh, vile creature, I would I had never seen her!"

"Ann Putnam, you are deluded."

"Deluded!" shrieked Ann Putnam, her eyes flashing with fire. "Could you all but see me in my sore afflictions, could you but know the fits I have, and witness the suffering of her victims, you would not call it delusion."

"Ann Putnam, Mr. Parris has so wrought upon your imagination, that you are insane."

At the attempt to impute anything evil to her beloved pastor, Ann Putnam's rage knew no bounds, and, in a voice choking with wrath, she declared that Mr. Parris was the most saintly man living.

"His zeal for the cause of Christ hath brought down upon him the wrath of the worldly minded. He is a saint—a glorious saint, and because he denounced Cora Waters for being the child of a player, you would malign him."

"Ann Putnam," interrupted Charles Stevens, "you have no right to impugn the motives of my mother, nor to assail our guest. The zeal of Mr. Parris has made a monster of him. He is a wicked, cruel, revengeful man, rather than a follower of the meek and lowly Lamb of God."

"I will not stay where my blessed pastor is

spoken so ill of!" declared Ann Putnam, and she
bounded out of the door, shaking the dust off her
shoes. At the gate, she paused and held her fist
in the air, and at the height of her masculine voice
screamed:

"I denounce you! I cry out against you,
Hattie Stevens! I will to do no more with you!"
and having performed that wonderful act of dis-
carding a former friend, she turned about and hurried over the hill.

"Charles, I am sorry you and your mother an-
gered her," said Cora.

"Why, Cora?" he asked.

"She can do us ill."

"Ann Putnam is an evil woman and a fit follower of such a man as Parris," declared Charles.
"My mother did a noble act in denouncing him."

"It is time, Charles," interrupted Cora. "I feel,
I know that if evil befalls you, I am the cause.
I must go away. I cannot remain here to prove
the ruin of those who befriended me. I must go
away."

"Where would you go?"

"I know not where; but I will go anywhere, so
that I may not prove the ruin of my friends. The
wild heathen in the forest could not be more cruel
than these people."

"Cora, you shall not go!" cried Charles. "No,

you shall not. I will protect you and mother.
I have friends, friends true and strong, friends of
whom they little dream. They live in the forest
and will come to my aid by the hundreds to fight
my battles."

"Do you mean the Indians?"

"Yes. Two years ago I saved the life of Ora-
cus, a young chief, and made him my friend. An
Indian, once a friend, is the truest of friends.
Oracus and his warriors would die for me."

"Do not appeal to the Indians, if you can avoid
it," the girl plead. Charles assured her if she did
go away, it would not remove the wrath of the
minister from them, and she decided to remain.

Mr. Parris hated Rebecca Nurse more than any
other person in Salem. He was now about to ac-
complish his designs.

Until the day of trial, Rebecca Nurse lay in
jail, with great, heavy fetters, which she could
scarcely carry, upon her. Her husband, family
and friends did all in their power to procure her
release on bond; but witchcraft was not a bailable
offence.

They tried to secure mercy for the old woman
from Mr. Parris; but he was inexorable. When
Mr. Parris, a few months before, was publicly
complaining of neglect in the matter of firewood
for the parsonage, and of lukewarmness on the part

of the hearers of his services, "Landlord Nurse" was a member of the committee who had to deal with him, and he and his relatives were among the majority, who were longing for Mr. Parris' apparently inevitable departure. So when, through the machinations of the pastor, the good woman was arrested, they appealed to him in vain for mercy.

The meeting-house, in which the trial was held, was crowded with spectators. Neighbor jostled neighbor, and terrible, awe-inspiring whispers ran over the throng. Prayer was offered, and the court opened, and Rebecca Nurse, weak and sick, old and infirm as she was, was made to stand up before that tribunal to plead to the charge of witchcraft. When her son would have supported his aged mother, he was driven away.

Mr. Parris was the first witness called. The law of evidence, or at least the practice in Salem at that time, was quite different from the present. Hearsay testimony was freely admitted in the case of Goody Nurse. Mr. Parris stated that he was called to see a certain person who was sick. Mercy Lewis was sent for. She was struck dumb on entering the chamber. She was asked to hold up her hand, if she saw any of the witches afflicting the patient. Presently she held up her hand, then fell into a trance. While coming to herself, she

said that she saw the spectres of Goody Nurse and
Goody Carrier having hold of the head of the sick
man.   The testimony of Mr. Parris was given in a
calm and deliberate manner calculated to impress
the jury with truth.   Never did an assassin whet
his dagger with more coolness or with more malice
drive it to the heart of his victim, than did this
sanctimonious villain weave the net of ruin about
his victims.

Thomas Putnam, the husband of Ann Putnam,
stated that both his wife and child were bewitched
and had most grievous fits, all of which they
charged to Goody Nurse.   He described his wife
as being sorely attacked and striving violently with
her arms and legs, and presently she would begin
to converse with Good-wife Nurse, saying:

"Goody Nurse, begone! begone! begone!   Are
you not ashamed, a woman of your profession, to
afflict a poor creature so?   What hurt did I ever
do you in my life?   You have but two years to
live, and then the devil will torment your soul, for
this your name is blotted out of God's book, and
it shall never be put in God's book again.   Begone!   For shame!   Are you not afraid of what
is coming upon you?   I know what will make you
afraid, the wrath of an angry God.   I am sure that
will make you afraid.   Begone!   Do not torment
me.   I know what you would have; but it is out

of your reach; it is clothed with the white robes of Christ's righteousness."

After this, she seemed to dispute with the apparition about a particular text of Scripture, while she kept her eyes closed all the time. The apparition seemed to deny it, and she said she was sure there was such a text, and she would tell it, and then the shape would be gone. Said she:

"I am sure you cannot stand before that text."

Then she was sorely afflicted, her mouth drawn on one side, and her body strained for about a minute, and then she said:

"I will tell. I will tell, it is,—it is,—it is the third chapter of the Revelations."

Such stuff could not in this day be admitted in any intelligent court of justice.

Ann Putnam, the wife of Thomas Putnam, was next to testify against Goody Nurse. She said:

"On March 18th, 1692, being wearied out in helping to tend my poor afflicted child and maid, about the middle of the afternoon I lay me down on the bed to take a little rest; and immediately I was almost pressed and choked to death, that, had it not been for the mercy of a gracious God and the help of those that were with me, I could not have lived many moments; and presently I saw the apparition of Martha Corey, who did torture me so, as I cannot express, ready to tear me to

pieces, and then departed from me a little while;
but before I could recover strength, or well take
breath, the apparition of Rebecca Nurse fell upon
me again with dreadful tortures and hellish temptations to go along with her, and she brought to me
a little red book in her hand, and a black pen,
urging me vehemently to write in her book; and
several times that day she did most grievously
torture me, almost ready to kill me.   And on that
same day Martha Corey and Rebecca Nurse, the
wife of Francis Nurse senior, did both torture me,
with tortures such as no tongue can express."

"Did you suffer from Rebecca Nurse again?"
the witness was asked.

"Yes."

"When?"

"On divers times.   On the 20th, which was the
Sabbath day.   After that, she came and sat upon
my breast and did sorely torment me and threaten
to bear the soul out of my body, blasphemously
denying the blessed God, and the power of the
Lord Jesus Christ to save my soul, and denying
several passages of Scripture, which I told her of,
to repel her hellish temptations."

The afflicted children were present, and when
the unfortunate prisoner, tired and sick, bent her
head, they began to scream and bent their heads
also.   When she gazed at Abigail Williams, the

girl was seized with a convulsion, and so were the others, so that the trial had to be suspended for a few minutes, until quiet was restored.

Charles Stevens, who was present, remarked, loud enough to be heard:

"If they had a stick well laid about their backs, I trow it would cure them of such devil's capers."

"Have a care, Charles. Take heed of your hasty speech," said a by-stander.

Mrs. Putnam, fearful that her first deposition would not convict the woman, who had dared speak boldly against her beloved pastor, again took the stand and testified:

"Once, when Rebecca Nurse's apparition appeared unto me, she declared that she had killed Benjamin Houlton, John Friller, and Rebecca Shepherd, and that she and her sister Cloyse, and Edward Bishop's wife, had killed John Putnam's child. Immediately there did appear to me six children in winding-sheets, which called me aunt, which did most grievously affright me; and they told me they were my sister Baker's children of Boston, and that Goody Nurse, Mistress Corey of Charlestown and an old deaf woman at Boston murdered them, and charged me to go and tell these things to the magistrates, or else they would tear me to pieces, for their blood did cry for vengeance. Also there appeared to me my own sister

Bayley and three of her children in winding-sheets, and told me that Goody Nurse had murdered them."

This evidence was followed by the afflicted children bearing testimony to being grievously tormented by defendant, who came sometimes in the shape of a black cat, a dog, or a pig, and who was sometimes accompanied by a black man. Louder next related his experience of being changed to a horse and ridden to a witches' ball, and of seeing Rebecca Nurse ride through the air on a broomstick. The West Indian negro man John, the husband of Tituba and servant of Mr. Parris, was next put on the witness stand. The magistrate asked him:

"John, who hurt you?"

"Goody Nurse first, and den Goody Corey."

"What did she do to you?"

"She brought de book to me."

"John, tell the truth. Who hurt you? Have you been hurt?"

"The first was a gentleman I saw."

"But who hurt you next?"

"Goody Nurse. She choke me and brought me de book."

"Where did she take hold of you?"

"Upon my throat, to stop my breath."

"What did this Goody Nurse do?"

"She pinch me until de blood came."

At this, Ann Putnam had a fit and was carried out. Abigail Williams was called to the stand and asked:

"Abigail Williams, did you see a company at Mr. Parris' house eat and drink?"

"Yes sir; that was their sacrament."

"How many were there?"

"About forty. Goody Cloyse and Goody Good were their deacons."

"What was it?"

"They said it was our blood, and they had it twice that day."

"Have you seen a white man?"

"Yes sir, a great many times."

"What sort of a man was he?"

"A fine, grave man, and when he came, he made all the witches to tremble."

"Did you see the party of witches at Deacon Ingersol's?"

"I did."

"Who was there?"

"Goody Cloyse, Goody Corey, Goody Nurse and Goody Good."

Then the examining magistrate turned to the old, infirm and unfortunate prisoner, and asked:

"What do you say, Goody Nurse, to these things?"

The old, sick woman, summoning up all her energies, answered:

"I take God to be my witness, that I know nothing of it, no more than the child unborn."

The jury did not consider the evidence strong enough for hanging an old lady, who had been the ornament of their church and the glory of their village and its society, and they brought in a verdict of "not guilty."

The momentary rejoicing of the triumphant defendants was drowned by the howls of the afflicted and the upbraiding of Mr. Parris. One judge declared himself dissatisfied; another promised to have her tried anew; and the chief justice pointed out a phrase used by the prisoner, which might be made to signify that she was one of the accused gang in guilt, as well as in jeopardy. It might really seem as if the authorities were all scheming together, when we see the ingenuity and persistence with which they discussed the three words "of our company," as used by the accused.

The poor old woman offered an explanation, which ought to have been satisfactory.

"I intended no otherwise than as they were prisoners with us, and therefore did then, and yet do judge them not legal evidence against their fellow-prisoners. And I, being something hard of hearing and full of grief; none informing me how the court took up my words, therefore had no opportunity to dcelare what I intended when I said they were of our company."

The foreman of the jury would have taken a favorable view of this matter, and have allowed full consideration, while other jurymen were eager to recall the mistake of the verdict; but the prisoner's silence from failing to hear, when she was expected to explain, turned the foreman against her, and caused him to declare:

"Whereupon these words were to me a principal evidence against her."

Still it was too monstrous to hang the poor old woman. After her condemnation, the governor reprieved her, probably on the ground of the illegality of setting aside the first verdict of the jury, in the absence of any new evidence; but Mr. Parris, the power behind the people, caused such an outcry against executive clemency to be raised, that the governor withdrew his reprieve.

Next Sunday after the sentence, there was a scene in the church, the record of which was afterward annotated by the church members in grief and humiliation. After the sacrament, by a vote, it was unanimously agreed, that sister Nurse, being convicted as a witch by the court, should be excommunicated in the afternoon of the same day.

Charles Stevens, impelled by a morbid curiosity,

18

went to the church that afternoon.   The place was
thronged.   Parris, with the triumphant gleam of a
devil on his hypocritical features, was in the pulpit
with the elders.   The deacons presided below.
The sheriff and his officers brought in the witch
and led her up the broad aisle, her chains clanking
as she stepped, and her poor old limbs scarcely able
to bear their weight.   As she stood in the middle of
the aisle, the Reverend Mr. Noyes pronounced her
sentence of expulsion from the church on earth
and from all hope of salvation hereafter.   Having
freely given her soul to Satan by a seven years'
service for diabolical powers, she was delivered
over to him forever.   In conclusion, Reverend Mr.
Noyes said:

"And now, vile woman, having sold yourself to
the Devil, go to your master amid the hottest
flames of hell!"

She was aware that every eye regarded her with
horror and hate, unapproached under any circumstances; but she was able to sustain it.   She was
still calm and at peace that day, and during the
fortnight of final waiting.   When the fatal day of
execution came, she traversed the streets of Salem,
between the houses in which she had been an honored guest, and surrounded by well-known faces,
and then there was the hard, hard task, for her
aged limbs, of climbing the rocky and steep path

THE SHERIFF BROUGHT THE WITCH UP THE BROAD AISLE, HER CHAINS
CLANKING AS SHE STEPPED.

on Witches' Hill to the place where the gibbets stood in a row, and the hangman was waiting for her. Sarah Good and six others of whom Salem chose to be rid that day went with her.

It was the 19th of July, 1692, when, at a signal, all eight swung off into eternity, and Reverend Mr. Noyes, in his zeal, pointing to the swaying bodies, · said:

"There hang eight fire-brands of hell!"

Mr. Parris, unable to conceal his triumph, declared these the most holy words ever uttered by lips not divine.

The bodies were put away on the hill like so many dead dogs; but during the silent watches of the night, Charles Stevens and the sons and grandsons of Rebecca Nurse disinterred her and brought her remains home where a coffin had been prepared. Mrs. Stevens and Cora Waters dressed the body in most becoming robes. All kissed the cold dead face of one they loved, as she lay in a rear room, the windows blinded and a guard outside. Then the body was hurriedly buried in a grave prepared in the field, where soon after the afflicted husband slept at her side.

Considering such horrible events, one can but conclude that superstition was having full sway.

CHAPTER XV.

'Tis a bleak wild, but green and bright
In the summer warmth and the mid-day light,
There's the hum of the bee and the chirp of the wren,
And the dash of the brook from the older glen.
There's the sound of the bell from the scattered flock,
And the shade of the beach lies cool on the rock,
And fresh from the west is the free-wind's breath.
There is nothing here that speaks of death.
—BRYANT.

SHORTLY after the arrest and incarceration of Goodwife Nurse, Reverend Deodat Lawson, an eminent Boston divine, came to Salem village. All land travel at that time was on horse-back. He lodged at the house of Nathaniel Ingersol near the home of the minister Mr. Parris. The appearance of a foreigner in the village was at once the signal for making a new convert, and the afflicted put themselves on exhibition to convince him that evil spirits were abroad. He had been but a short time at the house of Ingersol, when Captain Walcut's daughter Mary came to see him and speak with him. She greeted him with a smile, and hoped he had had a pleasant journey.

It was now growing late, and she stood in the door bidding all good-evening, preparatory to going home. Suddenly the girl gave utterance to a wild shriek and leaped into the house, holding her wrist in her left hand.

"What is the matter?" asked Mr. Lawson.

"I am bitten on the wrist," she cried.

"Surely you cannot be bitten, for I have seen nothing to bite you."

"Nevertheless, I am bitten. It is a witch that hath bitten me."

The candle had been burning all the while in the apartment, and Mr. Lawson knew that no one could have been in the room without his knowledge.

"Some one hath grievously bitten me!" the girl sobbed.

Mr. Lawson seized the candle and, holding it to her wrist, saw apparently the marks of teeth, both upper and lower set, on each side of her wrist. He was lost in wonder and, placing the candle on the mantel, remarked:

"It is a mystery."

"Yea, verily it is," Lieutenant Ingersol answered; "but you have not seen the beginning of the wonders of witchcraft in this village. Satan surely hath been loosed for a little season."

"I have heard much of the sore afflictions of the children at the home of Mr. Parris," remarked Mr. Lawson.

" And they are sorely afflicted, as I can bear testimony. After tea we will walk over to his house."

Mr. Lawson assented, and Mary Walcut was sent home. After an early tea, Mr. Lawson went to the parsonage, which was but a short distance. Mr. Parris met them at the door. His white, cadaverous face, prominent cheek bones, aquiline nose, piercing eyes, and wild, disheveled hair giving him a strange, weird appearance. He greeted Reverend Mr. Lawson warmly and thanked him for coming all the way from Boston to preach for him next Lord's Day.

"I am so sorely tried with my many afflictions, that I cannot compose my mind for sermonizing."

"I have heard somewhat of the afflictions and troubles that beset you," Rev. Deodat Lawson answered.

"Verily you cannot have heard more than has occurred. I am maligned, misunderstood and beset everywhere by the enemies of God."

"Meet it with prayer and humiliation," answered Mr. Lawson.

"I do—I do—and, verily, the Lord is making my enemies my footstool. Many are already in prison, and many more will yet go to the gallows." The pastor gnashed his teeth in silent rage, while his eyes gleamed with hate.

"How are the afflicted children?" asked Mr. Lawson.

"No better. Abigail come hither."

Abigail Williams, the niece of the pastor, came from an adjoining room. She was a girl of twelve, with a fair face, but cunning eyes, which deprived her of the innocence of childhood. Mr. Lawson at once entered into conversation with her, but had not proceeded far, when she uttered a shriek and, turning her face to the ceiling, whirled about in a circle, while her eyes, rolling back in her head, snapped like flashes of light. Her mouth was drawn to the left side of her face and her whole frame convulsively jerked till she fell to the floor, where she writhed and struggled, and blood-stained froth issued from her mouth, while Mr. Lawson gazed upon her appalled. Then she sprang to her feet and hurried violently to and fro through the room in spite of the efforts to hold her. Sometimes she made motions as if she would fly, reaching her arms up as high as she could, and bringing them down at her side, crying:

"Whish! whish! whish!"

Presently she began talking in a strange, hysterical and half inaudible manner.

"There is Goodwife Nurse!" she cried. "Do you not see her? Why, there she stands!" and the girl pointed to a corner of the room that was vacant. Her eyes seemed riveted on some object that kept moving about. After a short silence, Abigail Williams said:

"There, she is offering me the book to sign; but I won't take it, Goody Nurse! I won't! I won't! I won't take it! I do not know what book it is. I am sure it is not God's book. It is the Devil's book, for aught I know."

Then she remained a moment with her eyes closed and arms folded across her breast, after which she ran to the fire, and began to throw firebrands about the house, and run into the fireplace, against the back of the wall, as if she would go up the chimney. They caught hold of her and pulled her out.

"It is nothing uncommon," Mr. Parris explained. "In other fits, the children have sought to throw themselves into the fire."

Mr. Lawson did not tarry long at the house of the pastor; but returned to the home of Lieut. Ingersol.

When Sunday came, Mr. Lawson went to the church to preach. Several of the afflicted people were "at meeting," for it was thought proper that the afflicted should be in the house of God. So long as one was able to go to church, they were taken, regardless of any mental affection they might have. Mrs. Pope, Goodwife Bibber, Abigail Williams, Mary Walcut, Mary Lewes and Doctor Grigg's maid, all of whom were persons bewitched, are reported by reliable historians as being present at this "Lord's Day service." There was also present Goodwife Corey, who was subsequently arrested for a witch.

While at prayer, Mr. Lawson was interrupted by shrieks and struggles on the part of the afflicted, and a voice near said:

"Fits!"

He kept on praying for the Lord to relieve them of their torments, while Charles Stevens, who was in the house, declared that a whip would relieve them. After the prayer, a psalm was sung, as usual, and then Abigail Williams, turning to the preacher, said in a loud, coarse voice:

"Now stand up and name your text!"

After he had named his text, she said:

"It is a long text."

He had scarcely begun his sermon, when Mrs. Pope, one of the afflicted women, bawled out:

"Now, there is enough of that."

"These mad people ought to be kept away from the house of worship," declared Charles Stevens to a neighbor.

Rev. Mr. Lawson, unaccustomed to these interruptions, was greatly annoyed and had to pause
frequently in his sermon. Goodwife Corey was
present at the time, and Abigail Williams, in the
midst of the sermon, cried out:

"Look! look, where Goodwife Corey sits on the
beam, suckling her yellow bird betwixt her fingers!"

At this, Ann Putnam, the daughter of Thomas
Putnam, said:

"There is a yellow bird sitting on Mr. Lawson's
hat, where it hangs on the pin in the pulpit."

Those who sat nearest the girls tried to restrain
them from speaking aloud; but it was in vain;
for, despite all precaution, they would occasionally
blurt out some ridiculous nonsense, which the
people attributed to the results of witchcraft.

"Charles Stevens, what say you, now that your
eyes have witnessed these abominations?" said
John Bly.

"I say, if I had my way, I would cure them,"
answered the youth.

"How would you, pray?" Bly asked.

"With a good whip about their shoulders."

"Beware, Charles Stevens, how you speak so
lightly of these afflictions, lest you bring on yourself the same condemnation of those on Witches'
Hill."

There are some spirits so bold, that they over-
awe and intimidate even an enraged populace.
Martin Luther's very audacity saved him, on more
than one occasion, and something like the same
spirit enabled Charles Stevens to overcome or over-
awe the deluded populace of Salem.

A few days after the execution of Goody Nurse,
he was passing the meeting house, when he was
accosted by the West Indian negro, John.

"You not believe in witches?" said John.

"No."

"Goody Nurse brought me de book."

"John, I believe you lied. I believe you have
perjured yourself and sent your soul to endless
torment," answered Charles Stevens. John was a
cunning rascal and thought to give him a proof
positive of the powers of witchcraft. He fell
down in a fit, and Charles applied his cane to him
until he ran howling away effectually cured, while
Charles, disgusted with the black-skinned African,
left him and hurried out of the village.

Charles Stevens' favorite walk was across the
brook and among the great old oak trees beyond.
His mind was greatly harassed and, like all great
minds when perplexed, sought solitude. He went
farther and farther into the woods and sat down
upon a large stone. The recent trial of Goody
Nurse, her conviction and execution moved his

soul. He could not understand how people, civilized and enlightened, could be so deceived by what, to him, was so apparent.

Charles knew that all were not dishonest in their belief. He even believed that some of the actors in this tragedy were sincere, but had been over-persuaded by Mr. Parris, whom he set down as the prime mover in it all.

He sat for a long time, much longer than he supposed, reflecting on the past, and planning for the future, when he was startled by hearing footsteps coming toward him. He raised his head, and saw a young Indian brave, with his blanket wrapped about his shoulders, carrying a bow in his hand. His head was ornamented with a bunch of feathers, and his face was painted with all the gorgeous hues of savage barbaric art. He recognized Charles Stevens, for, advancing toward him with a smile, he extended his hand saying:

"My white brother is not happy. What has made him sad?"

The Indian was a good judge of human character, and in the face of the young white man he read a look of sorrow.

"The white men of Salem are very wicked, Oracus," said Charles. "Not only are they wicked to their red brothers, but to their white brothers, as well. They have taken the old and helpless, the weak and forlorn, and put them to death."

The young savage folded his arms across his massive chest and stood for a long time in silence. His eyes were upon the ground, and his stolid features were without show of emotion. His people had suffered wrongs at the hands of the white men; but in this one he had ever found an earnest, true friend.

There existed between Charles and the brave a bond of brotherhood as enduring as life. The young chief inquired what had been done at the village, and Charles proceeded to tell him all, in as few words as possible, of the arrest, trial and execution of Goody Nurse and others. When he had completed the terrible story, the young chief drew his blanket about his shoulders and said:

"I am your friend, and if your white brothers prove false, remember your red brother will be true."

"I believe you, Oracus."

"I have shown one white brother through the paths, away from his enemies, and you will always find Oracus in his forest home ready to befriend you."

"The time may come when I will need your aid," said Charles Stevens.

After a long interview, he rose and started home.

He was near the great bridge which spanned the brook, when he suddenly came upon a tall, powerful man, whose sallow face and cavalier-like manner showed him to be a citizen of the southern colonies. Charles instantly recognized him as Mr. Joel Martin, the man whom he had seen on that night with Mr. Parris, Bly and Louder, coming to arrest Cora's father.

"You are Charles Stevens?" the Virginian said, halting before the youth.

"I have no desire to deny my name, for it is that of an honest man; I am Charles Stevens," he answered.

"Do you know who I am?"

"I suspect you are one whom I saw at my house, though your name I have not learned."

"I am Joel Martin, and by profession an overseer on a Virginia plantation. There were but two of us, my brother and I. He was an overseer of an adjoining plantation, when one day a slave escaped. He pursued him and was slain."

"I have heard the story," interrupted Charles.

"You have? and from his own lips?"

"I have; and I do not blame the man who was seeking liberty. He was a white man, as you yourself are. He had committed no crime, save that he was arrested as one of Monmouth's insurgents and had been captured while in the ranks of the rebel."

Martin's eyes flashed with fury and, in a voice that was hoarse, he whispered:

"You aided him to escape; but it shall not avail. I have for years followed on his trail, and I will not let go my hold on him, until I have dragged him to the scaffold. No; the blood of my brother cries out for vengeance, and I will follow him day and night through the trackless forests, until I have brought the renegade to justice. He cannot conceal himself so deep in the forest, he cannot hide himself among the savage tribes, nor burrow so deep in the earth, but that I will find him." .

Charles Stevens turned away and was walking toward home, when the tall Virginian, by a few quick strides, overtook him and, laying his hand on his shoulder, said:

"You do not care to hear these threats; but I have not done with you yet. Listen; I want to say more. If you seek to thwart me, I will kill you. Do you hear?"

"I have no fear of you, Mr. Martin," cried Charles Stevens, turning on the tall, swarthy southerner a glance which made him quail. "Your profession is brutality. You are a stranger to mercy; yet I will defy you. I fear you not, and, if you seek my life, you had better take heed for your own."

Charles boldly walked away, leaving the discomfited Virginian to fume and rage alone. The shades of night were falling fast over the village of Salem, as Charles hurried homeward, and he was amazed as he came in sight of the house, to see a great throng of people going away from the door. The young man quickened his pace, hardly knowing whether he was asleep or awake. A negro slave came running toward him crying:

"Massa! Massa! Massa!"

"What has happened?" asked Charles.

"Um tuk um away! Dey tuk um off!"

"Who?"

"Yo mudder."

"My mother! Oh, God!" Charles Stevens ran swift as a roe buck toward the crowd, which had now almost reached the jail.

"What does this mean?" he demanded of John Bly, whom he met near the jail.

"Your mother is a witch," Bly answered.

"You lie!" cried Charles, and with one swift, sure blow, he laid the slanderer senseless at his feet.

"Hold, Charles Stevens! Hold! Be not rash, or she may fare worse," whispered a kind voice at his side, and, turning, he saw the sad face of John Nurse. He had drunk the bitter cup to its dregs and could advise. The world seemed swimming before the eyes of Charles Stevens. He tried to rush to that throng, whom he saw dragging both his mother and Cora Waters to the jail; but in vain. His feet refused to carry him. He strove to utter an outcry; but his voice failed, and all became darkness.

19

CHAPTER XVI.

Come, rest in this bosom, my own stricken deer,
Though the herd have fled from thee, thy home is still here:
Here is the smile that no cloud can o'ercast,
And a heart and a hand all thy own to the last.

—MOORE.

WHEN Charles Stevens regained consciousness,
he was lying on a bed, and kindly faces were bending over him. He was conscious from the first of
an oppressive weight of trouble, but could not
realize what had occurred. As one awakening
from a troubled dream, he strove to gather up his
scattered faculties and recall what had happened.
Like a blast of doom, the awful truth burst upon
him, and he leaped to his feet. He was at the
home of Landlord Nurse, and the pale, sad, horror-
stricken faces about him were the old gentleman
and his sons and daughters. They caught Charles
before he reached the door.

"My mother!" cried the young man.

"No; you can do her no good by an act of
rashness!" John Nurse answered.

"Tell me all about it. I will sit here and listen to it all," said Charles, when he discovered that he could not break away from his friends.

"Your mother and Cora Waters have both been cried out upon as witches, warrants were issued, and they were arrested. Now collect your faculties and act on your coolest judgment. Think what you will do."

Charles Stevens bowed his head in his hands and reflected long and earnestly on the course to pursue. He recalled the words of Oracus, the brave young chief, who could muster a hundred warriors. He was cunning and might devise some plan of escape, and Charles was not long in resolving what to do. He would not act hurriedly. He would be desperate; but that desperation would have coolness and premeditation about it.

He promised his friends to be calm, assuring them he would be guarded in his speech, and then begun seeking an interview with his mother and Cora. It was three days before the interview was granted. He found them occupying loathsome cells, each chained to the wall. The interview was long, and just what such an interview could be, full of grief and despair. Charles tried to hope. He tried to see a ray of sunlight; but the effort only revealed the swaying forms of those hung on Witches' Hill.

Even if he summoned Oracus and all his braves, would they be strong enough to break down that door of iron, or cut the chains asunder! Charles, in his desperation, resolved to rescue the beloved ones or die in the effort. He went away weeping.

He did not return home. That home was desolate, lonely and so like the tomb, that he dared not go near it. At the home of his kind friend, he wrote to relatives at New Plymouth, Boston, New York, Virginia and the Carolinias. To all he appealed for help, for Charles was determined to move heaven and earth or rescue his mother and Cora; but he did not depend on those distant relatives and friends so much as the dusky friends in the forest. He knew that before answers could come to his letters, he would be dead, or would have succeeded in his efforts. Even if he should be killed in an abortive attempt, however, he hoped that his relatives would resume the warfare for the prisoners.

"Where is Cora's father?" he asked himself. "Could I but find the Waters brothers, I would have two friends and allies to aid me. Oh, Heaven, give me light! Give me light!"

Charles Stevens, like all true Christians, in this dark hour went to God for aid. Kneeling, he prayed as he had never prayed before. He seemed to take hold of the throne of grace and, with a faith strengthened and renewed, drew inspiration for his desperate resolve from the only living fountain. Armed with his rifle and pistols, he left the village and went into the forest. The forest inspires man with reverence and love for God. The giant trees, the deep glens, the moss and ferns and cool shades seem to breathe of eternity. Charles Stevens had always loved the dark old woods, and never had they seemed so friendly as on this occasion, when they screened him from the frowns of man.

Solitude offered him its charms. The zephyrs sought to soothe his sorrows by their gentle whispers, and the birds sang for the peace of his troubled spirit, while the babbling brooks strove to make him gay; but who can be gay when loved ones are menaced with a terrible danger? Charles Stevens saw little of the beauty of nature. His eyes were searching the forests for dusky forms, which he hoped to meet. Those dusky sons of the forest were not often desirable sights; but Charles was as anxious to see the feathers and painted faces of these heathens, as if they were brothers.

He spent the day in wandering through the woods, forgetting to take any nourishment, for he had brought no food with him, and, in fact, he had not thought to eat since the arrest of his mother and Cora.

He was weak and faint, and his hands trembled. He was not hungry; but his strength was giving way, and he realized that he had been foolish not to provide himself with food.

Evening came, and he sank down on the mossy banks of a stream and took a few draughts of water to revive him. The stars came out one by one.

By the merest chance, he raised his despairing eyes and, gazing across the stream to the woods beyond, saw a light. Charles struggled to his feet and gazed like one to whom life has suddenly been restored.

"Perhaps it is Indians!"

He plunged into the creek, waded across and started through the woods toward the light. It was much further away than he had at first supposed, and he was several minutes in reaching the camp fire.

Ten dusky sons of the forest were seated about the camp fire, while two men in the garb of civilization were roving about. Charles felt some misgivings at first on discovering men of his own color in the camp. He crawled from tree to tree, from log to bush, until he was near enough to see the features of the men. When he first got within sight they stood with their backs toward him and he could not see their faces; but at last one turned about so that the glare of the fire-light fell full on his face, and, with a cry of joy, Charles Stevens bounded to his feet,. crying:

"Mr. Waters! Mr. Waters!" and dashed toward the camp.

A pair of strong arms encircled his waist, and the young man heard a voice say:

"White man go too soon!"

He had been seized by a sentry; but Mr. Waters and Oracus hastened to him, and he was released. The other white man was the brother of Mr. Waters, and Charles, bewildered, overjoyed, yet faint and weak, was half led and half carried to the camp. He found himself making hurried explanations, while a savage was broiling venison steaks before the fire for him.

"We know all," said Mr. George Waters.

"What! do you know they have been cried out upon?" asked Charles.

"We do."

"Do you know they are in prison?"

"We have heard it all," said Mr. Waters, calmly.

"How could you have heard it?" asked Charles.

"We have faithful friends, who inform us of everything."

"Were you going to take action for their rescue?" asked Charles.

"We were concerting plans when you came; but you must have food."

Charles Stevens gazed on the calm face of the man before him, and could but wonder at his coolness.

"Mr. Waters, do you know that your own daughter is one of the accused?"

"I know all."

"How can you be so calm, knowing all as you do?"

"I am calm for my daughter's sake. The only hope of liberating her, of saving her life, is by cool, deliberate and well matured plans."

"Are your plans formed?"

"Yes."

"When will you act?"

"On to-morrow night. Oracus will have all his warriors ready by that time, and we will require crow-bars, hammers and axes, to break in the door of the jail. Meanwhile, if you expect to aid us, you will have to take some refreshments, food and drink, and get some sleep. You don't look as if you had slept for weeks."

"I scarcely have."

"Your conduct is foolish. If you love your mother, you should give the full strength of body and mind to her rescue."

Charles ate some broiled venison and went to sleep.

So exhausted was he, that he did not awake until the noise of breaking camp aroused him.

Another white man was in camp. His hands were fastened behind his back and he was tied to a tree. His sallow complexion and angular features were familiar to Charles Stevens. The prisoner was Joel Martin.

"Two of the Indians captured him last night," explained George Waters. "He was prowling about in the woods, and they seized him."

"What are you going to do with him?" Charles asked.

"We will do him no hurt unless we are forced to," said Mr. Waters.

"I trust you will not be forced," said Charles Stevens.

"So I pray; yet we must protect ourselves and those whom we would rescue."

"I see that many more Indians are in camp than were here yesterday."

"Yes."

"Are they friends?"

"They are the braves of Oracus, and will follow where he leads."

Charles Stevens passed an anxious day. A part of the time he was near enough to Joel Martin to hear him muttering:

"I have no fear of George Waters, galley

slave.   You may turn me over to your heathen
cut-throats; yet I will defy you.   If I live, I will
yet drag you to justice for the murder of my
brother."

"Mr. Martin, you have forgotten that the word
of God says, 'Vengeance is mine and I will repay,
saith the Lord,'" put in Charles.

"I will be the instrument of vengeance."

"You are in the power of Mr. Waters."

"For the present I am."

"Don't you think you should be careful how
you threaten him, seeing he has you at his mercy."

Charles could not intimidate the bold Virginian.
He was furious, and no threat of punishment could
move him.

During the day, a dozen more Indians came in.
The red men now numbered eighty, and by the
afternoon the entire party was moving toward
Salem.

At dusk they were but five miles from the village.   Here a halt was called, and, after a short
consultation, Oracus detailed five of his braves to
guard Mr. Martin, and with the others moved on
over the hills and through the woods toward Salem.

"What will they do with him?" Charles asked.

"Release him when we leave the village."

"Mr. Waters, would you not be justified in
killing him?"

"No."

"Why not? He will murder you if he can."

"No one is justified in slaying a prisoner, and I shall never do it. No more blood will be on my hands, unless it be in defence of her. For her, I slew the other, and only for her will my arm ever be raised against my fellow man."

"Not even in self defence?"

"No, as God is my judge, my hand shall never be raised even to defend this miserable life. I live but for my child, and when she is gone, I care not how soon I am called. I have known only sorrow since——"

He did not finish the sentence, but turned away.

It was late in the night when the party entered Salem. The houses were dark and silent. No light was visible from any window, and it seemed a deserted hamlet. Earnestness without excitement was evinced. Everything was done in perfect order. The men moved first to the blacksmith shop, where several supplied themselves with axes, heavy crow-bars and sledges.

"Explain to your warriors that, under no circumstances, are they to shed blood," said Mr. George Waters.

While Oracus was giving this order to his braves, Mr. Waters, by the aid of a lighted pine knot, found a pair of cold chisels, which he appropriated.

Then the party moved off toward the jail in perfect order. There was no undue haste, or nervous excitement. All seemed as cool as if they were going as invited guests to a banquet.

The Indians' moccasined feet made scarcely any noise upon the ground, as they moved forward. Mr. Henry Waters carried in his hand a stout iron bar, and twenty Indians bore on their shoulders a heavy log of wood.

At a word of command from Oracus the others deployed as flankers and guards. They had strict orders to harm no one; but, should they find any attempting to approach them, they were to seize and hold such persons.

The jail was reached. The long, low wall of stone, with gates of iron, loomed up like some sullen monster before the determined men. Mr. Henry Waters thrust the heavy iron bar he carried under the iron gate, and tore it off its hinges.

Then George Waters and Charles raised their sledges, while the savages with the heavy log of wood ran it like a monster battering-ram against the door. At the same instant they struck it with their sledges.

The crash was deafening, and the jail trembled to its very centre. Again, and again, and again did those crashing thunder-bolts fall upon the iron door. The unfortunate inmates, not knowing the object of this terrible attack, set up a howl which was heard above the thunder crashes. The door, stout as it was, could not long withstand that assault. It gave way with a crash, and fell into the hall way.

The terrified jailer tumbled out of his bed, only to find himself seized and held by a pair of

THE JAIL TREMBLED TO ITS VERY CENTRE.

painted sons of the forest. Others who attempted to interfere were seized and held in grasps of iron.

No sooner was the door of the jail burst off its hinges, than George Waters and Charles Stevens, each with a chisel and hammer, rushed in to cut the chains of the prisoners.

"Mother! mother! where are you?" cried Charles.

He had to call several times before the frightened woman could answer. Then from out the darkness there came a feeble response. He groped his way along in the darkness. He found a cell door, tore it open and reached her side.

. At this moment some one lighted a torch within the jail. A scene, wild, weird and terrible burst upon their view. The prisoners were almost driven to madness by the sudden appearance of the savage and civilized liberators.

Charles Stevens, with chisel and hammer, quickly cut the chains of his mother and hastened to liberate Cora. Her father held the light, while he cut the iron band.

"Free! free!" cried the excited Charles. "Let us away before the town is roused!"

"No," answered Mr. George Waters; "not while a prisoner remains to suffer the wrath of prejudice."

Then with chisel and hammer he went from one to another and cut the iron bands which bound them.

Oracus and Henry Waters joined him in the work of liberation, until all were freed.

This required several moments of time, and the confusion and uproar which they were compelled to make was rousing the town.

Mr. Parris, half-dressed, ran barefoot through the town, waving his long arms in the air, and shouting that the fiends of the air had conspired to liberate the prisoners. His words and his wild, fanatical manner tended rather to increase the fear of the people of Salem, than diminish it. Then there went out the report through the village that the Indians had attacked the town, and the people, roused from their midnight slumbers, magnified the numbers of the assailants ten to one.

"Cora! Mother!" whispered Charles, "this way!"

He took a hand of each and started to run from the jail down the street.

Others followed.

"Fly! all of you! Fly for your lives!" cried Henry Waters, who, now that his work was done, flung aside his iron bar and sledge.

At a word of command from Oracus his warriors formed a hollow square about the escaping fugitives, and moved off as rapidly as they could.

Everybody was bewildered. Everybody running into the street was asking:

"What has happened? What has gone amiss?"

"They are rescuing the prisoners," shouted Mr. Parris, wildly. "Don't you see them hurrying away with them."

He ran to the sheriff and cried:

"Bestir yourself! Do you not see they are taking your prisoners away?"

"I have no deputies," answered the sheriff. "They number hundreds, and the Indians are with them."

"Nonsense! They are only disguised, and are not a dozen. Come! I will go with you."

Four or five by-standers, being thus emboldened, offered to go themselves and aid in recovering the prisoners.

"Come! I will lead you!" cried the eager preacher, allowing his zeal to overcome his discretion.

They ran after the escaping party, and Mr. Parris, either being more zealous than the others, or more swift of foot, outran them and, eluding some of the Indians, who tried to intercept him, ran to where Charles Stevens was half leading and half dragging his mother and Cora from the village.

"Fire-brand of hades! you shall not escape me," cried Mr. Parris seizing Cora's shoulder with a clutch so fierce as to make her cry out.

Charles released both his mother and Cora, and, seizing Mr. Parris by the throat, hurled him to the ground, and raised a hammer to brain him; but at this moment a strong hand seized his arm, and the calm, kind voice of Mr. Waters said:

"Stay your hand, Charles. Do the man no harm."

Next moment, a pair of dusky hands seized Mr. Parris, and he was hurried away to the rear. Mr. Henry Waters caused a couple of guns to be fired in the air in order to intimidate their pursuers. This had the desired effect, and the mention of Indians was sufficient to drive all to the defense of their homes.

The fugitives reached the forest before the sheriff and Mr. Parris could get an armed party in pursuit.

They followed them to the brook, and fired a volley at them, but in vain. The number of accused who escaped on that night, has been estimated at from twenty to one hundred.

20

CHAPTER XVII.

OUT OF THE FRYING PAN INTO THE FIRE.

Though high the warm, red torrent ran,
Between the flames that lit the sky ;
Yet, for each drop, an armed man
Shall rise, to free the land, or die.
                                        —BRYANT.

THE liberated prisoners went whithersoever they pleased. Some went to Boston, others to Plymouth, many to New York, New Jersey and Maryland, while a few returned to England. They were wearied with their experience in the New World, and were content to spend their days in England.

Charles Stevens retained a firm hold on his mother and Cora, until it was quite evident that their pursuers had, for the present, at least, given up the chase. They went on in the forest until they were joined by the five savages left to guard Joel Martin. Martin was no longer with them. Charles did not inquire what had become of him, for he was wholly engrossed in the safety of Cora and his mother.

The Indians and the Waters brothers were engaged in a consultation. Charles took no part in the consultation, for he knew nothing to advise. Then the Indians accompanied them for a few miles through the woods. The forest was dark and sombre, and they had only the silent stars to light their path, until the tardy moon, rising at a late hour, filled the landscape with silver light.

Day dawned, and they were in a wild, picturesque wood, with towering hills and stupendous oaks on every side. Here they halted again for consultation. Oracus, after giving them all the provisions he had with him, took his warriors and stole off into the forest.

George Waters and his brother urged the escaped prisoners to eat some dried venison and parched corn and sleep. They did. Indian blankets on the ground afforded them beds, and their only covering was the sky.

Charles slept until the afternoon was almost spent, and then he was awakened by the tramp of horses feet. He started up and found three Indians with five horses, saddled and bridled. The Indians belonged to the braves of Oracus, and, without a word, they dismounted and turned over the horses to the Englishmen, and stole away into the forest.

A few moments later, the white people were

mounted and riding away through one of the narrow paths known only to the Waters brothers.

Charles Stevens' soul was too full for him to give heed to what course they took. His mother and Cora were free, though he little dreamed that they were escaping from one danger to another. They arrived one night at the home of Mr. Dustin, near Haverhill, in Massachusetts. When the frontiersman heard their story, he said:

"You are welcome, my persecuted friends, to the shelter of my roof, so long as it can afford you any protection; but the war clouds seem to grow darker and more lowering every moment, and I don't know how long my roof will afford protection to any one."

Charles Stevens had been so busy with his own cares and griefs, that he had forgotten that a terrible Indian war was raging on the frontier. This war was known as King William's war, in which the French joined with the Indians in bringing fire and sword upon the inhabitants of New England and New York. The French and English had long been jealous of each other, and a connected account need not be given here of all the disastrous occurrences which lead up to the terrible assault on Haverhill, where the fugitives from Salem were stopping.

We will mention, as first of the principal attacks

during the war of King William, the attack on Schenectady. This was made in pursuance of a plan adopted by Count Frontenac, then governor of Canada, as a means of avenging on the English Colonies the treatment of King James, deposed by William and Mary, which had inflamed the resentment of Frontenac's master, Louis XIV. While New York was torn with internal strife over Leisler, the governor of Canada fitted out three expeditions against the colonies, and in the midst of winter one was sent against New York. The attack on Schenectady was the fruit of this expedition. It was made by a party consisting of about two hundred French and fifty Caughnewaga Indians, under command of Maulet and St. Helene, in 1689 and 1690.

Schenectady was built in the form of an oblong square with a gate at either extremity. The enemy found one of the gates not only open, but unguarded. Although the town was impaled and might have been protected, there was so little thought of danger, that no one deemed it necessary to close the gate. The weather was very cold, and the English did not suppose an attack would be made.

It was eleven o'clock and thirty minutes on Saturday night, February 8th, 1690, when the enemy entered, divided their party, waylaid every

portal and began the attack with a terrible war-
whoop. Maulet attacked a garrison, where the
only resistance was made. He soon forced the
gate, slew the soldiers and burned the garrison.
One of the French officers was wounded in forcing a
house; but St. Helene came to his aid, the house
was taken, and all in it were put to the sword.

Naught was now to be seen, save massacre and
pillage on every side, while the most shocking
barbarities were practised ont he unfortunate inhabitants.

"Sixty-three houses and the church were immediately in a blaze," says a contemporaneous writer.
Weak women, in their expiring agonies, saw their
infants cast into the flames, or brained before their
eyes. Sixty-three persons were murdered and
twenty-seven carried into captivity.

A few persons were enabled to escape; but,
being without sufficient clothing, some perished in
the cold before they reached Albany.

About noon next day, the enemy left the desolate place, taking such plunder as they could carry
with them and destroying the remainder. It was
the intention of Maulet to spare the minister, for
he wanted him as his own prisoner; but he was
found among the mangled dead, and his papers
burned. Two or three houses were spared, while
the others were consigned to the flames.

NAUGHT WAS TO BE SEEN, SAVE MASSACRE AND PILLAGE ON EVERY SIDE.

Owing to the wretched condition of the roads and the deep snows, news of the massacre did not reach the great Mohawk castle, only seventeen miles distant, for two days. On receipt of the terrible news, an armed party set out at once in pursuit of the foe. After a long tedious march through the snow and forest, they came upon their rear, and a furious fight followed, in which about twenty-five of them were killed and wounded.

A second party of French and Indians was sent against the delightful settlement of Salmon Falls, on the Piscataqua. At Three Rivers, Frontenac had fitted out an expedition of fifty-two men and twenty-five Indians, with Sieur Hertel as their leader. In this small band he had three sons and two nephews. After a long and rugged march, Hertel reached the place on the 27th of March, 1690. His spies having reconnoitred it, he divided his men into three companies, leading the largest himself. Just at dawn of day the attack was made. The English stoutly resisted, but were unable to withstand the well-directed fire of their assailants. Thirty of the bravest defenders fell. The remainder, amounting to fifty-four, were made prisoners. The English had twenty-seven houses reduced to ashes, and two thousand domestic animals perished in the barns that were burned.

The third party, which was fitted out at Quebec

by the directions of Frontenac, made an attack upon
Casco, in Maine. The expedition was commanded
by M. De Portneuf. Hertel, on his return to
Canada, met with this expedition, and, joining it
with the force under his command, came back to
the scene of warfare in which he had been so un-
happily successful. As the hostile army marched
through the country of the Abenakis, numbers of
them joined it. Portneuf, with his forces thus
augmented, came into the neighborhood of Casco,
about the 25th of May, 1690. On the following
night, an Englishman who entered the well-laid
ambush was captured and killed. This so excited
the Indians that they raised the war-whoop. Fifty
English soldiers were sent from the fort to ascertain the occasion of the yelling, and were drawn
into the ambuscade. A volley from the woods on
either side swept them down, and before the remainder could recover from the panic into which
they were thrown by the volley, they were assailed
with swords, bayonets and tomahawks, and but
four out of the party escaped and these with severe
wounds.

"The English seeing now that they must stand
a siege, abandoned four garrisons, and all retired
into one which was provided with cannon. Before
these were abandoned, an attack was made upon
one of them, in which the French were repulsed

with an Indian killed and a Frenchman wounded. Portneuf now began to doubt of his ability to take Casco, fearing the issue; for his commission only · ordered him to lay waste the English settlements, and not to attempt fortified places; but, in this dilemma, Hertel and Hopehood (a celebrated chief of the tribe of the Kennebec), arrived. It was now determined to press the siege. In the deserted forts they found all the necessary tools for carrying on the work, and they began a mine within fifty feet of the fort, under a steep bank, which entirely protected them from its guns. The English became discouraged, and, on the 28th of May, surrendered themselves as prisoners of war. There were seventy men and probably a greater number of women and children; all of whom, except Captain Davis, who commanded the garrison, and three or four others, were given up to the Indians, who murdered most of them in their most cruel manner; and, if the accounts be true, Hopehood excelled all other savages in acts of cruelty."

These barbarous transactions produced both terror and indignation in New York and New England, and an attempt at a formidable demonstration against the enemy was made. The general court of Massachusetts sent letters of request to the several executives of the provinces, pursuant to which, they convened at New York, May 1st, 1661. As

the result of the deliberations, two important measures were adopted. Connecticut sent General
Winthrop with troops to march through Albany,
there to receive supplies and to be joined by a
body of men from New York. The expedition
was to proceed up Lake Champlain to destroy
Montreal. There was a failure, however, of the
supplies, and this project was defeated. Massachusetts sent forth a fleet of thirty-four sail, under
William Phipps. He proceeded to Port Royal,
took it, reduced Acadia, and thence sailed up the
St. Lawrence, with the design of capturing Quebec.
The troops landed with some difficulty, and the
place was boldly summoned to surrender. A
proud defiance was returned by Frontenac, as his
position at that time happened to be strengthened by
a re-enforcement from Montreal. Phipps, learning this, and finding, also, that the party of Winthrop, which he expected at Montreal, failed, gave
up the attempt, and returned to Boston, with the
loss of several vessels and a considerable number of
troops, for a part of his fleet was wrecked by a storm.

It was in the midst of such trying scenes and
devastation on the part of the French and savages,
that superstition and fanaticism broke loose in
Salem and produced a reign of terror far greater
than that caused by the savages on the frontier.
It was from such scenes to such scenes that Charles

Stevens, his mother and friends fled. Mr. Dustin lived near Haverhill, in Massachusetts, and when they appealed to him for shelter and protection he said:

"To such as I have you are welcome; but, I assure you, it is poor. The savage scalping-knife may be more dangerous than the fanatic's noose in Salem."

They had been at Haverhill but a few weeks, when, as Charles and Mr. Henry Waters were one day returning from a hunt, they discovered a man trailing them.

"It's a white man," Charles remarked.

"So I perceive, and why should he trail us?" Henry Waters asked.

"I know not; but let us ascertain."

They halted at the creek near Haverhill, and were sitting on the banks of the stream, when a voice from the rocks above demanded their surrender.

Looking up, they found themselves covered with three rifles. Three white men, one of whom they recognized as Mr. Joel Martin, the Virginian, stepped out from behind the rocks and advanced toward them, assuring them that any effort to escape, or resist would result in instant death.

"I have you at last, murderer!" cried Martin, seizing Henry Waters.

"No, you mistake——" began Charles; but Henry Waters signed him to keep quiet. The Waters brothers, as the reader is aware, were twins and looked so much alike, that it was difficult to distinguish one from the other.

Charles was not slow to grasp at the idea- of Henry Waters. He would suffer himself to be taken to Virginia in his brother's stead, where he would make his identity known and establish an alibi; but there was danger of the revengeful Martin killing his prisoner before he reached Virginia, and Charles said:

" Will you promise, on your honor as a Virginian, not to harm the prisoner until he reaches a court of justice?"

The Virginian gave his promise, and then the three led Mr. Waters hurriedly away, mounted horses, hastened to Boston and took a vessel for Virginia.

Charles Stevens went to Mr. George Waters and told him what had happened. Mr. Waters' face grew troubled; but he said nothing.

That night there was an alarm of savages in the neighborhood and Charles Stevens and Mr. Waters went with a train-band to meet the foe. In a skirmish, Mr. Waters was wounded, and it was thought best for him to go to Boston for medical treatment.

"I have friends and relatives there," Charles said, "and we might be safe."

Next day the four secretly set out for Boston, where they lodged for awhile with some relatives of Charles and his mother, who kept their presence a secret.

Before concluding this chapter, it is the duty of the author, although stepping aside from the narrative, to relate what befell their brave friends, the Dustins, during the progress of King William's war. The atrocities committed upon the colonists by the French and Indians were equal to any recorded in the annals of barbarous ages. Connected with these were instances of heroic valor on the part of the heroic sufferers, which are not surpassed. On March 15th, 1697, the last year of King William's war, an attack was suddenly made on Haverhill by a party of about twenty Indians. It was a rapid, but fatal onset, and a fitting *finale* of so dreadful a ten years' war. Eight houses were destroyed, twenty-seven persons killed, and thirteen carried away prisoners. One of these houses, standing in the outskirts of the village and, in fact, over the hill, so as to be almost out of sight of the people in the town, was the home of Mr. Dustin, the house which had afforded shelter to the fugitives from the Salem witchcraft persecution.

On that fatal morning, Mr. Dustin had gone to

the field to commence his spring work. The season was early, and the plow and shovel had already begun to turn over the rich, black soil. The industrious farmer had but just harnessed his horse, when the animal began to sniff the air, and, turning his eyes toward some bushes, Mr. Dustin discovered two painted faces, with heads adorned by feathers.

At the same moment, a rattling crash of firearms and the terrible war-whoop announced the attack on Haverhill. He unharnessed his horse, seized his gun, which he always kept near at hand, and galloped away like the wind toward the house, pursued by arrows of the Indians.

Reaching the house before the Indians, he cried to his family to fly, and he would cover their retreat.

"Mrs. Neff, take Mrs. Dustin and fly for your lives," he cried.

Mrs. Dustin had an infant, but a few days old, and was confined to her bed. Mrs. Neff was her nurse. The husband made an attempt to remove his wife; but it was too late. The Indians, like ravenous wolves, were rushing on the house. Mrs. Dustin turned to her husband and said:

"Go, Thomas, you cannot save me, go and save the children."

Moved by her urgent appeal, he leaped on his

horse and, with his gun in his hand, galloped away after the children, seven in number, who were already running down the road. The first thought of the father was to seize one, place it on the horse before him, and escape; but he was unable to select one from the others. All were alike dear to him, and he resolved to defend all or perish in the effort. They had reached a point below the town, where the road ran between two hills in a narrow pass. A party of Indians, eleven in number, had seen the children and were running after them. Mr. Dustin spurred his horse between the children and the savage foe, and shouting to his darlings to fly, and bidding the oldest carry the youngest, he drew rein at the pass and cocked his gun. Thomas Dustin was a dead shot, and his rifle was the best made at that day.

Facing the savages, he fired and shot the leader dead in his tracks. His followers were appalled at the fate of their brawny chieftain, and for a moment hesitated. Mr. Dustin hesitated not a single instant, but proceeded, without a moment's delay, to reload his gun. Five of the Indians fired at the resolute father, as he rode away after his flying children.

"Run! run! run for your lives!" he shouted.

The Indians, with a whoop of vengeance followed the father. He had four balls in his gun, and, wheeling his horse about, he fired this terrible charge at them. Though none were killed instantly at this shot, three were wounded, two so severely that they died next day. The Indians abandoned the pursuit of the resolute father, who continued to fight as he retreated, and turned their attention to less dangerous victories, so Mr. Dustin escaped with his children.

Mrs. Neff, the nurse in attendance on Mrs. Dustin, heroically resolved to share the fate of her patient, even when she could have escaped. The Indians entered the house, and, having made the sick woman rise and sit quietly in the corner of the fire-place, they pillaged the dwelling, and set it on fire, taking the occupants out of it. At the approch of night, Mrs. Dustin was forced to march into the wilderness and seek repose on the hard, cold ground. Mrs. Neff attempted to escape with the baby, but was intercepted. The infant had its brains beaten out against a tree, and the body was thrown into the bushes. The captives of Haverhill, when collected, were thirteen miserable, wretched people. That same day they were marched twelve miles before camping, although it was nearly night before they set out. Succeeding this, for several days they were compelled to keep up with the savage captors, over an extent of country of not less than one hundred and forty or fifty

THE RESOLUTE FATHER CONTINUED TO FIRE AS HE RETREATED.

miles. Feeble as she was, it seems wonderful that Mrs. Dustin should have borne up under the trials and fatigues of the journey; but she did.

After this, the Indians, according to their custom, divided their prisoners. Mrs. Dustin, Mrs. Neff and a captive lad from Worcester fell to the share of an Indian family consisting of twelve persons. These now took charge of the captives and treated them with no particular unkindness, save that of forcing them to extend their journey still further toward an Indian settlement. One day they told the prisoners that there was one ceremony to which they must submit after their arrival at their destination, and that was running the gauntlet between two files of Indians. This announcement filled Mrs. Dustin and her companions with so much dread, that they mutually resolved to make a desperate attempt to escape.

Mrs. Hannah Dustin, Mrs. Mary Neff the nurse, and the lad Samuel Leonardson, only eleven years of age, were certainly not persons to excite the fear of a dozen sturdy warriors. The Indians believed the lad faithful to them, and never dreamed that the women would have courage enough to attempt to escape, and no strict watch was kept over them.

In order to throw the savage captors off their guard, Mrs. Dustin seemed to take well to them, and on the day before the plan of escape

21

was carried out, she ascertained, through inquiries made by the lad, how to kill a man instantly and how to take off his scalp.

"Strike him here," the Indian explained, placing · his finger on his temple, "and take off his scalp so," showing the lad how it was done. With this information, the plot was ripe. Just before dawn of day, when the Indians sleep most profound, Mrs. Dustin softly rose from her bed of earth and touched Mary Neff on the shoulder. A single touch was sufficient to awake her, and she sat up. Next the lad had to be aroused. Being young and wearied, his slumbers were profound. An Indian lay near asleep. Mrs. Dustin seized his tomahawk, and Mrs. Neff seized another Indian's weapons. The nurse shook Samuel. The lad rose, rubbed his eyes and went over to where the man lay, who had instructed him in the art of killing. He seized his hatchet and held it in his hand ready. At a signal from Mrs. Dustin, three blows fell on three temples, and with a quiver three sleepers in life had passed to the sleep of death. Once more the hatchets were raised, and six of the twelve were dead. The little noise they were compelled to make disturbed the slumbers of the others, and the three hatchets, now red with blood, fell on three more. Mrs. Neff, growing nervous and excited, cut her man's head a little too far forward, and he started up with a yell. The blood blinded him, however, and she stabbed him.

The yell had roused the others, and a squaw with a child fled to the woods, while the tenth, a young warrior, was assailed by Mrs. Dustin and the lad and slain ere he was fully awake. Ten of the twelve were dead, and the escaped prisoners, after scuttling all the boats save one, to prevent pursuit, started in that down the river, with what provisions they could take from the Indians. They had not gone far, when Mrs. Dustin said:

"We have not scalped the Indians."

"Why should we?" asked Mrs. Neff.

"When we get home and tell our friends that we three slew ten Indians, they will demand some 'proof of the assertion, and the ten scalps will be proof."

Samuel Leonardson, boy like, was anxious to have the scalps of his foes, and so they overruled Mrs. Neff and, turning about, went back to the camp which was now deserted save by the ghastly dead, their glassy eyes gazing upward at the skies.

"This is the way he told me to do it," said Samuel, seizing the tuft of hair on the head of the man who had instructed him in scalping. He ran the keen edge of a knife around the skull and, by a quick jerk, pulled off the scalp.

Being novices in the art, it took them some time

to remove the scalps from the heads of all; but the bloody task was finally accomplished and putting the scalps in a bag, they once more embarked in the Indian canoe and started down the stream.

"With strong hearts, the three voyagers went down the Merrimac to their homes, every moment in peril from savages or the elements, and were received as persons risen from the dead. Mrs. Dustin found her husband and children saved. Soon after, she went to Boston, carrying with her a gun and tomahawk, which she had brought from the wigwam, and her ten trophies, and the general court of Massachusetts gave these brave sufferers fifty pounds as a reward for their heroism. Ex-Governor Nicholson, of Maryland, sent a metal tankard to Mrs. Dustin and Mrs. Neff, as a token of his admiration. That tankard is now (1875) in the possession of Mr. Emry Coffin, of Newburyport, Massachusetts. During the summer of 1874, one hundred and seventy-seven years after the event, citizens of Massachusetts and New Hampshire erected on the highest point of Dustin's Island an elegant monument, commemorative of the heroic deed. It displays a figure of Mrs. Dustin, holding in her right hand, raised in the attitude of striking, a tomahawk, and a bunch of scalps in the other. On it are inscribed the names of Hannah Dustin,

Mary Neff and Samuel Leonardson, the English lad." *

Haverhill was a second time attacked and desolated during King William's war, and other places suffered. The treaty at Ryswick, a village near the Hague, in Holland, soon after, put an end to the indiscriminate slaughter in Europe and America. At this insignificant little village, a peace was agreed upon between Louis XIV. of France and England, Spain and Holland, and the German Empire, which ended a war of more than seven years' duration. Louis was compelled to acknowledge William of Orange to be the sovereign of England. That war cost Great Britain one hundred and fifty millions of dollars in cash, besides a hundred millions loaned. The latter laid the foundation of England's enormous national debt, which, to-day, amounts to five thousand millions of dollars.

Prior to the treaty at Ryswick, a Board of Trade and Plantations was established in England, whose duty it was to have a general oversight of the affairs of the American colonies. It was a permanent commission, the members of which were called "Lords of Trade and Plantations." It consisted of seven members, with a president, and was always a ready instrument of oppression in the

---

* Lossing's "Our Country," vol. iii., p. 418.

hands of the sovereign, and became a powerful promoter of those discontents in the colonies, which broke out in open rebellion in 1775.

The peace of Ryswick was of short duration. Aspirants for power again tormented the people with the evils of war. King James II. died in France, September, 1701. He had been shielded by Louis after his flight from his throne to France, and now the French monarch acknowledged James' son, James Francis Edward (known in history as the pretender) to be the lawful king of England. This act greatly offended the English, because the crown had been settled upon Anne, James's second Protestant daughter. Louis, in addition, had offended the English by placing his grandson, Philip of Anjou, on the throne of Spain, so increasing the influence of France among the dynasties of Europe. King William was enraged and was preparing for war, when a fall from his horse, while hunting, caused his death. He was succeeded by Anne, and a war ensued, which lasted almost a dozen years and is known in history as Queen Anne's War. We have, however, too long dwelt on the general history of the country. It will be essential to our story that we return to the village of Salem where superstition was reigning, while the chief characters of our story were resting in security at Boston, not daring to go abroad by day.

CHAPTER XVIII.

SUPERSTITION REIGNS.

The awful tragedy was through,   ·
And friends and enemies withdrew.
Some smite their breasts and trembling say,
" Unlawful deeds were done to-day. "
                                    —PAXTON.

AFTER the escape of Mrs. Stevens and Cora Waters, a wave of superstition swept over the village of Salem with such irresistible fury, that it seemed in greater danger than the frontier settlements did from the French and Indians. The Nurse family and all their relatives came in for a greater share than any other. Mrs. Cloyse was second of the family to be accused by Parris and his minions. Mrs. Cloyse drew ill-will upon herself at the outset by doing as her brother and sister Nurse did. They all absented themselves from the examinations in the church, and, when the interruptions of the services became too flagrant, from Sabbath worship. They declared that they took that course, because they disapproved of the permission given to the profanation of the place and the service. At last Mrs. Cloyse, or Goody Cloyse, as she was called in the records of the day, was arrested. Mary Easty and Elizabeth Proctor were also arrested. Mary Easty, sister of Mrs. Nurse, was tried and condemned. On her condemnation and sentence, she made an affective memorial while under sentence of death, and fully aware of the hopelessness of her case, addressing the judges, the magistrates and the reverend ministers, imploring them to consider what they were doing, and how far their course in regard to accused persons was inconsistent with the principles and rules of justice.

"I ask nothing for myself," she said. "I am satisfied with my own innocence and certain of my doom on earth and my hope in Heaven. What I do desire, is to induce the authorities to take time, and to use caution in receiving and strictness in sifting testimony; and so shall they ascertain the truth, and absolve the innocent, the blessing of God being upon your conscientious endeavors."

No effect was produced by her warnings or remonstrances. Before setting forth from the jail to the Witches' Hill on the day of her death, she serenely bade farewell to her husband and many children, and many of her friends, some of whom afterward related that "her sayings were so serious, religious, distinct and affectionate as could well be expressed,' drawing tears from the eyes of all present."

The subject of witchcraft grew more interesting after the execution of Mary Easty, and to examine Elizabeth Proctor and Sarah Cloyse, or Cloyce, as Mr. Bancroft spells the name, the deputy governor and five magistrates went to Salem. It was a great day. Several ministers were present. Parris officiated, and, by his own record, it is plain that he himself elicited every accusation. His first witness John, the West India negro servant, husband to Tituba, was rebuked by Sarah Cloyse as a grievous liar. Abigail Williams, the niece to Parris, was also at hand with her wonderful tales of sorcery. She swore she had seen the prisoner at the witches' sacrament.

Struck with horror at such bold perjury, Sarah Cloyse called for water and swooned away before it could be brought her. Upon this, Abigail Williams, her brother's wife, Sarah Williams, Parris' daughter and Ann Putnam shouted:

"Her spirit is gone to prison to her sister!"

Against Elizabeth Proctor, Abigail Williams related stories that were so foolish that one wonders how any sensible person could believe them. Among other things she told how the accused had invited her to sign the Devil's book.

"Dear child!" exclaimed the accused, in her

agony, "it is not so. There is another judgment, dear child," and her accusers, turning toward her husband, declared that he, too, was a wizard: All three were committed. Examinations and commitments multiplied. Giles Corey, a stubborn old man of more than four-score years, could not escape the malice of his minister and his angry

neighbors, with whom he had quarrelled. Parris had had a rival in George Burroughs, a graduate of Harvard College, who, having formerly preached in Salem village, had friends there desirous of his return. He was a skeptic on the subject of witchcraft, and Parris determined to have his revenge on him, and, through his many agents and instru-

LIEUT.-GOV. STOUGHTON.

ments, had him accused and committed. Thus far there had been no success in obtaining confessions, though earnestly solicited. It had been strongly hinted that a confession was an avenue of safety. At last, "Deliverance Hobbs owned every thing that was asked of her," and left unharmed. The gallows was to be set up, not for those who professed themselves witches, but for those who rebuked the delusion.

On May 14th, the new charter and the royal governor arrived in Boston. On the next Monday, the charter was published, and the parishioner of Cotton Mather, with the royal council, was installed in office. The triumph of Cotton Mather was complete. A court of oyer and terminer was immediately instituted by ordinance, and the positive, overbearing Stoughton was appointed by the governor and council as its chief judge, with Sewall and Wait Winthrop, two feebler men, as his associates. By the second of June, the court was in session at Salem, making its experiment on Bridget Bishop, a poor and friendless old woman. The fact of witchcraft was assumed as "notorious." To fix it on the prisoner, Samuel Parris, who had examined her before her commitment, was the principal witness to her power of inflicting torture. He had seen it exercised. Then came the testimony of the bewitched, and a ~~terrible mess of stuff~~ it was. One, ~~on reading it,~~ might suppose that all the inmates of Bedlam had been summoned into court to give their personal experience in the land of insanity.

Many of the witnesses testified that the "shape" of the prisoner often grievously tormented them, by pinching, choking, or biting them, and did otherwise seriously afflict them, urging them all the while to write their names in a book, ~~which "the spectre" called:~~ "Our book."

Sarah Williams, (who was devotedly attached to Mr. Parris and his cause,) swore that it was the shape of this prisoner, with Cora Waters, which one day took her from her wheel and, carrying her to the river side, threatened to drown her, if she did not sign the book mentioned, which she yet refused to do.

Others said that the witch "in her shape," that is, appearing to them in a spiritual body invisible to any save the parties before whom she would appear, boasted that she had ridden John Bly, having first changed him into a horse. One testified to seeing ghosts of dead people, who declared that Bridget Bishop had murdered them.

While the examination of the accused was in progress, the bewitched seemed extremely tortured. If she turned her eyes on them, they were struck down. While they lay in swoons or convulsions, the poor old woman was made to touch them, and they immediately sprang to their feet. Samuel Parris had his minions well trained. On any special action of her body, shaking of her head, or the turning of her eyes, they imitated her posture and seemed under some strange spell.

Evidence was given that one of the bewitched persons persuaded a man to strike at the spot where the "shape of this Bishop stood," and the bewitched cried out:

"You have tore her coat," and it was found that the woman's dress was torn in the very place.

Deliverance Hobbs, who had confessed to being a witch, now testified that she was tormented by the spectres for her confession. And she now testified that this Bishop tempted her to sign the book again, and to deny what she had confessed.

"It was the shape of this prisoner," she declared, "which whipped me with iron rods, to compel me thereunto, and I furthermore saw Bridget Bishop at a general meeting of the witches, in a field at Salem village, where they partook of a diabolical sacrament in bread and wine, then administered."

John Cook testified: "About five or six years ago, one morning, about sunrise, I was in my chamber assaulted by the shape of this prisoner, which looked on me, grinned at me, and very much hurt me with a blow on the side of the head, and on the same day, about noon, the same shape walked into the room where I was, and an apple strangely flew out of my hand."

→ Samuel Gray testified: "About fourteen years ago, I waked on a night, and saw the room wherein I lay full of light. Then I plainly saw a woman, between the cradle and the bedside, which looked upon me. I rose, and it vanished, though I found all the doors fast. Looking out at the

entry door, I saw the same woman, in the same
garb again, and I said, 'In God's name, what do
you come for?' I went to bed and had the same
woman again assaulting me. The child in the
cradle gave a great screech, and the woman disappeared. It was long before the child could be
quieted; and, though it was a very likely, thriv-
ing child, yet from this time it pined away, and,
after divers months, died in a sad condition. I
knew not Bishop then, nor her name; but when I
saw her after this, I knew her by her countenance
and apparel and all circumstances, that it was the
apparition of this Bishop, which had thus troubled
me."

John Bly testified:

"I bought a sow of Edmund Bishop, the husband of the prisoner, and was to pay the price
agreed upon to another person. This prisoner,
being angry that she was thus hindered from fin-
gering the money, quarrelled with me; soon after
which the sow was taken with strange fits, jump-
ing, leaping and knocking her head against the
fence. She seemed blind and deaf and could not
eat, whereupon my neighbor John Louder said he
believed the creature was overlooked, and there
were sundry other circumstances concurred, which
made me believe that Bishop had bewitched it."

The examining magistrates asked Bly:

"Have you ever been transformed by the prisoner?"

"I have," Bly answered.

"When was it?"

"Last summer. One night, as I was coming home late, the shape of the prisoner came at me. She shook a bridle over my head and I became a horse. Then she mounted me, rode me several leagues and the bridle was removed, and I lay in my bed."

John Louder, another acquaintance of Charles Stevens, was next called. John had had his experience with witches. He was an ardent admirer of Mr. Parris, and one of his emissaries. Louder, Bly and, in fact, all of Parris' tools were ignorant, bigoted and superstitious. They could be made to believe anything the pastor would tell them. Louder testified:

"I had some little controversy with Bishop about her fowls. Going well to bed, I did awake in the night by moonlight, and did see clearly the likeness of this woman grievously oppressing me; in which miserable condition she held me, unable to help myself till near day. I told Bishop of this; but she denied it, and threatened me very much. Quickly after this, being at home on a Lord's Day, with the doors shut about me, I saw a black pig approach me, at which I, going to kick, it vanished

away. Immediately after sitting down, I saw a
black thing jump in at the window and come and
stand before me. The body was like that of a
monkey, the feet like a cock's; but the face was
much like a man's. I was so extremely affrighted,
that I could not speak. This monster spoke to
me and said:

"'I am a messenger sent-unto you, for I understand that you are in some trouble of mind, and if
you be ruled by me, you shall want for nothing in
this world.'

"Whereupon, I endeavored to clap my hands
upon it; but I could feel no substance; and it
jumped out of the window again; but it immediately came in by the porch, though the doors were
shut, and said:

"'You had better take my counsel.'

"Whereupon, I struck at it with my stick, but
struck only the ground-sel, and broke my stick.
The arm with which I struck was presently disen-
abled, and it vanished away. I presently went
out at the porch door and spied this Bishop, in her
orchard, going toward her house; but I had not
power to set one foot forward unto her. Whereupon, returning into the house, I was immediately
accosted by the monster I had seen before, which
goblin was now going to fly at me; whereat I did
cry out:

" 'The whole armor of God be between me and you!'

"So it sprang back and flew over the apple tree, shaking many apples off the tree in its flying over. At its leap, it flung dirt with its feet against my stomach, whereon, I was then struck dumb, and so continued for three days together."

The records of the case on trial shows that William Stacy testified:

"I received money of this Bishop for work done by me, and I was gone but a matter of three rods from her, when, looking for my money, I found it unaccountably gone from me. Some time after, Bishop asked me if my father would grind her grist for her? I demanded why not?

" 'Because folks count me a witch.'

"I answered:

" 'No question but he will grind for you.'

"Being gone about six rods from her, with a small load in my cart, suddenly the off wheel stumped and sank down into a hole, upon plain ground, so that I was forced to get help for the recovering of the wheel; but, stepping back to look for the hole which might give me this disaster, there was none at all to be found. Some time after, I was waked in the night; but it seemed as light as day, and I perfectly saw the shape of this Bishop in the room, troubling me; but upon her

22

going out, all was dark again. When I afterward charged Bishop with it, she did not deny it, but was very angry. Quickly after this, having been threatened by Bishop, as I was again in a dark night, going to the barn, I was very suddenly taken or lifted from the ground, and thrown against a stone wall. After that, I was hoisted up and thrown down a bank, at the end of my house. After this, again passing by this Bishop, my horse with a small load, striving to draw, all his gears flew to pieces, and the cart fell down, and I, going to lift a bag of corn, of about two bushels, could not budge it."

The foregoing is a sample of the testimony on which people were hung. We have given these, that the reader may see what firm hold Mr. Parris and superstition had on the people. We could give page after page of this testimony; but the above is sufficient. If the reader wants a fuller account of the trials of Bishop, Martin or any of the unfortunates who suffered death at Salem during the reign of superstition, we refer them to the collections of Cotton Mather in his "Invisible World." From that book we quote the following information, as elicited by the examination in case of Susanna Martin, at Salem, June 29th, 1692:

Magistrate.—"Pray, what ails these people?"

Martin.—"I don't know."

Magistrate. — "But what do you think of them?"

Martin.—"I don't desire to spend my judgment upon it."

Magistrate.—"Don't you think they are be-witched?"

Martin.—"No; I do not think they are."

Magistrate.—"Tell us your thoughts about them."

. Martin.—"No; my thoughts are my own, when they are in; but when they are out, they are another's. Their master——"

Magistrate.—"Their master? Whom do you think is their master?"

Martin.—"If they be dealing in the black art, you may know as well as I."

Magistrate.—"Well, what have you done to-ward this?"

Martin.—"Nothing at all."

Magistrate.—"Why, 'tis you, or your appear-ance."

Martin.—"I cannot help it."

Magistrate.—"If it be not your master, how comes your appearance to hurt these?"

Martin.—"How do I know? He that appeared in the shape of Samuel, a glorified saint, may ap-pear in any one's shape."

No wonder that a writer having occasion to examine into the evidence a few years ago, and commenting on it, should exclaim:

"Great God! and is this the road our ancestors had to travel in their pilgrimage in quest of freedom and Christianity? Are these the misunderstood doctrines of total depravity?"

Reverend Mr. Noyes seemed to rival Mr. Parris in the persecution of witches.

"You are a witch. You know you are," he said to Sarah Good, while urging her to confession.

"You are a liar," the poor woman replied, "and, if you take my life, God will give you blood to drink."

Confessions became important in the prosecutions. Some, not afflicted before confession, were so, presently, after it. The jails were filled; for fresh accusations were needed to confirm the confessions. Mr. Hale says:

"Some, by these their accusations of others, hoped to gain time, and get favor from the rulers. Some of the inferior sort of people did ill offices, by promising favor thereby, more than they had ground to engage. Some, under these temptations, regarded not as they should what became of others, so that they could thereby serve their own turns. Some have since acknowledged so much. If the confessions were contradictory; if witnesses uttered apparent falsehoods, 'the Devil,' the judges would say, 'takes away their memory, and imposes on their brain.'"

Who, under such circumstances, would dare to be skeptical, or refuse to believe the confessors? Already, twenty persons had been put to death for witchcraft. Fifty-five had been tortured or terrified into penitent confessions. With accusations, confessions increased; with confessions, new accusations. Even "the generation of the children of God" were in danger of "falling under that condemnation." The jails were full. One hundred and fifty prisoners awaited trial, two hundred more were accused or suspected. It was also observed that no one of the condemned confessing witchcraft had been hanged. No one that confessed, and retracted a confession, had escaped either hanging or imprisonment for trial. No one of the condemned who asserted innocence, even if one of the witnesses confessed to perjury, or the foreman of the jury acknowledged the error of the verdict, escaped the gallows. Favoritism was shown in listening to accusations, which were turned aside from friends or partisans. If a man began a career as a witch-hunter, and, becoming convinced of the imposture, declined the service, he was accused and hanged.

Samuel Parris had played a strong hand and was more than successful. His harvest of vengeance

seemed to have no end. Witches' Hill became a
Tyburn-hill, and as many as eight were hung at
one time.

Matters had at last gone too far. The delusion
reached its climax in the midsummer of 1692, and
on the second Wednesday in October following,
about a fortnight after the last hanging at Salem,
the representatives of the colony assembled, and
the people of Andover, their minister joining with
them, appeared with their remonstrance against the
doings of witch tribunals.

"We know not," they said, "who can think
himself safe, if the accusation of children and
others under a diabolical influence shall be received against persons of good fame." The dis-
cussions which ensued were warm, for Mr. Parris
had defenders even in the legislature, who denounced Charles and Hattie Stevens "as murderers
and exercisers of the black art." The general
court did not place itself in direct opposition to
the advocates of the trials. It ordered by bill a
convocation of ministers, that the people might be
led in the right way, as to the witchcraft. The
reason for doing it and the manner were such,
that the judges of the court, so wrote one of them,
"consider themselves thereby dismissed." As to
legislature, it adopted what King William rejected
—the English law, word for word, as it was en-

acted by a house of commons, in which Coke and
Bacon were the guiding minds; but they abrogated
the special court, and established a tribunal by
statute. Phipps had, instantly on his arrival,
employed his illegal court in hanging the witches.
The representatives of the people delayed the first
assembling of the legal court till January of the
following year. Thus an interval of more than
three months from the last executions gave the
public mind security and freedom. Though Phipps
conferred the place of chief judge on Stoughton,
yet jurors, representing the public mind, acted
independently. When the court met at Salem, six
women of Andover, at once renouncing their confessions, treated the witchcraft but as something
"so called," the bewildered but as "seemingly
afflicted." A memorial of like tenor come from the
inhabitants of Andover.

More than one-half of the cases presented were
dismissed; and, though bills were found against
twenty-six persons, the trials showed the feebleness
of the testimony on which others had been condemned. The minds of the juries had become enlightened, even before the prejudiced judges. The
same testimony was produced, and there at Salem,
with Stoughton on the bench, verdicts of acquital
followed.

One of the parties acquitted on this occasion was

an old acquaintance. Mr. Henry Waters, who
had been arrested for his brother and taken to Virginia, suddenly appeared in Salem. John Louder,
at once cried out against him and caused him to be
arrested. On being arraigned, he plead not guilty
and was put on his trial. John Louder was the
principal witness. He stated that one day he and
Bly were hunting and that defendant pursued them
and bewitched their guns. Then he testified that
he fired a silver bullet and wounded the defendant.
He also testified to his appearing before him on
the evening he went to stalk deer, and offering him
a book to sign. It was known that the accused
had suffered from a wound.

Mr. Waters then proceeded to explain:

"My name is Henry Waters, and, in early life,
my brother and I were players. We were members of the Church of England and detested the
Catholic Religion. The end of Charles II. was
drawing near, and we reasoned that James II., his
brother, would become heir to the throne. Our
only hope was to organize a strong party and seize
the throne for the Duke of Monmouth. I was sent
to the American colonies to secure pledges of sup-
port, and get the names of all who would resist
a papal monarch on my book. I came, leaving
my brother and his child in England. On the
way here, I was suddenly fired upon by an Indian

in ambush and wounded in the side. As these men were stalking a deer I passed along and affrighted the animal, so it ran away, and I was for this accused of being a wizard."

He was then asked by the examining magistrate, if he did offer a book to Mr. John Louder to sign.

"I did," he quickly answered.

"When was it?"

"At the time and place he states."

"What book was it?"

"I have it here," and he produced a small, red-backed blank book. "This has caused so much trouble. Examine it, and you will see it was to contain only the names of those who would resist the accession of the Duke of York to the throne."

The book was passed around to the Judge and Jury, and a smile dawned on the face of each, which was dangerous to the friends of the prosecution. That book would have hung Henry Waters during the reign of James II.; but now it was his salvation. He was one of the first acquitted. The delusion was on the wane. "Error died among its worshippers."

CHAPTER XIX.

THE WOMAN IN BLACK.

The greatest of thy follies is forgiven,
　　Even for the least of all the tears that shine
　　On that pale face of thine.
Thou didst kneel down, to him who came from heaven,
　　Evil and ignorant, and thou shalt rise,
　　Holy, and pure, and wise.

　　　　　　　　　　　　　　　—BRYANT.

CHARLES STEVENS, his mother and Cora and her wounded father found safety and shelter at the home of Richard Stevens in Boston. Richard Stevens was an uncle to Charles, and a man past middle life, but noted for his practical common sense. Like all others of this noted family, he never rose high in either social or political circles. They were simply farmers or small tradesmen, with more than average intelligence, patriotic and honest as their great projenitor, who came over with Columbus.

Richard Stevens knew that the delusion of witchcraft could not last. In his house, which was among the best in Boston, save those occupied by

346

the governors and officers, the fugitives, save Mr.
Waters, remained all during the latter part of 1692.
As soon as his wound was healed, George Waters,
mysteriously disappeared. He reached Williams-
burg, Va., just after his brother was acquitted.
He did not meet with Henry, for he had already
taken a ship for Boston.

George Waters went to Robert Stevens, where
he made himself known and learned of his brother's
acquittal.

"The mistake was soon discovered," said Robert
Stevens; "even before the case came on to be tried.
Hearing that you had been arrested, I went to see
you and discovered that they had the wrong man;
then I procured his release."

George Waters thanked Mr. Stevens for what he
had done.

"What are you going to do now?" asked Robert.

"I shall return to Boston."

"He will never cease to follow you."

"No."

Then Mr. Waters again became thoughtful, and
Robert asked:

"Are you going to slay him?"

"No. Did Charles Stevens write to you?"

"Yes."

"Concerning the pardon?"

"He did."

"And have you done everything?"

"Everything that can be done."

"Do you bid me hope?"

"Yes."

That night George Waters set out by land to return to New England. It was a formidable journey in those days, and required many weeks. There were large rivers to be crossed, and he had to go to the headwaters before he could swim them. Many days and nights did the lone traveller spend in the forest.

One afternoon he was suddenly aware of a man pursuing him. Instinctively, he knew it was his enemy Joel Martin. The man was alone, and George Waters, who was an expert marksman, could have waylaid and shot him. Martin came to seek his life, and, ordinarily, one might say that he was fully justified in killing him. George paused on the crest of a high hill, and with the declining sun full on him, watched the determined pursuer.

"Joel Martin is a brave man," thought Mr. Waters. "He is as brave as he is revengeful."

Martin was almost a mile away; but he clearly saw the figure of the horseman and supposed he had halted to challenge him to battle. Martin unslung his rifle and urged his jaded steed forward at a gallop, waving his weapon in the air.

"I might be tempted to do it," George Waters thought, and he took his gun from his back, threw it on the ground and rode away.

Joel Martin, who witnessed the strange proceeding, was puzzled to know what it meant. He came up to the gun of his enemy and saw him riding rapidly across the hills and rocks.

"Now he is at my mercy," cried Martin. "The fool hath thrown away his gun to increase his speed."

George Waters was fully a mile ahead of Joel Martin, when he heard the sharp report of a rifle followed by the crack of two or three muskets, accompanied by an Indian yell. Waters felt his heart almost stand still. He sought shelter in a dense thicket on the banks of a stream to await the shadows of night. He wondered what had become of Martin, and when he heard the yells of savages as he frequently did, he asked himself if they were not torturing the unfortunate prisoner to death.

When night came, he saw a bright fire burning further down the creek, and, leaving his horse tied to a bush, the brave Englishman crept through the woods, crawling most of the way. At last he was near enough to see a score of savages sitting about a camp fire. Near by, tied to a tree was the miserable Virginian. Mr. Waters saw that he had two wounds, and was no doubt suffering greatly.

His horse had been killed and afforded a feast for the savages, who evidently had not yet decided the rider's fate. Having feasted until their stomachs were overgorged, the Indians laid down upon the ground and fell asleep. Their prisoner was severely wounded and tied with stout deer-skin thongs, so that it would be utterly impossible for him to escape, and in the heart of this great wilderness the dusky sons slept in perfect security.

George Waters crept up closer and closer to the prisoner, and had to actually crawl between two sleeping savages, to reach him; then he slowly rose at the feet of Martin, who, unable to sleep for pain, was the only human being in the camp awake. The prisoner saw him approaching, saw him draw his knife, and expected to be killed by his enemy; but he made no outcry. Better be stabbed to the heart by George Waters than tortured by his fiendish captors.

George Waters cut the deer-skin thongs which bound him to the tree and, in a whisper, asked:

"Can you walk?"

"No."

"I will carry you."

He took the wounded man on his own broad shoulders, and carefully bore him from the camp. Not a word was said. Joel Martin's tongue seemed suddenly to have become paralyzed. George

Waters walked slowly, carefully, and silently. The Indians slept. When they were some distance from the camp, Martin, entertaining but one idea of Waters' plan, said:

"You have gone far enough with me. Stop right here and have it over with. I shall make no outcry."

"Joel Martin, you are a brave man, I know,——" began Mr. Waters; but Martin again interrupted him with:

"I shall make no outcry. You have a knife in your belt. Stab me, and be done with it."

"I shall not."

"Where are you going to take me?"

"To my horse."

Martin grumbled at the useless delay, but suffered himself to be carried to the horse.

"Can you ride?" Waters asked.

"Yes."

"I will help you to the saddle, and, if you think there is danger of your falling, I can tie you."

He assisted the wounded man into the saddle and took the rein in his hand, saying, "Hold, and I will lead."

"George Waters, where are you going with me?"

"To Virginia."

"Can it be that you intend to spare my life?"

"I have no occasion to take it,"

The crestfallen Virginian said no more. All night long they journeyed through the forests and across plains. At dawn of day they were among the mountains. They rested and George Waters kept watch over the wounded man while he slept.

By the middle of the afternoon, they were on the march again. Mr. Martin's wounds were inflamed and sore, and he was in a fever. Next day they reached the village of some friendly Indians, and remained there two weeks, until the wounded man was able to proceed. George Waters went with him until they were in sight of a village on the upper James River.

"I can go no further, Mr. Martin," said George Waters.

"I understand," he returned, dismounting from the saddle.

"Can you make your way to those houses?"

"Yes."

"I will take you nearer, if necessary."

"It is not."

George Waters cut two stout sticks with forks to place under his arms as crutches. Martin watched his acts of kindness, while a softer expression came over his face. He was about to go away, but turned about and, seizing Waters by the hand, cried:

"God bless you! You are a man!"

Not willing to risk himself further he turned away, and George Waters re-entered the forest. He reached Boston early in 1692, just after the acquittal of his brother and others of the charge of witchcraft.

Everybody realizing that the madness had run its course, Charles Stevens and his mother went back to their home at Salem, confident that they need fear no more persecutions from Parris, whose power was gone.

Next day after his arrival, while going down a lonely path near the village C h a r l e s suddenly came upon Sarah Williams. Her eyes were blazing with the fires of hope, fanaticism and disappointed pride.

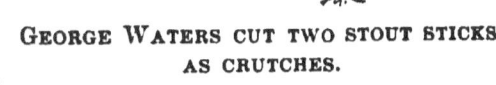

GEORGE WATERS CUT TWO STOUT STICKS AS CRUTCHES.

"Charles! Charles!" she cried. "Nay, do not turn away from me, for, as Heaven is my witness, I did not have your mother cried out upon!"

"Sarah Williams, I am as willing as any to forget the past, or, if remember it I must, only think

23

of it as a hideous nightmare from which, thanks to Providence, we have escaped forever."

"Charles, let us be friends."

"Far be it from me to be your enemy, Sarah Williams."

"Can you not be more, Charles?" said the handsome widow, her dark eyes on the ground, while her cheek became suffused with a blush.

"What mean you, Sarah Williams?"

"You used to love me."

The young man started and said:

"You mistake."

"I do not. You told me you did in the presence of Abigail Williams. At the same time you confessed to killing Samuel Williams in order to wed me."

Charles Stevens was thunderstruck, and could only gaze in amazement on the bold, unscrupulous woman, who had trained under Parris, until she was capable of almsost any deception to carry her point.

"Sarah Williams, what you say is a lie!" he declared, in a voice hoarse with amazement and indignation.

"We shall see! We shall see!" she answered, in a hoarse, shrill voice. "I will prove it. See, I will prove it and hang you yet. Beware! I do not charge you with witchcraft, but with murder.

Either take the place you made vacant by the death
of Samuel Williams, or hang!"

As least of the two evils, Charles Stevens intimated he preferred to hang, and, turning abruptly
about, he left her. Next day he was met by Bly
and Louder in the village, who interrogated him
on his recent trouble with Sarah Williams about
the dead husband. Knowing both to be outra-
geous liars, and unscrupulous as they were bold, he
sought to avoid them; but they followed him
everywhere and interrogated him, until he was
utterly disgusted and finally broke away and went
home.

Charles Stevens did not tell his mother of the
threat of Sarah Williams, for he considered it too
absurd to notice. Three or four days later, when
he had almost ceased to think of the matter, he
and his mother were startled from their supper, by
hearing a loud knock at the front door.

"Sit you still, Charles, and I will go and see
who this late visitor is."

She rose and went to the door and opened it.

Three or four dark forms stood without.

"Is Charles Stevens in?" asked one.

"Yes, sir."

"I want to see him."

"Who are you?"

"Don't you know me, Hattie Stevens? I am

the sheriff," said the speaker boldly, as he, unbidden, entered the house.

"You the sheriff! What can you want here?"

Turning to the men without, he said in an undertone:

"Guard the doors."

The dumfounded mother repeated:

"You the sheriff! What do you want here?"

"I want to see that precious son of yours, widow Stevens, and I trow he will guess the object of my visit."

"My son! Surely he hath done no wrong. He hath broken no law."

"Where is he?"

The voice of the sheriff was pitched considerably above the ordinary key, and Charles Stevens, hearing it in the kitchen, became alarmed, and hastened into the front apartment, saying:

"I am here. Is it me you want to see?"

"Yes, Charles Stevens, I arrest you in the king's name."

"Arrest me? Marry! what offence have I done that I should be arrested by the king's officers?"

"It is murder!" he answered.

"Murder!" shrieked both the mother and son.

"Verily, it is," answered the sheriff. Then he produced a warrant issued on the complaint of

Sarah Williams, charging Charles Stevens with the murder of one Samuel Williams.

Charles could scarcely believe his ears, when he heard the warrant read. He had for a long time known Sarah Williams to be a bold, scheming woman; but that she would proceed to such a bold, desperate measure as this seemed impossible.

"I am innocent!" he declared, while his mother sank into a chair and buried her face in her hands.

"It is ever thus. The most guilty wretch on earth is innocent according to his tell," the sheriff answered.

Charles Stevens besought the man not to confine him in jail, but was told there was no help for it, and he was hurried away to prison, leaving his mother overcome with grief in her chair.

. . . .

It was some days before the news of Charles Stevens' arrest reached Boston. The prosecution was interested in keeping the matter from the friends of the accused, for the Stevens family were known to have many friends in high places in the colonies, and they might interfere in the coming trial.

Cora Waters lived for weeks in ignorance of the peril of the man she loved. Her father had come home, her uncle was with them again, and she was almost happy. Poor child of misfortune, she had never known real happiness.

Bleak winter was taking his departure and a
smiling spring promised to be New England's
guest. Hope and peace and newness of life always come with spring. Spring gladdens the heart
and rejuvenates the aged.

One morning, while the frosty breath of winter
yet lingered on the air, Cora Waters, who was an
early riser, saw a large ship entering the harbor.
The wind was dead against the vessel; but she was
skillfully handled and tacked this way and that
and gradually worked her way into the harbor. A
wreath of smoke from one of her ports was followed
by the heavy report of a cannon, which salute was
answered by a shot from the shore.

"The ship will soon be in," the girl declared.
"I will go and see it."

In small seaport towns, such as Boston was at
that day, the appearance of a ship caused as much
excitement as the arrival of a train on a new rail-
road in a western village does to-day. Many people were hastening down to the beach where the
boat would bring in passengers. Some were expecting friends. Others had letters from loved
ones across the sea; but Cora had no such excuse.
It was simply girlish curiosity which induced her
to go with the crowd to the beach.

Boats had been lowered from the vessel, which,
having no deck, could not get into shore and was

forced to cast anchor some distance off. The boats, filled with passengers, were rowed ashore.

Cora stood with a careless, idle air gazing on the gentlemen and ladies as they disembarked. None specially excited her interest. Many were there greeting relatives and friends; but she had no friend or relative, and what were all those people to her?

She was about to turn away, when a face and pair of dark-blue eyes attracted her attention. She involuntarily started and stared impudently at the stranger, her heart beating, and her breath coming in short quick gasps.

"That face—that face! I have seen in my dreams!" she thought.

It was the pale face of a woman, still beautiful, although her features showed lines of suffering and anxiety. She was dressed in black from head to foot, and a veil of jet black was wound round her head. For a few moments, she stood looking about and then came directly to Cora and asked:

"Young maid, do you live in this town?"

"I do, for the present," Cora answered, though she instinctively trembled, for that voice, too, sounded like a long-forgotten dream. What strange spell was this which possessed her? The woman asked:

"Can you direct me to a house of public entertainment?"

"Come with me."

Cora knew that the lady had suffered with seasickness, and was anxious to reach land. She hastened with her to a public house kept by a widow Stevens, whose husband was a distant relative of Charles. As they walked up the hill toward the house, the woman continued to ply Cora with questions:

"Are you a native of America?" she asked.

"No."

"England is your birth-place?"

"It is."

"Have you been long here?"

"I was quite a child when I came," she answered.

"Have you lived a long while in this town?"

"Only a few months," she answered.

They had nearly reached their destination, when Cora saw her father coming toward them. At sight of his daughter's companion, the face of the father became white as death, and, bounding forward, he pulled her aside, saying:

"No, no! Cora, you shall not go another step with her!"

At sound of his voice, the woman in black seized his arm and cried:

"George! George! George!"

"Away! away!"

"No, no! Now that I have found you, I will not let you go. You may kill me, cut off my hands, and still the fingers will cling to you. Oh, God! I thank thee, that, after so many years, thou hast answered my prayers!"

"Woman, release me!"

"George! George!"

Cora was lost in a maze of bewilderment. She was conscious of the strange woman in black clutching her father's arm and calling him George, while he strove to drive her away.

A great throng of people gathered about them. Mr. Waters became rude in his efforts to break away. At last he flung her off, and she fell, her forehead striking on the sharp corner of a stone, which started the blood trickling down her fair white brow. The woman swooned. Sight of blood touched the heart of George Waters, and, stooping, he raised the inanimate form in his arms, as tenderly as if she had been an infant, and bore her to a public house and a private room.

When the woman in black recovered consciousness, she and George Waters were alone, and he was tenderly dressing the wound he had made.

"George," she said with a smile, "you will let me talk with you now?"

"Yes."

"George, you believed me guilty when you abandoned me at Edinburgh?"

"Yes."

"You do yet?"

"I do."

"George, Joseph Swartz told you a falsehood."

"No, no, woman, do not——"

"Hold, George; let me show you his dying confession. Let me show you the testimony of a priest."

She took up a small, red leather bag, such as was used in those days by ladies, undid the strings and, opening it, drew forth some papers, which she handed to him.

"Do you know the writing?" she asked.

"This is Joseph Swartz, my best and truest friend."

"No, no; read his death-bed confession, and you will see he was your malignant foe."

He read the paper through, and his hands trembled with excitement, astonishment and rage. He was about to say something, when she interrupted him with:

"No, no; don't, don't, George. He is dead— let us forgive. If you want more proof, I have it. See Father Healey's statement. He took Joseph Swartz's confession."

Glancing at the paper, he threw it aside and cried:

"Honore! Honore! Forgive me! I should have believed you, not him. I stole your child and, like a foolish man, ran away, without questioning you."

"I have been sixteen years seeking these proofs. I would not have come without them. You are forgiven, for, now that you have the proof, you believe."

When George Waters went out of the room, he was met by his daughter, Cora, who asked:

"Father, who is she—the woman in black?"

"An angel—your mother!"

"May I see her?"

"Yes, at once," and he led her to the apartment.

CHAPTER XX.

CONCLUSION.

How calm, how beautiful comes on
The stilly hour, when storms are gone;
When warring winds have died away,
And clouds, beneath the glancing ray,
Melt off, and leave the land and sea
Sleeping in bright tranquillity,
Fresh as if day again were born,
Again upon the lap of Morn.

—MOORE.

IN his dungeon cell, Charles Stevens learned that the veil of mystery which, like a threatening cloud, had enshrouded the life of Cora Waters was lifted, and the sunlight, for the first time, streamed upon her soul. She knew a mother's love. Her parents, estranged since her infancy, were again united. Such incidents are told in song and story, but are seldom known in reality. Charles heard the story in all its details related by his mother on one of her visits. He also learned that the colony of Virginia, by royal sanction, had granted a pardon to Mr. George Waters for the "death of one James Martin, late overseer to Thomas Hull."

364

"I am glad they are happy, mother," the unhappy prisoner said.

"It is the reward which in the end awaits the just," she said.

"They have forgotten me."

"Charles, why say you that?"

"Had not Cora Waters forgotten me, surely she would have visited me while sick and in prison."

"They have just heard of it," she answered.

"Just heard of it!" he repeated, amazed. "I have lain here pining in this dungeon for three long weeks, and you tell me they have but just heard of it."

"I am assured they have."

"Mother, that seems impossible. Why, I thought all the world knew it."

"But few know of it, my son. It seems to be the scheme of the prosecution to keep the matter secret. You have not written. You have sent no message?"

"No, mother."

"Then, pray, how could they learn of it save by the merest accident? A passing stranger bore the news."

Charles Stevens heaved a sigh.

"Perhaps 'tis so; but it seemed that my groans and sighs must be heard round the world, yet neither Cora Waters nor Adelpha Leisler, at whose side I stood a comforter in the dark hours of trouble, has seen fit to offer me one word of consolation."

"I trow, Charles, that Adelpha knows it not. Cora is coming."

"Who hath told you?"

"A friend from Boston brings information that the Waters brothers, with the newly found wife and mother and Cora, are coming to Salem to do all in their power to aid you."

Charles sadly shook his head and said:

"My poor friends can do nothing for me."

"They can at least offer you consolation and comfort."

"Yes; but what more?"

"That is much."

"True; and I will appreciate it. I could not think that Cora would forget me. Neither would Adelpha, if she knew."

His mother after waiting some time for her son to resume, at last said:

"Charles, if your choice were left you, which of the two, Adelpha or Cora, would you wed?"

Charles, smiling, answered:

"Mother, it is not for one living within the shadow of the scaffold to think of marriage."

"Charles, can you really think your case so serious?"

"I do mother. I know it."

"Oh, Charles, surely they will not condemn you! They have no proof. You are innocent."

"I am innocent, mother; but that is no reason that evidence will not be produced against me."

"Yet it will be false."

"False, of course; yet many have been hung on testimony false as Satan himself."

"Oh, Charles, what shall we do?"

"Trust in the Lord, mother. When all earthly help is gone, we can only look to God for aid. I have prayed to him that, if it be his will, this cup might pass; yet his will, not mine, be done. If I must die a martyr to that woman's falsehood, I pray he may give me sufficient strength to endure the trial."

The mother fell on the neck of her son, crying: "You shall not die! Oh, my son! my son!" .

Charles comforted his mother as well as he could, and she took her leave. All was dark and gloomy. He knew that malice and hatred pursued him, caught his throat and would not let go its hold, until it dragged him to death. He was buried in the midst of his gloomy reflections, when the door of his cell opened, and a jailer, entering, said:

"Another visitor for you, Charles Stevens."

"Another visitor? Who can it be?" he asked.

"It is I," and Samuel Parris entered.

For a moment, Charles Stevens was struck dumb at the audacity of the pastor of Salem in venturing to enter the cell of one whom he had wronged. Though the power of Mr. Parris was on the wane, it was not wholly gone. He took advantage of the confusion of Charles Stevens to signal the jailer to leave them, and he went out, closing the iron door behind him. Folding his arms on his breast, Parris gazed on the prisoner.

Charles Stevens, about whose waist was a thick belt of leather, fastened by a chain to the wall, sat on a miserable cot, his face bowed in his hands. He did not look up at the white, cadaverous face and great, blazing orbs, which gleamed with fury upon him, although he knew full well that those eyes were on him.

"Charles!" the deep sepulchral voice at last spoke.

"Well?"

"Look up."

With a sigh, the young prisoner raised his head. Every movement he made was accompanied by the rattling of chains.

"Charles, you will not believe me, when I tell you I am sorry for this."

"No; I will not."

"Nevertheless, I am.. Charles Stevens, you do not know me; the world misjudges me, and all future generations will do the same. Some things which I have done may seem harsh; yet I was commanded of Heaven to do them."

"Samuel Parris, if you have come to upbraid me, to gloat over my captivity and add to my misery, do so. I am powerless and cannot resist you; but I do entreat you not to blaspheme your Maker."

The great eyes of Parris gleamed with sullen fire; his thin lips parted; his breath came short and quick, and for a few moments he was unable to answer. At last, becoming calmer, he said, in his deep sepulchral voice:

"Charles, you do not like me?"

"I confess it."

"I have rebuked you for your sinful associations, and the wicked dislike rebuke. The devils said to the Saviour, when he would cast them out, 'Let us alone; we have naught to do with thee.' Everywhere in this life, the sinner says, 'Leave me alone;' yet it is my calling to go forth and snatch brands from the burning. Charles, why will you not denounce the child of that player?"

"She hath done no wrong."

"Do you love her?"

"That is a question you have no right to ask, or expect me to answer."

"I have read it in your heart."

24

"I have no answer."

"What have you to say in extenuation of your conduct hitherto?"

"Nothing."

"Why did you return to Salem?"

"It is my home."

"Did you anticipate this accusation?"

"No."

"And what do you expect now?"

"Death."

"Have you no hope of escaping?"

"None."

"But you seem calm and collected."

"Why should I not?"

"Most men fear death."

"True."

"And do not you?"

"I would rather live."

"What would you consent to do to save your life?"

"Nothing dishonorable."

"What I am about to propose is by no means dishonorable, but honorable and fair in every particular."

"Proceed."

"You are charged with the death of Samuel Williams. Whether you be guilty or not, it is quite clear that Williams is dead. Now it is the

"CHARLES STEVENS, DO YOU SEEK DEATH?"

duty of some one to care for the widow. She is young——"

"Hold, Mr. Parris! If you are going to propose that I shall wed Sarah Williams, spare your words; I will not."

"Charles Stevens, do you seek death?"

"None should wed where the heart is not. That bold, unscrupulous woman has already won my contempt."

"Have a care!"

"Go tell her that Charles Stevens prefers death on the gibbet to becoming her husband."

Mr. Parris gazed on the helpless prisoner for several minutes, his thin lips curled with a sneering smile.

"Charles Stevens," he said in low measured tones, "you are a fool. Do you know what it is to die? Have you counted the cost of a leap in the dark?"

"No sane man courts death; yet to the Christian, who hath kept God's commands, the monster is robbed of half his terrors. God has wisely constituted us so that we dread death. If we did not, we would not be willing to endure the misfortunes, disappointments and ills which afflict us from the cradle to the grave; but the Christian can say welcome to death in preference to dishonor. I thank my God, Samuel Parris, that I can, with the prophets of old, say, O, grave, where is thy victory?"

"Charles Stevens, have you ever thought that, after all, this, too, may be a delusion? That the Bible may be only the uninspired work of man, and that there may be no beyond—no God, save in nature?"

"So you have turned atheist?" cried Charles. "Perhaps you have been one all along?"

"Charles Stevens, one cannot help their doubts."

"One need not be a hypocrite, Mr. Parris. One can even drive doubts away. The true Christian never doubts and never fears. Pray for faith, have faith in your prayers, believe and ask God to help your unbelief, and doubts will disappear."

"Charles, you are too young, too wise to die. Accept Sarah Williams and live."

"Never! Away, hypocrite! Schemer, begone!"

The pastor, quite humbled, turned and went from the prison. There was a malignant gleam in his great wicked eyes, which boded the unfortunate prisoner no good.

For several weeks longer, Charles Stevens languished in prison. Cora, her father and mother came to Salem and visited him. When Cora Waters gazed on the young man, from whom she had parted a few weeks before in the full vigor of his young life and strength, and saw him emaciated, weak and pale, so that she scarcely knew him, she broke down and wept. The two were left alone in the cell. Then Charles told her how uncertain were his chances of life, and how impending his prospects of death. He could not quit this life without telling her that he loved her, and that he wished to live to make her his wife. Though that pleasure was forever denied him, it would make his last days more agreeable to know that his love was returned.

What answer could she make? She, whose fondest hope this had been, said nothing; but, with heart overflowing, she threw her arms about the prisoner and burst into tears. Had she won him only to lose him? Was he to be snatched from her side at the very moment that she found him her own?

"No, no, no! they shall not! they shall not!" she sobbed.

From that day, Cora shared the imprisonment of her lover, so far as the jailer would permit. She added to his comfort and assured him that her undying love would follow him to the grave. Their hopes rose and sank as the day of trial drew near.

The fatal day came at last, and Charles was arraigned before the court of oyer and terminer on charge of the murder of one Samuel Williams.

He plead not guilty and made every preparation for defense. . It was like fighting a masked battery; for they knew not what the evidence would be against them. The trial opened, and Sarah Williams, to make the scene more effective, came dressed in black and looking very pale. She was called to the stand and, between tears and sobs, told her sad story of how her loving husband had one day quarrelled with the defendant, and the latter had threatened him. Was any one else present? Yes. John Bly and Mr. Louder were both present when he threatened to kill her husband. Charles Stevens remembered having a slight altercation when he was quite a boy with Mr. Williams; but it was such a trivial matter that he had forgotten it till now. Then she told that her loving husband feared he would be slain by Charles Stevens, and that he went away to New York city on a voyage, and that the same day Charles Stevens had come to her house, and had asked her whither her husband had gone, and she had every evidence to believe he went after him.

There were other witnesses, who swore that about this time Charles Stevens left the town and was gone away for some time. Charles remembered that on that occasion he had taken a journey to Rhode Island.

Then came two strangers, evidently sea-faring

men, of the lowest order. They were brutal, unscrupulous and had lived the lives of buccaneers, as was afterward proved. Both swore that they knew defendant, although he had never seen either before. They saw the defendant slay Samuel Williams on Long Island, near the beach, and both gave a graphic account of his dragging the body along the sand and hurling it into the water, where the tide bore it away. Their statements were corroborative.

Bly and Louder were next produced, who gave evidence that the defendant had confessed to them that he had slain Samuel Williams, and that defendant was greatly enamored of the murdered man's wife.

Mr. Parris and others testified to having seen him in the company of Sarah Williams on divers of times, and that he had shown great fondness for her.

"What have you to say to this evidence?" asked the chief justice to the prisoner.

"I can only say they are all grievous liars."

"The jury will take notice how the defendant assaults men of unquestioned character. Even the minister is assailed."

There was a murmur of discontent, in which even some of the jury joined.

Judges, jury and prosecutors were all against

Charles, and his trial must result in conviction. The people were excited at the dastardly murder, and began to complain at the delay in the trial, which wore tediously on day after day for nearly a week.

At last the evidence was all in, and the last argument made. There was everything against the prisoner. The prosecution had been so skillfully planned and executed, that there could be but one result. Charles Stevens was very calm, while Cora was carried away in a fainting condition. Mr. Waters went to the prisoner to speak with him.

Charles' face was white as death; but his mind was clear and showed not the least agitation.

"There can be but one result," the prisoner said. "An acquittal is impossible. Be good to Cora and mother, and keep them both away on that day. It would be too much for them. They would not forget it to their dying hour."

Mr. Waters assured him that his last requests should be granted, and spoke a few words of consolation and hope. So many good people of late had perished on the gibbet, that hanging was no longer ignominious. The best and purest had died thus.

The jury had been out but a few moments, when a great hub-bub arose without, and voices could be heard crying:

"Wait! wait! stay your verdict!"

A crowd of men rushed into the court room with a tall young man, whose weather-beaten face indicated a seafaring life, at the head of them. His cruel gray eyes, bold manner, as well as the pistols and cutlass at his belt, gave him the appearance of a pirate.

"I am not dead, I trow! Who said I was dead?" he asked.

"Samuel Williams! Alive!" cried a score of voices.

"Who said I was murdered?"

Sarah Williams rose with a shriek and stared at her husband, as if he had been an apparition, while all the witnesses, including the Rev. Mr. Parris, were covered with confusion. The jury was recalled and Samuel Williams himself took the stand. He stated:

"I left my wife, because I could not live with her, and, marry! I would prefer hanging to existence with her. I went to New York, where Captain Robert Kidd was beating up recruits to sail as a privateer in the *Adventurer* to protect commerce against the French privateers and sea-robbers. I enlisted and then, with one hundred and fifty men, Kidd did good service on the American coast, and we went to the Indian Ocean to attack pirates. Our plunder from the pirates made us long to gain

more booty, and Kidd became a pirate himself.
Armed with cutlasses and pistols, we were made
to board many vessels, English as well as other
nationalities. We went to South America, the
West Indies, and finally came to New York, where
Captain Kidd, one dark night, landed on Gardiner's
Island, east of Long Island, with an enormous
treasure of gold, jewels and precious stones, which
he buried in the earth. From there we came to
Boston. A pardon had been granted for all, save
Kidd, who was yesterday arrested and sent to
England to be tried.* I heard that a man had
been arrested for my murder, and I hastened to
save him."

The romantic story of the returned pirate produced the most profound sensation among the
people in the court room. The jury had just voted
on a verdict of guilty, when they were recalled,
and instructed to give a verdict of acquittal, which
they did. Mr. Parris retired in humiliation and
disgrace. Cora fainted in her rescued lover's arms,
while Mrs. Stevens, falling on her knees, thanked
God that the light of Heaven at last shone on the
path so long dark. Cora's mother came to take
her from the liberated prisoner; but he would not

---

* Kidd was subsequently tried, condemned, and hung
in chains ; but his treasure on Gardiner's Island has not to
this day been found.

give her up, holding her until she regained consciousness, when all went home together, a happy
and united family.

Almost in the twinkling of an eye, the delusion
was dispelled, and many who had been wrong
hastened, so far as in them lay to make reparation.
The bigoted and fanatical, if we may not say
hypocritical preachers, were displaced by God-
fearing, righteous ministers, who were more liberal,
exercising common sense, and possessing humanity
as well as godliness, which is ever essential to a
good minister. They were liberal, even to the
player's child as well as to the players themselves.

George and Henry Waters both became citizens
of Salem, and Charles and Cora were married three
months after the acquittal of the former. Their
lives were eventful, with as much happiness as is
commonly allotted to mortals of earth, and they
left nine children, all brought up in the fear of the
Lord, and lovers of liberty.

Witchcraft prosecutions were doomed, and
shortly after the acquittal of Charles Stevens in so
singular a manner, they altogether ceased to prose-
cute. The imprisoned witches and wizards were
reprieved and set free. Reluctant to yield, the
party of superstition were resolved on one conviction. The victim selected was Sarah Daston, a
woman eighty years old, who, for twenty years,

had borne the undisputed reputation of a witch. If ever there was a witch in the world, she, it was said, was one. Her trial was conducted at Charlestown in the presence of a great throng. There was more evidence against her than any tried at Salem; but the common mind disenthralled of the hideous delusion asserted itself, through the jury by a verdict of acquittal.

Cotton Mather, who was thoroughly imbued with the delusion, to cover his confusion, got up a case of witchcraft in his own  parish. He averred that miracles were wrought in Boston. Cotton Mather does not seem to have been blood-thirsty, though he was more anxious to protect his vanity than his parishioners, and his bewitched neophyte, profiting by his c a u t i o n s, was afflicted by veiled spectres. The imposture was promptly exposed to ridicule by one who was designated as "a malignant, calumnious, and reproachful man, a coal from hell." It was the uncultured, but rational, Robert Calef. Cotton Mather wrote and spoke much on the subject of witchcraft, long after the delusion had vanished.

The inexorable indignation of the people of

COTTON MATHER.

Salem Village drove Parris from the place. Noyes confessed his error and guilt, asked forgiveness and devoted the remainder of his life to deeds of charity. Sewall, one of the judges, by rising in his pew in the Old South meeting-house on a fast day, and reading to the whole congregation a paper, in which he bewailed his great offence, recovered public esteem. Stoughton and Cotton Mather never repented. The former lived proud, unsatisfied and unbeloved. The latter attempted to persuade others and himself that he had not been specially active in the tragedy. His diary proves that he did not wholly escape the impeachment of conscience, for it is stated that Cotton Mather, who had sought the foundation of faith in tales of wonders himself, "had temptations to atheism and to the abandonment of all religion as a mere delusion."

As when a storm clears away, it leaves the atmosphere clearer, so the common mind of New England became more wise. By employing a cautious spirit of search, eliminating error, rejecting superstition as tending toward cowardice and submission, the people cherished religion as a source of courage and a fountain of freedom, and forever after refused to separate belief from reason.

The actual fate of Mr. Parris is not certainly known. Some have intimated that he died of a

loathsome disease, others that, like Judas, he took
his own life; but we are assured that he received
his share of earthly torment for his base hypocrisy
and cruel wrongs.   Most of the people who pre-
tended to be afflicted afterward made confessions
admitting their error.   Efforts were made by the
legislature to make amends for some of the great
wrongs done at Salem; but such wrongs can never
be righted.   The victims of Parris' hate and ava-
rice have slept for two hundred years on Witches'
Hill, and there await the trump that shall rouse
the dead, when the just shall be separated from
the unjust.

Salem Village is peaceful, happy and quiet.   In
the gentle murmur of waves, the whisper of breezes
and the laugh of babbling brooks, about the quaint
old town, all nature seems to rejoice that the age
of superstition has passed.

THE END.

Witches Hill.

HISTORICAL INDEX.

www.ingramcontent.com/pod-product-compliance
Lightning Source LLC
Chambersburg PA
CBHW051511100726